M000309422

# The Raft
# The River
## and
## The Robot

Copyright © 2012 L.B. Graham

THE RAFT, THE RIVER, AND THE ROBOT is a work of fiction. Names,
characters, places and incidents are either products of the authors'
imaginations or used fictitiously. Any resemblance to actual events, locales,
or persons, living or dead, is entirely coincidental. All rights reserved. No
part of this publication may be reproduced or transmitted in any form or
by any means, electronic or mechanical, without permission in writing
from the author or publisher.

A font used in this book is copyright © 2009 by Matt McInerney
(matt@pixelspread.com), with Reserved Font Name: "Orbitron." This
Font Software is licensed under the SIL Open Font License, Version 1.1,
and is also available at http://scripts.sil.org/OFL.

www.lbgraham.com

# The Raft
# The River
## and
## The Robot

# L. B. Graham

A *not yet* BOOK

*The stars over us was sparkling ever so fine; and down by the village was the river, a whole mile broad, and awful still and grand.*

Mark Twain

# The Raft

# Rabbit

The sled was piled high with firewood, and HF pulled it through the gently falling snow. Jim usually did most of the work, but HF tagged along without complaint on these excursions, taking over cheerfully enough when Jim got tired and it was his turn to pull for a while.

Not long after Atticus started letting Jim go into the woods alone to gather firewood a few winters back, he took HF along one day. He stayed close by, studying Jim's labors like he studied everything. When Jim finally asked HF if he'd like to help load the sled and take a turn pulling it, HF said, "I reckon so. It don't look too hard."

HF was pale and freckled, scrawny with a mop of dark hair. Back then, he'd been more or less the same size as Jim, but Jim had several inches on him now. Jim was as tall as Atticus, in fact, and it looked as if he would end up being taller. Of course, that didn't mean a whole lot, since Atticus wasn't especially tall.

Atticus wasn't very big and didn't say very much, but he had presence. When he talked, Jim and HF listened, especially when he talked about how to survive as a groundling. Atticus had a lot to say about that. That's why he'd been reluctant at first to let Jim and HF go off alone together; he worried that they'd forget the things he had taught them.

Jim and HF were out alone today, and as long as they stuck to the woods, safety wasn't a big issue. Still, they tended to operate quietly when they were outside the cabin. They had room for more wood on the sled, but with Atticus sick, Jim didn't want to be gone too long and let the fire die down. Even when the cabin felt boiling hot to Jim, Atticus shivered with fever under his blankets.

Right about the place where the incline leading up to the cabin grew suddenly steeper, a rabbit darted in front of the sled. HF stopped short in his tracks and looked over at Jim, who was already swinging the .22 around and heading out after it. Jim didn't like the idea of Atticus lying cold in the cabin, but with any luck this wouldn't take long and there'd be fresh meat in the stew tonight.

The rabbit, though, sensed danger and moved fast. Jim slipped on the icy hillside, his hopes of a quick catch diminishing. He sprang up and raced onward, HF trailing close behind.

The rabbit zigzagged through the trees, maintaining a course that sloped down, toward the river. Jim hadn't expected that. There was no escape for the rabbit that way—only exposure from loss of natural cover followed by a divide the animal could not cross. And yet, the open ground between the edge of the woods and the river created complications for Jim too. At the edge of the wood, the rabbit bolted out from under the snowy trees down the open bank until it was about midway between the tree line and the river. It stopped, perhaps only now realizing that it couldn't keep going the direction it was headed. It sat, paralyzed by the decision to run right or left. Jim stopped too, lingering under the barren branches of a tall beech. He raised his rifle.

The shot wasn't difficult. In fact, it was absurdly easy, but Jim hesitated. He knew Atticus wouldn't approve. To fire his rifle at the edge of the river would be to cross the line. HF knew it, too. He had come up alongside and was staring at Jim as though in silent reproach. Jim tried to ignore the unblinking eyes and think.

He understood the prohibition, of course. Atticus didn't make rules without having a good reason. Though packs were unlikely on the island, they weren't unheard of. Across the river, on the mainland, packs were a little more likely—more so on the Illinois side, which still had the remnants of a road, than on the Missouri side. But even if a pack saw Jim from across the river, what would they do? Would they really take all the trouble to find a way across the river, just to cause him trouble?

But of course, it was not the packs but the hunters that Atticus was chiefly concerned about. Still, what were the odds that a hunter would be flying directly overhead at just that moment? Jim's chances of shooting the rabbit and retrieving it without danger were high. But that was precisely Atticus's point. No groundling ever expected a hunter to be just about to fly overhead or worse, to already be aground and close by. But they could be, and that was the problem.

Some hunters, Atticus said, left the hives just to hunt animals, but many of them would prefer to hunt a groundling if they could. Atticus said the way to be sure no hunter ever came after them was to always behave as though a hunter was nearby, and to never do anything that would unnecessarily expose them to risk. Taking the shot at the river's edge was a risk. Retrieving the rabbit was another.

Still, Jim thought, eyeing the immobile rabbit through his sight, the risk was very small, and fresh rabbit would taste very good. He slid his finger over the trigger, applying a little pressure, but still the prohibition held him back, even if only barely.

"Hovercraft," HF said, leaning in to whisper.

Jim lowered the gun and looked up, instinctively. Sure enough, HF's sensitive hearing had picked up what his hadn't—a small hovercraft. It zipped out from above the trees on his left, flying low and almost noiselessly over the river toward the far shore.

Jim and HF watched, not daring to move, in case a hunter was watching or the hovercraft was equipped with motion detection capability. The rabbit bolted right, its mind made up now. For a moment, Jim was sure that the hovercraft would turn around and that they would be seen so close to the wood's edge, but it kept right on going toward the Missouri shore.

Then he saw why.

The hovercraft swept in an arc over the wood on the opposing shore, and a large buck with gorgeous antlers broke out from under the trees and ran alongside the river. The hovercraft flew low, after it, and a shot rang out across the water. The buck leapt up the small bank and disappeared back into the trees, and Jim knew the hunter had missed. The hovercraft banked to the left and likewise disappeared, not into the trees but over them.

For a long moment, Jim and HF stayed where they were. Jim feared that as soon as he began to retreat, the hunter would come zooming back into view. Few hunters would keep after a deer—even such a splendid one—when a groundling was in view. Still, as the moment stretched on, the hovercraft did not reappear.

At last, Jim looked at HF and motioned with his head back up the hill. They turned and started moving back slowly, looking behind more than they looked ahead, but the hovercraft did not reappear. When they were about twenty-five yards in from the edge of the wood, Jim started running back up the slope, retracing his steps to the sled. HF ran beside him, going as silently up the hill as he had run down it.

When Jim had taken up the rope to pull the sled, and they were back on their way to the cabin, HF broke the silence. "I sure am glad you didn't shoot that rabbit, Jim. Our goose woulda been cooked for sure."

"Yeah," Jim said, straining to pull the sled faster. He didn't feel it was necessary to tell HF he'd been just about to take the shot. He probably knew already. HF didn't say a whole lot, but he saw more than most. Jim didn't think HF would say anything to Atticus. He didn't think like that. A real brother might have ratted him out, but HF could never be a real brother, even if Jim had come to think of him that way.

As they crested the last big ridge and the slope started to level out again, Jim saw the cabin up ahead. He would help HF start stowing the wood and then go inside. Then he would see what he would see.

# Atticus

Jim opened the door to the cabin slowly. The hinges creaked, but not as loudly as they would have otherwise. He slipped in, saw right away that Atticus was sleeping, and shut the door even though he knew HF would be close behind him. The creaking of the door opening again might wake Atticus, but the sound couldn't hurt him like the cold could.

He walked to the fire and used the poker to shift the logs. When he had redistributed the wood, he added another log and used the bellows to stoke the embers. His face glowed with the heat of the fire; he had to slide backwards to keep working on it. Still, he knew that the heat he found almost unbearable scarcely touched Atticus in his feverish state. He stoked the fire still hotter.

The door opened with a loud creak, as Jim had feared it would, and HF slid quickly in. He went right to the chair between Atticus' bed and the wall. Except when he went out with Jim, HF had stationed himself there, day and night, since Atticus had come down with the fever. As faithful as any dog, HF sat in that chair for hours on end swinging his legs rhythmically and staring straight ahead, speaking only when he was spoken to.

Atticus stirred with the opening and closing of the door, but he did not wake. He shifted in the bed, turning from his back to his side. He had gotten tangled in his covers since Jim had gone out, and he struggled to hike the blanket up over his shoulder, shivering all the while. Jim glided from the fire to the bed, and with a few strong tugs, he straightened things out and covered Atticus up.

Jim sighed as he started gathering together the ingredients for their stew. Atticus had his days and nights thoroughly mixed up. He slept deeply during the day, while he tossed and turned and frequently moaned for water during the night. Jim was glad Atticus could get some good sleep, even if it was during the day, but he was starting to feel the effects of three nights with little real rest.

His attention was soon diverted by the sorry state of their stores. There were still plenty of onions. They would last until spring with plenty to spare. As for the potatoes, there were maybe twenty left, which should be enough, but it seemed lately that whenever Jim cooked potatoes, he had to cut out more than he could keep. They might still hold out, but it would be close.

The celery was almost gone. Just three stalks left, and one of them, Jim thought, could only charitably be called 'stubby.' And then there was the carrot. It was long and straight and glorious—and it was the last one. Jim had been saving it for the last week to have on his birthday, which was the next day, but as he washed and cut up the vegetables for the stew, he reached for the carrot anyway.

It was irrational to think that eating the last carrot tonight would revive Atticus and help break the fever, but it occurred to Jim that Atticus hadn't had any carrot in his stew since falling sick. He was determined to see what the carrot could do.

At first he only chopped up half of it. He thought perhaps he could hold half of it back and stretch it out so there would be some left for his birthday dinner. But as he looked into the pot at the pitiful display the floating half carrot made, he decided there was nothing for it but to put it all in. There was no point using up half the carrot if no one could even tell it was in there.

The stew was almost ready, and Jim was stirring it with the wooden spoon and trying to decide if it was time to serve it up yet, when Atticus called softly from his bed, "Jim? That you?"

"Yes, Atticus," Jim said, letting the spoon sit in the stew and walking over to his father. "Supper's about ready."

Atticus' eyes opened and he smiled. "It smells wonderful."

HF leaned forward at the sound of Atticus' voice, and Atticus reached over and patted him on his knee.

"Good. I'll get your bowl in a minute," Jim said. "First, we should change your shirt."

"O.K." Atticus' eyes closed again. It seemed that with this fever, even keeping them open required too much effort.

Jim walked over to the chair he had stationed by the fire so he could dry Atticus' sweaty shirts when he took them off. If there had been less to do, he would have washed them before hanging them up, but with Atticus sick and spring around the corner, he just didn't have the time. He changed his father's shirts twice a day, drying one while he wore the other. He wished he could do the same for Atticus' sheets, but taking them off the bed seemed out of the question. Atticus clung to them like life itself.

When Jim returned to the bed, Atticus seemed unable to lift himself up far enough for Jim to do his work, so HF helped, reaching under Atticus' arms and lifting him. Jim peeled off the sweaty shirt he was wearing; Atticus shivered violently and his teeth chattered uncontrollably.

"Almost there," Jim said, slipping the next shirt over Atticus' head. He quickly worked his arms into the sleeves and pulled it down.

"Go on, HF, help him back down." Soon Atticus was lying back down, tucked in comfortably. "How's that feel?"

Atticus looked up at him again, forcing the smile back onto his face. "It's great, Jim. Thanks."

"I'll be back with your bowl, and then I'll prop you up, O.K.?"

"O.K."

Jim set the stew pot on the hearth, close enough to the fire so that the rest would stay warm until he could come back for it. Atticus hadn't had much of an appetite of late, but Jim knew he needed to eat.

Getting Atticus propped up wasn't as hard as Jim had feared it would be. Perhaps the dry shirt and the smell of the stew had done its work, but Atticus seemed a little livelier and more energetic, though Jim knew he might just be seeing what he wanted to see.

Atticus did eat, though. Jim knew he wasn't making that up at least. He got more than halfway through the bowl Jim had served, and that was more than he'd eaten since the fever had struck three days before. Jim was encouraged, and while he knew it might have nothing to do with the carrot, he was glad he had thrown it in.

Since falling ill, Atticus usually fell back to sleep immediately after eating. But this time he stayed awake, so Jim returned to his seat beside the bed to eat his own bowl of stew. What's more, Atticus seemed strong enough to talk, at least a little bit.

"I'm sorry, Jim," he said as Jim dug in. "I've lost track of time a bit. Is today your birthday?"

"Tomorrow," Jim said between bites.

"Oh," Atticus said. "That's good. If I'm better, maybe we can go hunting. It would be good to have meat for your birthday."

"Meat would be good," Jim said, agreeing. He knew they wouldn't be hunting tomorrow, even if his father's fever broke soon. Atticus would probably be in no shape to even get out of bed the next day, let alone hunt, but this revival of spirits was encouraging. "We almost had meat tonight."

"Oh?" Atticus said, watching Jim wolf down his stew.

"Rabbit," Jim said, deciding as he did that saying anything about the hunter would only make Atticus worry, even though the moment of danger had passed. "It got away, though."

"Rabbit," Atticus said, smiling wearily at the thought of it. "Wouldn't that be great?"

"He was a scrawny feller," HF added.

"But still," Atticus said, "Rabbit."

"Yes," Jim agreed.

"Even a little squirrel would go down well right now."

Atticus must be delirious if he was salivating over squirrel. Ordinarily, he scoffed at wasting ammunition on a creature so small when there was always plenty of bigger game to be killed. The thought of bigger game made him think of the buck across the river. He wondered if the hunter had gotten it, and if so, if he'd just left the carcass in the wood. Hunting for those who lived in a hive was different than it was for groundlings. It was sport, not survival.

Atticus spoke dreamily, "Just think, Jim, a little meat with onion, carrot, potato, maybe some radishes and parsley…" his voice trailed off, and Jim found himself almost mesmerized by the picture and scent of the stew Atticus described. He didn't have the heart to mention that they had just used their last carrot or that there hadn't been any radishes in weeks.

Jim finished his dinner and set down his bowl. "Sounds good."

"Yes," Atticus said, his voice fainter than it had been even just a moment ago. "We'll have meat, and your birthday will be a great day."

Atticus closed his eyes, and Jim cleared the bowls to the sink, where he rinsed them using water from the bucket on the counter. By the time Jim was finished cleaning up, Atticus was asleep and snoring softly. Jim switched off the lamp in the corner, then went back to the fire to add another log.

HF remained quiet in his seat on the other side of Atticus' bed. His legs still swung, keeping time like a pendulum.

A few minutes later Jim lay in his own bed, his hands beneath his head, watching the flickering shadows that the fire cast on the cabin's ceiling. Outside, the owl that lived in the nearby elm had just begun his hooting. Jim lay listening, wondering as he often did, to whom or for whom the owl called.

Moonlight shone in at the window. Jim let this thoughts wander, and they drifted to the rabbit. He wondered if the little fellow was curled up, safe in its warren. Or perhaps, with its earlier fright behind it, it was somewhere out there, hopping along in the moonlight. There were as many predators in the wood by night as by day, if not more, so it was never really safe to be out. Still, no creature, great or small, escaped the need to feed.

Jim's eyes grew heavy and flickered shut.

He found himself down by the river's edge again. The moonlight glistened on the water's surface as it rolled ceaselessly on. He looked for the rabbit in the open space between the wood and the river, but it wasn't there.

A hovercraft came zooming up the river, a bright, penetrating floodlight sweeping back and forth across the water. Jim watched in horror as the hovercraft swung around and began to search the edge of the wood where he was hiding. The light settled upon him, but he was frozen in his tracks and could not run.

The hovercraft crept slowly forward, keeping its bright light on Jim. Soon, it hovered right over the shore, just ten or fifteen feet from where Jim stood. And there, behind the glass of the cockpit, Jim could see the face of the pilot.

The pilot grinned as he pointed his gun at Jim.


Jim gave a start and sat up in bed. He rubbed the sleep from his eyes and looked around at the cabin. He could tell by the light coming in from the window that it was well after dawn.

He slid down out of his bed and crossed to where HF still kept watch over Atticus. He moved up and felt Atticus' forehead. He had but one birthday wish, to find the fever broken.

It was, if anything, hotter than it had been the day before.

# Blessing

By the seventh day of the fever, Jim knew Atticus wasn't going to get better.

He couldn't have explained it. It wasn't that there was some medical sign that told him this. Nothing he observed said with certainty that the fever wouldn't still break, that Atticus wouldn't recover. He just knew. Atticus had been sick before, as had he, but this time … this time it was different. Atticus was dying.

Atticus seemed to know it too. There was no more talking of what they'd do when he was better. No more attempts to set Jim at ease with forced smiles amidst the pain. Instead, in his more lucid moments, a sense of urgency seemed to have come over Atticus. He talked—often incoherently—about what to plant where, and when, about how to keep the deer from getting the best of it, about where to set the traps in the spring, about where to get which fish and which spots were not safe enough, regardless of what could be caught there. Threaded through all this were repeated cautions about packs and hunters—cautions given and received many times before.

It saddened and disappointed Jim to think that Atticus didn't trust him to survive alone. Atticus had been fifty when Jim was born, and keenly aware of his own mortality. He had been training Jim to live independently on the land all his life. Now that Jim was fourteen, there wasn't a whole lot that Atticus did for them that Jim couldn't do himself.

But Jim kept his sadness and disappointment to himself. If Atticus was dying, he wanted it to be as peaceful a passing as he could make it. He listened whenever his father had the strength to speak, as though he was hearing whatever Atticus was saying for the first time.

He stopped leaving the cabin for anything, even firewood. HF seemed as reluctant to leave Atticus as he did, but when Jim sent him for the firewood, he went. He'd bring in an armload, stack it neatly by the hearth, then go back to his seat by Atticus' bed, returning to his silent vigil.

Jim didn't know if HF understood what was happening. HF had been with Atticus since Jim was born, but what he knew or understood about life and death, Jim just didn't know. Sometimes, HF came out with things that indicated a deeper awareness of the world than maybe even Jim had. Other times, Jim was stunned to discover what HF didn't—couldn't—understand.

Either way, Jim couldn't worry about HF now. With each passing day, Atticus slipped further away into a world of fitful sleep and fever dreams. The critical work Jim had been doing to prepare for the spring planting and harvesting, and the daily checking of the traps, even those things were neglected now. There was Atticus, and nothing else.

On the morning of the tenth day, Jim woke to find Atticus also awake. His breathing was shallow and a bit labored, but he seemed calmer than he'd been the last few days. When Jim pulled his chair up beside his father's bed, there was no flurry of urgent instructions, no reminders about what to do and how to do it.

Atticus moved a shaking hand over and set it lightly on Jim's hand. He seemed to have to gather strength to speak, and when he did, his voice was small and quiet. Jim had to lean forward to catch it. "Jim, there are things I meant to tell you. Just never seemed to be the right time."

It took Atticus a lot of time and strength to get the whole statement out, and Jim waited patiently through each word and each painful pause. He watched Atticus carefully, and seeing that he meant to go on, continued to wait.

"Find Florence. Go to the Caretaker," Atticus seemed unable to go further. His eyes closed, and he lay, for quite a while, just breathing. Jim glanced at HF, who sat in his chair, legs rocking. He couldn't tell if Florence meant anything to HF; it didn't ring a bell with Jim.

"All right, Atticus," Jim said. "I will. I'll go to the Caretaker."

Jim knew the name. Most groundlings in these parts had heard of him, even if like Jim they hadn't met him. Jim had always gathered that Atticus didn't just know about him, but actually knew him, but how or why he knew him wasn't exactly clear. What the Caretaker could do for Jim wasn't clear either.

As far as Jim knew, the Caretaker was just an old hermit who lived like a groundling but still had connections to the hives. At least that was how people talked about him. A man between worlds, not really a part of either. By sending Jim to see the Caretaker, Atticus couldn't be suggesting that Jim give up being a groundling and go to a hive, could he? Atticus had raised Jim to scorn the hives, even as he scorned them himself.

"The Caretaker," Jim began. "Where is he, and why do you want me to go there?" His father's eyes drooped shut. He opened his mouth as if to speak, but nothing came out. Jim began to wonder if his father even knew what he was saying. "Is the Caretaker in Florence?" Jim asked, almost shouting in his father's ear. "Is Florence where he lives?"

With obvious effort, Atticus opened his eyes again. It seemed clear that he didn't have the energy to elaborate. Looking at Jim, he spoke words barely loud enough to be called a faint whisper. "Murphy will help. Go there first."

"All right," Jim said. He could do that. He knew where to find the Murphys. As likely as not, he would have gone to them first anyway with the news of Atticus' passing. He was reassured by the fact that his father had given such a sensible directive; perhaps his directive about the Caretaker wasn't just feverish babbling. Maybe it was rational as well.

"Are we going to the Murphys', Jim?" HF said.

"Not yet, HF."

Jim waited for more instructions, but no more came. Soon he could tell from his father's breathing that he had fallen back asleep. From the sound of those quick, shallow breaths, Jim feared that maybe this was it. Maybe Atticus would wake no more.

He was wrong, though. That evening, as the sun was going down and the bright orange rays slipped through the barren branches of the trees outside and through the western-facing windows, Atticus woke again. Jim, who had been nodding off himself, came quickly alert when he saw his father's eyes open.

Atticus didn't try to reach over this time, but he did raise his hand just enough to motion for Jim to lean closer, which he did. The dying man's lips moved, but Jim didn't hear anything, so he leaned in even further, until his head was just above his father's chest and his ear was near his mouth.

Atticus's trembling fingers reached out for Jim's head. Gently, they slipped through Jim's short, curly hair. Jim's eyes closed as he felt Atticus softly stroking his scalp with his fingertips. Tears rose unbidden, but he held them back. Atticus had taught him to be strong, to face the world as it was, whatever came. He wouldn't cry, not now.

"Grow strong. Be courageous. Live well." Atticus said at last.

It was short, but clear, and when Atticus' hand let go, Jim raised his head to look at his father. Atticus looked at him, his eyes shining with tears of his own, and a look that spoke of inexpressible pride. Jim was speechless. Atticus didn't cry either, but he was crying now. For a long moment, the two just stared at each other.

Atticus turned his head the other way so he could see HF where he was sitting on his chair. "Go with Jim. Help him."

Then, looking back at Jim, Atticus added. "Take care of each other."

Atticus didn't speak again.

The orange light faded, and darkness fell on the cabin and the three inside it. Neither Jim nor HF moved from their seats, even when the fire burned low. Atticus' breathing grew shallower, slowed, and sometime late in the night, long after the moon had risen above the trees, stopped.

Jim pulled the blankets up and covered him, feeling his own exhaustion come over him now that it was over. He rose, walked over to his bed and lay down.

HF didn't speak or move. He sat, his legs swinging as always, and kept watch over Atticus through the night.

# One Battery

It was late when Jim woke. Much later than usual. He realized that the fire had almost gone out and jumped up to stoke it, worried that Atticus would be cold. Halfway to the fireplace he stopped, realizing with a sinking feeling that Atticus no longer cared how hot the fire was. He crawled back into bed and rolled over so his back was turned to his father's bed and the rest of the cabin. He curled up under his covers to stay warm.

He must have fallen asleep again, because the next thing he knew the squeak of the door's hinges woke him. He sat up and looked quickly around. HF was no longer sitting beside Atticus.

By the time Jim had slipped his boots on and made it to the door, HF was coming back through the crisp midmorning air, carrying firewood. When HF saw Jim standing at the door, he said, "It gets powerful cold without that fire, Jim."

Jim stepped aside and then closed the door as HF came in. Then, after he had deposited the wood carefully by the hearth, as usual, he returned to his customary chair and sat quietly back down.

Now awake and up, Jim wanted to be active, so he set about doing what was necessary. He found their largest candle, set it on a plate, lit it, and then rested it on his father's chest, as was the custom. He should have done this the previous night and sat with the body overnight, keeping the vigil, but he had been too tired.

He ate what was left of the previous day's stew with a warm biscuit, then sat beside Atticus for a while, unable to focus on anything. Various memories fluttered through his consciousness, but mostly he just felt numb. In the end, he got up, grabbed the best shovel, and went outside to start digging the grave.

The cold ground would make it hard, but not impossible to dig. An early thaw at the beginning of the month had lasted almost a week before temperatures dipped back below freezing. Now, with March just around the corner, the promise of consistently warmer weather was in the air.

Jim stopped in his tracks, his hand gripping the cold, smooth handle of the shovel. It was already early March, not late February at all. It had been a week since his birthday. The turning of the calendar from February to March had passed during the haze of his father's final days. He would double check the old calendar on the wall of the cabin when he was back inside to be sure, but Jim was pretty sure it was already the second day of March.

He paused, wondering if he should tell HF to come too. If Jim left him inside, he would probably just sit by Atticus' bed the whole time, and Jim didn't know if HF understood Atticus was gone. In the end, he decided to leave HF alone.

Not too far ahead, there was a small piece of ground where the sun shone through, pretty much all year round, even when the trees had their leaves. Jim thought that was as good a place as any to lay Atticus to rest. He stopped there, felt a brief twinge of regret that he'd be digging up one of the few lush patches of grass anywhere near the cabin, but dismissed it quickly and got to work.

It was slow going, and he found himself fighting both tears and the soil. By early afternoon, though, he had a grave that was not quite six feet deep, but deep enough to serve the purpose. Jim wiped the sweat from his face on his shirt and thought for a moment about trying to keep going and make it deeper, but the ache in both his arms and his legs told him he was spent. He drove the shovel into the pile of loose dirt and turned back to the cabin.

He stood for a long time at the foot of his father's bed. There was a lot of wax on the plate, but the candle had plenty of life left in it. He knew he was supposed to let it burn out, but that would take the rest of the day. If he did that, he wouldn't be able to bury Atticus until the next day.

No, even as he thought about it, he had already decided he wanted to be off early with HF the next morning. Since it still got dark relatively early, he would need to leave at first light if he wanted to make it to the Murphys' by supper. He bent over and blew out the candle. He would bury Atticus now.

He looked over at HF and said, "I'll need your help."

HF glanced up. "That hole's mighty big for plantin,' Jim. What do we aim to grow in there?"

Jim looked over HF's shoulder and out the window, realizing that with just a slight turn of his head, HF had a clear view of the spot in the glade where he had dug the grave. "It's for Atticus. We need to bury him."

The rhythmic rocking of HF's legs seemed to slow, but the expression on his face never changed and he did not blink. "Why would we want to go and do a thing like that?"

"Don't you know?" Jim said, feeling the sudden pull of tears once more. "He's dead, HF."

"Sure, I know that," HF said.

"Then we need to bury him," Jim said, growing impatient.

"Why don't we just fix him?"

Jim stared, dumbfounded. "We can't fix him, HF. You can't fix dead."

HF thought about that for a moment. Jim wondered what was going through his head, but he was in no way prepared for what HF said next. "When your Mama died, Atticus told me that folks break down sometimes, just like robots. I figured he didn't fix her because he didn't have the right parts. Reckon we could fix Atticus, if we had the right parts?"

"No," Jim said, aggressively swiping the backs of his hands at the tears that were flowing freely down his cheeks. "We can't."

"Maybe we could take him somewhere and see," HF said, a little more insistent.

Jim could see that HF was getting agitated, and he knew he should try to be patient, but he snapped, yelling at him anyway. "It doesn't matter where we take him. He's dead! I told you, you can't fix dead!"

"There ain't no cause to holler," HF said, fixing an unblinking stare on Jim.

Jim took a deep breath. Atticus never shouted at either of them, and he would have been disappointed in Jim for shouting at HF now, merely because he didn't understand death—especially since Jim wasn't really sure he understood it much better himself. "I'm sorry."

"No harm done, I reckon," HF said, and then he was silent for a while. When he spoke again, his voice was quieter—plaintive and almost desperate. "Maybe a new battery ... in there?"

HF reached down and pointed to the place where the candle sat on Atticus' motionless chest.

Jim just shook his head. "No, HF," he said softly. "People only get one."

HF's shoulders slumped, and he hung his head. Jim could see that he understood now. Atticus was gone, and he would not be back. As he blew out the candle and set it on the table, Jim explained what they needed to do with the body, and HF listened, nodding.

Together they lifted Atticus and carried him outside. Everything about him seemed stiff now, except the thin wisps of white hair that fluttered erratically in the wind. Jim didn't like looking at the face. He didn't think it looked much like Atticus anymore.

They carried him out and placed him in the grave silently. They stooped down and lowered him in. Jim knew he had to be buried, but when it came to it, he felt bad putting him in. Still, he guessed that sooner or later, everybody ended up in a hole somewhere, one way or another.

He handled the shovel, but somehow it didn't seem right just to cover Atticus up without saying anything. Neither Atticus nor Jim had been very big on talking, but this seemed like a moment when something should be said. Jim looked down at the pile of loose dirt beside him, and bending over, picked up a handful.

As he let the dirt fall from his hand in a steady stream on Atticus' body, he said, almost without thinking, "Dust to dust."

No sooner had Jim said it, and no sooner had he started to wonder why he'd said it, than a sudden and vivid memory overcame him. He could see Atticus, standing by a grave, saying those very words. In that same vivid memory, Jim could feel hot tears on his own cheeks as he stood by the grave and listened. He could feel strong hands on his shoulders. Not

Atticus' hands, though; Atticus was standing at the head of the grave, a few feet away.

As strong and as vivid as it was, the memory disappeared as suddenly as it came. Jim stumbled back, his mind racing. Was that his mother's grave? He was little; he knew that much. Who else would Atticus have been burying that Jim would have wept for? And who was holding his shoulders? In the memory those strong hands were vastly comforting, but whose were they?

Jim shook off the memory and the questions as if shaking off a daze, and he reached for the shovel. There was already too much turmoil inside to go digging into random memories. He focused on the job at hand and soon found himself musing over how easy and how much less time it took to put the dirt back in the grave, compared with how hard and how long it had taken to get it out. Soon, the grave was filled in with a small mound over it to mark the spot.

Jim started back toward the cabin, but HF didn't move. Jim stopped, about halfway to the door, and called back. "Come on, HF," he said. "There's no point watching over him now." Reluctantly, HF turned away from the grave and followed Jim inside.

With Atticus settled, he could think about what to take with him to the Murphys'. He'd need to think carefully about that. He didn't know what it might take to go to the Caretaker, to find Florence. He didn't even know if Florence was upriver or downriver—or even if it was on the river at all. Still, if it was going to be any kind of journey, he'd want to travel light. A change of clothes or so and his .22 were essential. He'd also need some extra ammunition and a flashlight, and he could make a big batch of biscuits tonight for the crossing and beyond. HF could carry a pack too, so they could take the big tarp in case they needed a shelter from bad weather.

He would also need to take some of Atticus' more basic tools. He could leave the ones he didn't know how to use, of course, and that would lighten the load, but he knew he should take the main ones. Besides, the tools were the one thing from his life in the hive that Atticus had held onto all these years. It didn't seem right leaving them all behind.

Jim walked to the window and gazed out at the grave. He felt bad that he was leaving it unmarked. He would need to take care of that when he came back.

It occurred to Jim then, for the first time, that coming back was optional. The cabin had been home because Atticus was there. Now Atticus wasn't there—nor, for that matter, was he anywhere else Jim could go. Jim looked around at the cabin. There were millions in the world just like it, and many better. The world lay open before him. All those empty cities and towns, warehouses and stores, cabins and farms—all left behind as people migrated to the hives, most of them essentially intact. He could go anywhere. Nobody said that he had to return here.

Still, Jim suspected that he would come back. He knew the routines of life here, and that was something. Besides, there would be Atticus' grave to mark and probably other things that he would realize he should have done only after he was gone and it was too late to do them.

He would go, he would honor Atticus' final wishes, and then he would come home—and maybe somewhere along the way, he would figure out what life was to be without Atticus in it.

# Across The Island

Jim stopped to wipe the sweat from his brow. The sun was bright today, even through the trees. When they'd left the cabin, just after dawn, he'd been able to see his breath in the air. Now it was well above freezing, perhaps even above 40, and he found himself peeling off his outer fleece and tying it around his waist before shouldering his .22 again.

There were other signs that a second thaw was underway. Though he and HF were trudging through a few inches of snow, it was slushier than it had been, and here and there he could see small rivulets of water running downhill underneath it. Above, on some of the trees, buds were evident, and Jim knew that within a few weeks there'd be more trees full of leaves than bare.

That thought gave Jim pause. He'd started forward again, but for the first time since he'd decided to head to the Murphys', he was reconsidering his choice. If he was right, if only a few weeks would bring leaves to most of the trees on the island, then why not wait for better cover? He didn't need Atticus to remind him it was safer to move about when visibility from the skies was limited.

What harm would it bring to go back and wait? As far as he knew, the Caretaker wouldn't be any more difficult to find in spring, and whatever help Murphy could give him could wait too. He glanced at HF, keeping pace on his right side, and considered asking him what he thought. He didn't, though, because he knew what he really wanted was to ask Atticus. Asking HF couldn't change that.

Thinking about Atticus made him want to keep going. He was underway now, and he suddenly felt very strongly that he needed to keep moving forward. Cooking the biscuits last night and packing, planning his route in his head so he could minimize the number of road crossings he'd need to make and steer clear of the really open places on the island, all of it had given him something to think about, something to do, and things that kept his thoughts from Atticus and the mound of dirt in the glade by the cabin were welcome.

If he went back now, then what would he do? There was plenty of work, of course, but at the end of each day, he'd be in the cabin, by the fire, alone. Sure, HF would be there, but that wasn't the same. He'd feel the loneliness, the emptiness of loss, even more than he already did.

No, it had felt too good to set out that morning, to put the cabin behind him and move out. Not just for what he was leaving behind, but also because the prospect of a larger journey to find the Caretaker was vaguely exciting. An air of mystery surrounded the Caretaker, and now he not only had permission to go in search of him, he had a commission to go—Atticus had sent him as almost his last wish. True, it might be safer in a few weeks, but it would never be entirely safe, so the slight difference waiting might make wasn't reason enough to turn back.

Up ahead, Jim could see the open swath the road cut through the wood. His pulse quickened, and not just because he knew a road always brought with it an air of danger. Ever since he was little, the feel of walking on a road—the hard pavement underfoot, stretching on and on in either direction beneath the open sky—had whispered to him of the past, of days when people walked and rode on them without fear of what lurked above or around the next corner. Roads made him think about the world before the hives, a world that was even older than Atticus, much older.

Jim slowed and approached the edge of the wood cautiously, as he'd been taught. HF had crossed roads with both Atticus and Jim many times, and he understood the need for caution and quiet. Jim stooped beside a tree, and for several moments, simply watched.

The road was up a slight embankment from the wood, but it wasn't terribly steep. In places, even on the island, the edge of the wood was much farther from the road and the ground from the wood to the road much more difficult to traverse. Here, the wood was close on both sides, and the slope up to the road easily crossed. When it came time to go, they would be out in the open for less than a minute, probably a lot less.

That was another advantage of coming the longer way. Not only did it reduce the road crossings to two, but the road here was about as cooperative for a crossing as could be found anywhere on the island. Granted, the second one wasn't as simple, but that crossing never was. Even so, an extra couple of hours en route was a small price to pay for cutting his time out in the open almost in half.

Jim turned to HF and whispered, "Well, are you ready?"

HF nodded.

Jim took up the two stones he'd selected along the way, and threw the first one onto the road as far to his left as he could. The second he threw onto the road as far to the right as he could. Stones were unlikely to draw out any hunters who might be lurking nearby, but they might well scare out into the open any animals lurking nearby, and if there were also a hunter, there was always the chance that the movement of the animal might pull him away too. At a minimum, throwing the stones decreased the chance that they'd startle some animal when crossing and increase the amount of activity on the road, thereby also decreasing the likelihood that they'd be spotted from above.

Jim waited until well after the stones had come to a stop. Nothing stirred in either direction. At least, he didn't sense anything stirring. He looked to HF, who often heard and saw more, but he shook his head to indicate that he too, had heard nothing. Jim nodded, rose, and ran out into the open.

Up the bank he sprinted, taking it in just a few steps. He was on and then across the road in a heartbeat, and then he was leaping down the slight embankment on the other side. He gained the wood with just a few strides, but he didn't stop there. If he'd attracted any attention, he wouldn't wait by the edge of the wood for it to find him. He ran, weaving through the trees, as fast as he could go.

HF ran behind him. If Jim outdistanced him, HF would let him know. Jim wasn't worried about that though, as HF could hold his own on foot. He'd take a straighter course than Jim, maybe, but he'd follow as well as he knew how.

Jim darted behind a large tree and stopped, panting as he gasped for breath. With his .22 in hand, he took a quick survey of the woods behind. He'd come far enough from the road that it was barely visible in the distance. He saw no movement in any direction, and again a quick glance at HF yielded only a barely perceptible headshake. If a hovercraft was lurking above, or if a hunter was on the ground, HF hadn't detected it either. Jim waited a little longer, then resumed his original pace—a steady walk.

There was always a sense of uncertainty after a crossing, but you couldn't look over your shoulder forever.

By mid-afternoon they had reached the second crossing, and it was a different animal entirely from the first. To reach it, they had moved parallel to some open fields and hills for almost an hour. Eventually they came upon a road and moved parallel to that too, until they came to the gas station and store built at the crossroads. The edge of the wood had crept up behind the property over time until it ran right up to the back of the building, and it was against the back wall of the gas station that Jim leaned as he considered the expanse of open space before him.

There was no point throwing rocks here. He would have to cross the open ground in front of the store to reach the intersection, then move diagonally right across the crossroads, which formed a giant 'X' beneath the open sky from where he was standing. Then there was about a hundred feet of open ground on the other side that he'd have to cross to reach the woods there, but once he did, he was home free.

Crossing at a crossroads was always tricky. In a situation like this, it would save him the double crossing of taking each of the roads that met here separately, which was a plus, but it was a longer crossing than either of them alone would have been. Besides, crossroads like this tended to lure hunters, since the more experienced ones knew how to play the game too.

Jim took a deep breath. The thrill he felt the last time he had pavement under his feet was gone now, replaced by a deeper sense of his vulnerability. He'd be out in the open much longer here than he had been there. Still, he reminded himself how unlikely it was that a hunter would be nearby; almost certainly, he told himself, he'd be out and across with nothing to fear in a matter of moments. Having consoled himself with that thought, he darted out from the side of the building and was on his way.

He pumped his arms and legs furiously; the gas station paving soon gave way to a section of grass and then he was in the intersection. He glanced quickly upward but saw no sign of movement above.

On the other side of the intersection he left the pavement behind for the last time that day. He was in the open field, now, and he ran with all he had in him for the wood and safety. HF motored along beside him, not trailing him as he had before. He wondered if HF also understood how much riskier this crossing was and had sped up, or if he, Jim, was simply not able to move as fast now as he had earlier.

And then, almost at the same time that he felt his body begin to complain that it couldn't keep going at that pace much longer, he entered the wood. As before, he didn't stop, but he did slow as he ran through the trees, deeper and deeper into the relative safety they provided.

This time, when he did stop to check behind him, he stopped for several minutes. He was tired from a day on the march, and he knew that if a hunter had seen him cross and decided the game was on, he didn't have the energy to elude him. That being so, he wanted to wait until he was sure he hadn't been seen before heading in the direction of the Murphys'. No need to risk the Murphy family if he had been spotted.

But again, no evidence presented itself that his movements had been detected, and after perhaps fifteen minutes of rest, he turned his back to the intersection and started forward. He was less than an hour from the Murphys', and barring some unforeseen setback, Jim was confident he'd be there well before dark.

The setback didn't come, and not long after he'd spotted the Murphys' house up ahead in the wood, he heard the sound of the twins playing. The boys were ten and full of energy, so it came as no surprise that they let out whoops that would have woken the dead when they saw him and HF approaching.

"Hey there Jim!" one of them shouted as the whoops died down.

"Hey there HF!" the other added.

"Howdy boys," HF said enthusiastically. The Murphys loved Jim and HF, and the twins especially treated them like royalty. "Glad to see you're still full of fun and fight."

Mr. Murphy poked his head out from the other side of the house, smiled, and started toward them, still carrying the split-ter he'd been using to add to their store of firewood. Closer by, the screen door bounced open and Mrs. Murphy and Sarah came out from inside. Mrs. Murphy was drying her hands on a towel and Sarah had a book clasped in her hands, but both smiled that same warm smile that, at least on Sarah, made Jim's cheeks hot and his knees weak.

"Jim, what a surprise," Mrs. Murphy said as she threw her arms around him.

"Hi, Mrs. Murphy," Jim said as he hugged her, and then he added with a slightly awkward wave at Sarah, "Hi, Sarah."

"Hey, Jim," Sarah said, returning the awkward wave.

"Where's Atticus?" Mr. Murphy said, as he approached the huddle, wiping the sweat from his forehead with his sleeve.

He already knew he would have to explain, and yet the question caught Jim off guard. "He was sick with a fever, for a long time," Jim started, stumbling over his words. "And then, two nights ago, he just…"

"Oh, Jim," Mrs. Murphy said, covering her mouth with a hand. The smiles had slipped off the rest of their faces too. Sarah, looked away, tears brimming in her eyes, and Mr. Murphy let the splitter slide to the ground and stared down at the heavy head where it rested.

Mrs. Murphy put her arms around him again, holding him close. "I'm so sorry."

Jim hugged her back, and for a long time, neither let go.

# The Murphys

Eventually, Mr. Murphy went back to splitting wood, and Mrs. Murphy and Sarah went inside to finish getting dinner ready. Mrs. Murphy apologized profusely that they had nothing but biscuits and gravy for dinner, but Jim insisted that biscuits sounded great to him. This wasn't exactly true, as he'd eaten nothing but cold biscuits all day, but it was true that dinner with the Murphys sounded good, no matter what they were eating. He didn't feel too bad about the partial lie.

In the meantime, he sat down on the wooden bench by the front door and watched the twins as they demonstrated how far they could each throw the heavy rock they'd unearthed earlier that day. When they had sufficiently impressed him, they regaled him with a story celebrating the triumph of Edgar over a black snake.

Edgar was their beagle, and apparently it had been engaged just a week before in an epic battle with a black snake of remarkable proportions and won. The twins were on the verge of running inside to bring the skin out to show Jim, despite Mrs. Murphy's clear instruction that they "remain outside" after their last noisy intrusion into the house, when Jim reassured them that he'd be delighted to examine it after supper. This struck them as a reasonable compromise, so they moved on to their next diversion, asking Jim and HF if they liked to box. They were pretty disappointed that neither one was eager for a bout, so they decided to box each other until dinner was ready.

At last they were called to the table, and Jim ate hungrily. Mrs. Murphy surprised them all by serving up the last of the salted pork—their sow Sadie had died the previous summer. There wasn't much left and once divided six ways, it didn't make but a few mouthfuls each, but the more Jim protested that he felt like he was taking food out of their children's mouths, the more all five Murphys insisted that he partake. In the end, one of the twins told him that he'd sock Jim in the face if he didn't shut up and eat, so Jim decided to dig right in.

When supper was over and the twins had been put to bed in the loft, Jim and HF joined the Murphys around the fire downstairs. Mr. Murphy was smoking his pipe while Mrs. Murphy was mending the knee on a pair of pants belonging to one of the twins. Sarah still had her book at hand, but Jim hadn't noticed her turning many pages, so he suspected she wasn't too attached to her reading just then. When he and HF took their seats among them, each of the Murphys looked over and smiled, as though to formally welcome them to their familial circle.

Mrs. Murphy set her work in her lap and looked at Jim. "I keep wishing we had come across at Christmas like we planned to at Thanksgiving."

"Atticus would have been mad if you'd tried," Jim said, shaking his head. "Six inches of snow most places and more in the drifts. He'd have wondered what had become of your common sense."

"Probably," Mr. Murphy said around his pipe stem.

"Still," Mrs. Murphy said, looking as if she didn't know exactly what it was she wanted to say. "You always think there's next time, but one day there isn't."

"It wouldn't have changed anything," Jim said, staring into the fire. "The fever'd still have come."

"I know," Mrs. Murphy said tenderly. "I guess I just wish I'd been able to say good-bye."

Jim looked at her and smiled. He wanted to reassure her, to show her that he appreciated the fact that she was trying to comfort him. He didn't feel comforted, but he did appreciate her trying. More than that, even, he appreciated not being alone at the cabin with HF.

The subject of Atticus' death seemed to linger even though they didn't discuss it further, and anxious to move on, Jim decided he might as well get on to the reason for his coming. "Atticus told me we should come to you all for help."

"Of course," Mrs. Murphy said, as though the thought of anything else would have been absurd.

Mr. Murphy, who'd been watching Jim carefully, got right to the point. "Help with anything in particular, Jim?"

Leaning forward as he turned to Mr. Murphy, Jim said, "Ever heard of a place called Florence, or know where I could find it?"

"Florence?" Mr. Murphy said. "Wasn't there a Florence in South Carolina?"

"I don't know," Jim said. He wasn't much on geography, but he knew South Carolina was another state, somewhere out in the east, he thought, and probably not what Atticus was talking about.

"Hmm," Mr. Murphy said, while Mrs. Murphy looked up from her sewing just long enough to repeat the word "Florence" and look bewildered. While they racked their brains, Jim noticed that Sarah had given up all pretense of reading and was just watching and listening to the conversation. When she saw Jim look over, she smiled shyly, and Jim almost didn't hear Mr.

Murphy when he said, "I can't think of a place called Florence around here. Why do you ask, Jim?"

"Atticus asked me to find it," Jim said, regaining his composure once he'd turned back to the elder Murphys. "He also told me to go to the Caretaker."

"The Caretaker!"

The exclamation had come from the loft behind them, and Mrs. Murphy moved quickly and decisively to let the twins know in no uncertain terms that they'd been put to bed and were to go to sleep, immediately. They assured her that they would, but Jim was skeptical of their sincerity. Fortunately, he had nothing to say that couldn't be said in front of any of them, so he didn't mind too much if the twins eavesdropped from the loft. He would have if he were them.

When the twins had been attended to, Mr. Murphy got back to the subject at hand. He glanced over at HF, sitting quietly beside Jim, his legs rocking back and forth, then turned back to Jim. "Atticus told you two to go to the Caretaker?"

"And to find Florence."

"Find Florence and go to the Caretaker," Mr. Murphy repeated, looking quizzically at Jim. "Well, I can tell you how to find the Caretaker, but I don't know what that has to do with any place called Florence. He's downriver, at the place that serves as the regional hub for Vista Corp."

Mrs. Murphy was now paying her sewing as much attention as Sarah was her book, which was none. She looked at her husband, concern on her face. "Are you sure he's still there? He'd have to be pretty old by now."

"I'm not sure of anything," Mr. Murphy said with a shrug. "But I'd guess that was what Atticus meant me to tell Jim when he sent him to us for help. It was Atticus who told me he was there in the first place. Didn't Atticus tell you this himself?"

"He was pretty weak at the end," Jim said. "He didn't have the strength to say much."

No one said anything for a while, and Jim thought maybe that was all there was to say. "Well, at least we know what direction to head out tomorrow. South it is, right HF?"

"Sure, Jim," HF said. "South it is."

"You two planning to walk there," Mr. Murphy said. "Just like that?"

"Well," Jim said, shrugging his shoulders, "I guess. Once I figure out a way across the river and we get off the island—"

"Island," Mr. Murphy scoffed.

"Frank," Mrs. Murphy said warningly with a sideways glance at her husband.

"I know Atticus always said—"

"It doesn't matter if this is an island or a peninsula," Mrs. Murphy said, unusually insistent. "Not tonight."

Turning back to Jim, finally, Mr. Murphy added, perhaps a little sheepishly. "So which river would you cross in your quest to go downriver, Jim?"

"Either one, I guess," Jim said. He'd never cared much about the running argument Atticus and Murphy had carried on for years, but tonight he felt a strong urge to defend Atticus. Still, he didn't want Mrs. Murphy mad at him, so he dropped it. "Either way, the rivers meet up and head south together. Whichever one we cross, it'll take us south just the same, won't it?"

"Sure," Mr. Murphy said. "But if you boys cross the Illinois— the river on our side of 'the Island'—then you'll be on the east bank when it joins the Mississippi. If you go back across to your side, then it will be the Mississippi that you're crossing, and you'll be on the west side."

"Does it matter?" Jim said, thinking all the while that Mr. Murphy should just go ahead and say whatever it was he obviously wanted to say. Unfortunately, adults didn't always work like that. They sometimes felt the need to "lead you to it." Atticus had done that a lot too.

"Well, the regional hub for Vista Corp.—the last known whereabouts of the Caretaker—is on the western side of the Mississippi, so I think if you decide to go by foot, that it would matter a lot.

"OK," Jim said, patiently. "I can cross back over to my side of the island and cross there."

"I don't think you should try to walk it," Mr. Murphy said after sitting and shaking his head silently for a while. "Before it was the regional hub for Vista, the area you'd be walking to was a pretty big city. Even if you could cross the river safely, it would take you a long time to walk it, and with all those buildings and the relative lack of cover, there'd be danger from packs and hunters."

"So what do you think they should do?" Mrs. Murphy asked, and Jim was glad somebody else wanted him to come to his point.

"Go by river," Mr. Murphy said.

"By river?" HF said. "I ain't much of a swimmer, Mr. Murphy."

Murphy smiled at HF. "I didn't mean you'd swim. I meant we could make a raft, and you two could float to the Caretaker."

"Wouldn't the river be just as dangerous?" This was the first thing Sarah had said, and for a moment, the other three just looked at her, and then Mr. Murphy, looking happy to have the chance to expand on the wisdom of his suggestion, took the objection up.

"It's all about how many nights he has to spend in the open," he said. "Once the raft is built and in the river, it'll take far less time for him to float there than it would take him to walk there, and that's the key."

"I don't have a raft," Jim said, unsure if he should interrupt Mr. Murphy with this statement of the obvious.

"We'll make one, my boy," Mr. Murphy said with a grin. "At the lodge."

This time the look Mrs. Murphy gave Mr. Murphy was searching indeed, and for a long moment, they just looked at each other, and Sarah and Jim watched the silent exchange. After what felt like a long time, Mrs. Murphy said. "Can't you build it here, Frank?"

Mr. Murphy answered, still looking at Mrs. Murphy. "We're more than four miles from the river here, most of it difficult and densely wooded ground. At the lodge, we'd be less than a hundred yards from the riverbank."

Mrs. Murphy didn't say anything, but the look on her face said she still wasn't at all pleased. Mr. Murphy continued. "It's the best way. There are plenty of fallen trees there, and the big room of the lodge will be a perfect place to do most of the work out of sight of any watchful eyes."

Mr. Murphy finished, and still he and Mrs. Murphy kept their eyes locked on one another. After a moment, Mrs. Murphy gave a slight nod, and Jim knew the matter was decided. It was Mrs. Murphy who spoke next. "How much time will you need?"

"Not sure," he said. "At least a few days, maybe a week. If Jim and HF can give me a hand tomorrow, we'll set you up right and proper, then we'll head out the day after next. That soon enough for you, Jim?"

For the first time in what felt like ages, Mr. Murphy was looking at him. Jim nodded, gratefully. "Sounds fine to me. I'd be glad to help you with whatever you need."

"Sure we will," HF said.

"But you don't have to put yourself out so much for us," Jim said.

Mrs. Murphy responded quickly and strongly. "Nonsense, Jim. Atticus sent you to us for help. We'll do whatever we can."

"Well, we appreciate that," Jim said.

"The timing should be pretty good," Mr. Murphy said after a moment's reflection. "The moon's waning now, but it should be pretty new when you head out. Not so bright you'll be easily seen, but bright enough to give you some visibility on the river."

"Well," Jim said, "A raft by moonlight it is."

"A raft can't bring you back up river, Jim," Mr. Murphy said, taking the pipe out of his mouth and fixing Jim with a sober look. "So if you're meaning to come back, you'll need to find another way. I can't help you with that."

"That's all right," Jim said. "We'll make our way downriver to the Caretaker, and then work it out from there."

Jim crept up into the loft with the twins when it was bedtime, and HF followed. "Where should I go, Jim?" he asked.

"Just over there in the corner is fine," Jim whispered. "So hush, now, it's time for bed."

The next day there were eggs for breakfast from the Murphys' chickens. He and HF worked hard helping Mr. Murphy with several odds and ends while Mrs. Murphy and Sarah cooked all day to send supplies with them for the time they'd be working on the raft. When night fell again, they didn't linger long by the fire. They meant to head out before dawn.

Sleep didn't come easily, and late in the night, Jim could hear Mr. and Mrs. Murphy talking quietly in their bed below. Mrs. Murphy was saying that she thought they should try to talk Jim out of going, but Mr. Murphy said that he thought "the boy" was old enough to do whatever he thinks he needs to do. It wasn't exactly the same thing as saying Jim could handle himself, but he was grateful Mr. Murphy took his side nonetheless.

Then he heard something that he almost wished he hadn't. It came from Mr. Murphy, who said in a teasing way, "You're just worried he'll decide not to come back, and Sarah will have to marry Stephen Dowling."

Before all the implications of this statement could register with Jim, Mrs. Murphy answered. "Yes, I have my hopes for Sarah and Jim. You can't blame me, can you?"

No answer was immediately forthcoming, and she continued. "The Dowling boy stinks—he's fat and has terrible hygiene. And –" she started, as though coming to a secondary but no less significant point, "I'd much rather my grandbabies look like Jim."

Their conversation drifted on from there as Mrs. Murphy admonished Mr. Murphy to be careful while they were gone, but Jim had lost interest in their exchange. He lay in the dark, no longer thinking about the complications of traveling on a river by raft at night.

Instead, Sarah's shy smile preoccupied him, and he thought maybe he'd miss it just a little.

# The Lodge

If Jim had thought that he and HF would steal away with Mr. Murphy in the wee hours of the morning while the rest of the family slept, he was mistaken. Mrs. Murphy was up before anyone else, making a big breakfast. Sarah soon joined her, and both twins asked for and received permission to go with them "as far as the big stump."

It wasn't long though, before it was just the three of them, navigating the wood by the waning moonlight. Jim and Mr. Murphy carried the canoe overhead and HF pulled a small board that had their supplies and a selection of tools on it by means of a rope handle. In less than an hour, they'd reach the bank of the Illinois River, and though it was fairly light, Jim was glad to set the canoe down.

"I wish I could just let you take the canoe," Murphy said. "But you wouldn't be able to get it back upriver, and I need it."

"It's all right, Mr. Murphy," Jim said. "I'm sure a raft will be just fine."

Murphy handed him an oar and said, "You'll be up front. Stay low as you go forward. Hold the gunwales as necessary, but try not to rock side to side too much."

Jim stepped in, crouching over, then made his way up to the front of the canoe. He knelt there with one knee on either side of the keel, but pretty close together. He set the paddle down on the bottom beside him and turned to watch as HF got in and came up pretty close behind so there'd be room for Murphy to pack their stuff in the broad middle.

"If I tumble out into the river," HF said, "will you come get me, Jim?"

"You won't fall out," Jim said, giving HF a reassuring look. HF didn't answer, but sat clutching the sides of the canoe.

When they were ready to embark, Murphy gave some instructions. "I'll push us out and then get in, Jim. When I tell you, paddle on the right. I'll steer. Just paddle on the right unless I tell you to stop."

"Got it," Jim said.

"When the current gets us, you'll know. Keep paddling and listen for my direction."

Jim raised his hand and gave Murphy the thumbs up, and when he'd turned back around to face the river, he felt the canoe lurch forward and then glide smoothly out into the water. It rocked back and forth as Murphy got in, but not as much as Jim expected. He could hear HF muttering something behind him, but Jim couldn't hear what he was saying. Soon he was being directed to paddle, so he raised his oar and started to pull with long, even strokes.

They moved on an angle away from shore, heading downriver. As they moved closer to the outskirts of the current, it felt like there was some resistance to their continued progress, and Jim could feel Mr. Murphy's stroke become quicker and harder. He picked up his pace too, and soon they seemed to break through into the current and were now being swept downstream far more rapidly.

"Keep going, Jim," came the encouragement from behind, and so he kept going. They were almost in the middle of the river now, but they were still angling left across the current. After a few more minutes, they seemed to slip out of its central pull, and the going got both easier and slower.

"Go ahead and take a break, and I'll paddle from here," Murphy said. Jim was glad for the rest. He slipped the oar out of the water and held it across his lap where it lay, dripping on his knees.

Murphy brought the canoe around so it was no longer moving on an angle. Instead it was headed more or less downriver, parallel to the eastern shore, which Jim could see was pretty close on the left. Jim could also see the big road that ran next to the river, and he wondered how far above the lodge they actually were. On the other side of the road here were only trees running up a hill.

From time to time, Murphy used his paddle to slow the canoe, but he didn't take them any closer to the shore, not yet. Jim figured he was either looking for some sign that the lodge was near, or perhaps he was surveying the shore for a place where he could put in and hide the canoe. Jim didn't mind either way. Though it was getting lighter, he thought they probably had a good half hour before the sun would come up. They had time before they needed to be off the river and under cover.

Up ahead, the trees on the hill beyond the road began to thin, and then Jim saw it—a huge timber building with lots and lots of glass windows, up the hill, commanding an impressive vista overlooking the river. So this is the lodge, he thought, and he took it in.

The canoe slowed and Murphy paddled them to shore directly. Near the river's edge were lots of overgrown, reedy bushes, and hiding the canoe was surprisingly easy. Soon they were loaded up and on their way.

The approach to the lodge made quite an impression on Jim. First there was the big road, running north and south almost right on the river's edge. Here it was wide enough for two cars to travel side by side, but he knew that not much further south, it became wide enough that four could have fit. Beyond the big road, though, was the long sloping hill of tall grass, bent over in the morning breeze, running up to the front of the lodge. Behind it, a great wood spread out as far as Jim could see.

One thing that Jim hadn't expected, were all the smaller, ancillary buildings. There was a kind of open pavilion, straight down from the lodge by the water, but even up the hill, surrounding the place, were maybe a dozen or more smaller out buildings beneath the tall trees. When Jim asked Murphy about then, he said they were cabins with identical floor plans inside, which, he presumed, people once rented if they wanted more privacy than the main building of the lodge afforded.

They followed the smaller private drive that headed up the hill toward the lodge. It ran around behind the large building and past the main entrance in the back to a large open area of cracked pavement. A big ancient truck sat rusted on the edge of it. Atticus had told Jim that in some places, groundlings had figured out how to fix up some of the these old vehicles so that they ran again, but Jim didn't figure that this one would ever budge from here, unless some act of God brought a flood of spectacular proportions down this river and swept it away.

Murphy led Jim and HF up to the front door—or really, the doorway, since there was no door there. Even with the approach of dawn, it looked very dark inside. Some hesitant light penetrated the entryway but seemed to hang shyly there; deeper in the room an eerie gloom prevailed. Murphy pulled a flashlight from the supplies he had packed, and Jim retrieved his. They stepped inside.

Jim felt the hairs stand up on his neck as they went in. It was such a big building, and he knew anyone or almost anything could have made a home inside it over the long years of its disuse. He trusted Murphy and intended to follow him wherever he went, but he thought maybe he should slip his .22 from where it hung on his shoulder into his hands.

As though sensing his apprehension, Murphy looked back, smiled broadly, and said, "Stay close, Jim."

Beyond the entrance hallway, a handful of wide stairs went down into a large open room. Other hallways led out of this room in several directions, but straight ahead were the great big windows that faced the river and already some light was coming in through those. So, despite its great size, this room was a bit brighter than the hall through which they'd entered. It smelled musty, but Jim couldn't see or smell anything that indicated the presence of any large animals.

Murphy led them over to the far side of the room, and they set their stuff down in a corner, next to but not directly in front of where the windows were. Murphy stood against the solid wall as he peered out the window, then he turned to Jim and HF. "I suggest we stretch out here and get some sleep. When the sun is higher in a few hours, there'll be enough light for me to give you the tour."

Jim glanced around the room again at all the different passageways heading out from this central place, and he wondered how far they extended. This room was very large, but the building as viewed from the outside was considerably larger.

"Most of the lodge has windows on this western wall," Murphy continued, "so we shouldn't need to drain our flashlight batteries too much."

"Sounds like a plan," Jim agreed, and he stretched out on the smooth wooden floor. He lay there thinking that it might not be wise for both him and Murphy to sleep, but as he drifted off, he reassured himself that at least HF was there, as alert as ever.

When he woke, he could see from the bright sunlight pouring in through the windows that at least a few hours had passed. Jim left Murphy snoring softly in the corner and went for a walk around the room to stretch his legs. HF followed him as he made his circuit. There was a huge fireplace surrounded by stone masonry at one end, and it looked like all kinds of things had been burned there over the years, including some of the wooden furniture in the style of the few remaining pieces left in the room.

Nothing else seemed worthy of note, except for a large square board, maybe ten feet by ten feet, lying on the floor and painted in black and white checkerboard fashion. It looked for all the world like a chess or checkerboard, and when Jim counted, sure enough there were eight rows with eight squares. Atticus had taught Jim chess when he was a boy, but that had been on a handheld electronic device he'd brought from the hive. When Atticus' last battery for it had died, that had been the end of that, since Atticus said the kind of battery it required wasn't one he had anymore or knew where to find, without leaving the island. He'd talked about making a 'real board,' but he never had. Jim had always envisioned something smaller, but he wondered now if this was what a real board looked like.

"What do you think, HF?"

"What do I think of what, Jim?"

"This place?"

"I think it's pretty big," HF said. "You could fit the whole cabin in this room."

Jim nodded. "I think maybe you could."

With little else to see in the big room and eager to explore, Jim woke Murphy and before long they'd set out on their expedition. Murphy took them first to see the large rooms on the ground floor in the northwest side of the lodge. One had obviously been a restaurant, for the kitchen ran along its northern wall, and the others had been banquet rooms, Murphy said, reserved for big occasions—weddings and the like.

Off the southern side of the main hall on the ground floor ran a corridor that had some supply closets, a place called a "Game Room" and another called a "Laundry," but Jim didn't recognize any of the games and the laundry machines were huge, like nothing he'd ever seen before. Jim found one other room on that hall fascinating. It was a big room with a huge concrete hole dominating the middle, labeled "Pool." Jim had heard of places in the hives where people gathered to swim, but having lived as a groundling his whole life, he'd only ever gone swimming in creeks, rivers and lakes.

He tried to imagine this pool full of water, but it was hard to do, as lots of broken plastic furniture had been thrown into it. What's more, the furniture was half covered with old, moldering leaves which Jim figured had blown in through one of the large paned windows on the western wall that had been broken and almost entirely lost somewhere along the way.

Most of the rest of the lodge consisted of the guest rooms. The interior halls that led to these rooms were the scariest places in the lodge. Unless the doors along the hall were propped open and the curtains on the big windows pulled back, the halls were very dark and stank from a lack of fresh air. Jim asked Murphy if they could leave the doors and curtains open, and Murphy didn't see why not. So, as they explored, Jim left a trail of open doors behind him, and he found the slightly less gloomy halls on the way back somewhat encouraging.

When they were back in the main hall at last, Jim said, "I would have liked to see this place when it was alive, you know, with people and light and stuff."

"Me too," Murphy replied. "Maybe, one day, it will live again."

# Distant Rumble

They ate a quick, light lunch, intent on rationing their supplies since they weren't really sure how long the raft building would take. Afterward, Murphy led them back to the main doorway, where they hung in the shadows for a few minutes, watching the skies.

"There's nothing for it, Jim," Murphy said, "we're going to be a little exposed today. Keep the .22 handy."

Jim nodded and then followed as Murphy jogged across the open space beyond the doorway toward the wood where the smaller cabins were sprinkled. Once under cover again, he slowed and explained what they were looking for—downed trees of a certain diameter, from which the raft would be built.

They spent the better part of the afternoon examining trees, and after they'd covered a lot of ground and looked at a lot of trees, they went back through and Murphy marked a dozen of them with a piece of white chalk he had in his pocket.

"We'll start with the one farthest from the lodge," Murphy said, as he led Jim and HF back through the wood toward it. "It'll be good for us, psychologically. We'll feel like we're rolling downhill at the end of the day."

Jim wasn't sure about that. It seemed to him unnecessary to wear themselves out on the hardest part of the job, right up front. And yet, when they'd cut the first log to length and dragged it as far as the edge of the wood, where they were to leave it until dark, he had to admit it felt good to know that none of the others would need to go so far. He found himself almost jogging as he moved out ahead of the others, leading the way to the tree that was second farthest away.

The slight euphoria couldn't last. Even with HF helping, it was heavy, hard work. A number of times, they had to take the bow saw and work some of the bigger limbs off to lighten the load and make the tree navigable through the wood. That was a break of sorts, but hard work too in its own right. Jim took his fair share of turns, knowing this was to be his raft and wanting Murphy to know he could do a man's job and work a man's day.

At last, with the sun already sinking below the horizon in the western sky, they sat on the twelfth tree, which lay with the others, just opposite the lodge. They waited, bodies weary, for the cover of dark to finish the job, and Murphy told stories of conversations he'd had with Atticus over the years. Jim knew some, but not all of them, and he laughed sometimes at the way Murphy described things. Whenever the laughter stopped, though, he ached. It was a deeper ache than the ache of fatigue that throbbed throughout the rest of his body.

When it was fully dark, they rose, took the first tree, and dragged it across to a long, narrow, grassy lane in front of the lodge. The plan was to cut them down enough to get them through the front door, then move them inside to the main hall where they could finish dressing the logs out of sight, using the bow saw, an adze, and a planer.

They wouldn't be able to complete the raft inside, of course, since they'd never get it out again if they did; there weren't any doors at the lodge that big. But Murphy felt that they could attach them in pairs so they could still be moved through the door at the back of the main hall, and then move them down to the river where he'd do the final job of securing them all together.

"We should set up and get started," Murphy said after they had moved the last tree, "but I'm beat. I think we'll just have to get up before dawn and have a go."

"That's all right by me," Jim said. He was weary too, and their small lunch hadn't quite kept the hunger pangs at bay. He was ready for food and sleep.

They went inside the lodge, ate their slightly less meager supper, and curled up in their corner of the main hall on the mattresses they'd dragged down from the guest rooms. Murphy seemed to fall asleep instantly, his light snores beginning right away. Jim turned on his side and saw HF, sitting on the floor by one of the big windows.

HF's face was partially illuminated by the moonlight as he gazed down on the big river, rolling quietly by.

Jim didn't remember falling asleep, but the next thing he knew, Murphy was shaking him awake. "I'm going to need your help."

Jim rose quietly, and he and HF followed Murphy to where they'd set the logs out front. Murphy explained what he wanted, and both Jim and HF got to work with a pair of handsaws, taking the smaller limbs off the logs. Murphy set to work on another tree, not far away.

When they finished working on the sixth tree, Murphy suggested they take a break. They sat inside the lodge, in the dark hall, eating, and then headed back outside.

"We won't be able to get them all done this morning," Murphy said. "But that's all right; I'll have plenty to do today with just these. Let's get them inside."

So they did, and before long, Jim was looking down at the six logs lying on the floor of the main hall. Even though this room and the lodge retained little of what he imagined had been its former glory, it was an oddly incongruous sight.

He didn't have long to contemplate it, though, for Murphy had a job for him and HF to do outside while he got to work here. He wanted them to scavenge floor planking from some of the smaller cabins, where the boards would be smaller and easier to work with. He thought a smooth surface for the top of the raft would be a much nicer way to travel than the convex and knobby surfaces of the logs.

"As long as we're making a raft, we might as well make it right," he said with a grin as he explained what he wanted the boards for.

"How long do you think it will take to get to the Caretaker?" Jim asked, wondering for the first time since the idea of building the raft had been broached, just how long he would actually be on it.

Murphy paused and thought for a moment. "You probably won't have much darkness left after the launch on the first night. Even so, I'd be surprised if you didn't get to the hub by the third."

Jim looked around at the six logs they'd dragged inside. He thought about the work they'd already done, and about the work they still had to do to get it ready to launch. It seemed strange that all this effort was going into a raft he'd only need for a few days.

"I'm sorry to be so much trouble," Jim said.

Murphy looked at him, his look suggesting something between amusement and puzzlement. "Where'd that come from?"

"This is a lot of work just to get us a few days downriver, isn't it?" Jim said. "We could probably have walked it in the time it'll take for us to make this and for us to use it—and you wouldn't have had to do all this."

"I don't have to do all this," Murphy said. "I want to, Jim. For you and HF. For Atticus."

"I'm grateful, Mr. Murphy," Jim said. "But still, it seems like a lot when we can't even bring the raft back and it'll just end up floating away downriver, or whatever, when we're done with it."

Murphy nodded. He scratched the scruff of his beard, appearing to mull this over. "Jim, when you cross a road, how long do you spend studying it? You know, checking it out, before you cross it?"

"A little while," Jim said, wondering at the change of topic. "Depends on the crossing."

"Do you ever spend more time studying the road than you do actually crossing it?" Murphy asked.

Jim understood. "Every time."

Murphy nodded. "Remember, Jim, time spent preparing wisely is always time well spent. If I could see a safer way for you to do this, and if it took months to prepare and only moments to execute, well, we'd do that and be glad to do it."

And that was the end of that. The rest of that day, and the next, Jim and HF worked out in a few of the cabins, prying up some of the looser floorboards and then stacking them neatly in piles by the edge of the wood.

On the first day, they didn't come back across to the lodge until the sun went down, but on the second day, they finished by late afternoon, and Jim knew there were still a couple of hours of daylight left. So, he sat with HF at the edge of the wood, looking at the lodge and listening to the echo of Murphy and his tools at work coming from within.

"What do you think, HF? Should we go now, or wait?"

"Might be safer in the dark," HF said, "but probably not much safer with all the ruckus he's makin'. A feller would have to be deaf or dimwitted to be anywhere around here and not know something fishy is going on in there."

Jim smiled. HF's hearing was very good. He wondered just how cacophonous the raft building sounded to him.

"Well, in that case," Jim said, "we might as well take these across now and be done with it."

It took three trips, and even though the project began with a lighter spirit after HF's pointed analysis, Jim found himself glad it was over when they were finished. There wasn't anything left in the plan that would require their going outside until time to take the raft pieces down to the riverside.

They entered the main hall and Murphy looked up from where he was working with a welcoming grin. Jim surveyed the state of things there, and he was struck by the fine job Murphy had done of planing the tops of the logs to flat surfaces.

When Murphy finished what he was working on, he walked Jim through the steps that remained. Tomorrow, he would start attaching the logs in pairs and then add a layer of flooring to each pair. Hopefully, if not tomorrow night, then by the night after, they'd be ready to launch.

As they sat contemplating this hopeful prospect, HF stood suddenly and moved to the row of windows on the western wall. Jim was about to ask him what he was doing when he heard a distant rumble echoing in through the open doorway.

Jim's first thought was of thunder, but the clouds he saw through the windows didn't look like rainclouds. And, as the rumbling grew louder, Jim could tell it wasn't thunder. In fact, he could tell that the distant rumble he was hearing wasn't a natural sound at all. It was the sound of a machine, or more likely, many.

All three of them were now at the window, peering anxiously out at the road at the bottom of the hill. The sound seemed to be coming from down the hill, not up in the sky, and from the north. They watched the road in that direction, as far as they could see.

"Motorcycles!" Murphy gasped as a bunch of two-wheeled vehicles rolled into view. Some had single riders, most had two, and more were coming behind them.

They weren't moving very fast, but they were coming at a steady pace. The motorcycle out in front rolled to a stop, and the rider raised his hand and pointed up the hill at the lodge.

Panic and fear crashed over Jim like a wave.

# The Pool

There was movement nearby, and a sound, but Jim seemed to be in a dream he couldn't escape. The strange collection of things Murphy had called motorcycles were still sitting on the main road, their riders looking up at the lodge and talking amongst themselves. Jim was unable to turn away. He stood at the window mumbling quietly, "Keep going, keep going, keep going."

Murphy jerked him away from the window and the spell was broken.

"Listen to me," Murphy said. "We need to move! Grab your .22 and help me get the rest of the tools."

Instinctively, Jim looked around for his pack first, but HF already had all their packs in hand. So he started gathering the tools that Murphy couldn't get, and soon he was rushing up the stairs to the landing of the hall that had the pool and game room on it. He followed Murphy down that hall, past several closets and rooms and then turned into the laundry.

Murphy pulled open a small round door in the front of a big square machine and started putting in the tools he was carrying. "They won't all fit here. Open that one."

Jim looked at the other big square machine Murphy had nodded toward, saw that it had a similar door, and soon he had put the tools he was holding in it.

When they'd shut the doors on their tool stashes, Murphy grabbed his pack from HF and started, still at a quick pace, back toward the main hall. "If they haven't started up the drive yet, we may be able to go out the main door and angle south-east up into the woods."

"If they have?" Jim asked.

"Working on that," Murphy said, then made a sign to be quiet as he stopped where the corridor emptied out into the main hall.

Jim listened, too. The motorcycles were rolling again, and the sound seemed to be coming closer. They hadn't gone on down the big road. They were coming up the drive to the lodge.

"Too late," Murphy said turning back down the hall toward the laundry. "They're coming."

Murphy ran quietly back down the hall, past all the rooms they'd just passed the first time, but this time past the laundry, too. He hesitated for a moment outside the pool, then ducked in through that door.

"Are we going out through the broken window?" Jim asked as they jogged beside the pool toward the windows on the far wall.

Murphy hovered there for a moment, alternating between looking back nervously at the door that led to the hallway and gazing out the window and craning his neck to see the private drive on the north.

"I don't see them," he said quietly, "but there are so many windows ... so much glass."

Now it was Jim's turn to look nervously back at the door. The people on the motorcycles had to have reached the door to the lodge by now. Even if they hesitated for a little while before coming in, how long could that "little while" last?

Murphy suddenly started away from the windows and across the concrete deck toward the side of the pool. "Come on, down here."

He turned toward Jim and started backing down a metal ladder into the pool. Jim rushed forward and stood at the edge, looking down at him. "What are you doing? We'll be trapped."

Murphy looked up, put his finger to his lips and stared Jim down. He took the finger he'd used to silently shoosh him and pointed adamantly toward the bottom of the pool, where he stood with his feet buried in leaves. Then he pointed at the debris in the middle of the pool, and Jim thought he understood.

He handed down the .22 and then went down that ladder in a hurry, and HF came right down after. Soon, he and HF were burrowing under the broken pieces of plastic furniture, and Murphy was moving leaves up over them. Then Murphy himself slid under a long plastic piece and started gathering what leaves he could reach to cover himself. Jim could see it wasn't a great job, but he wasn't sure how Murphy could both get under the leaves and cover himself at the same time and it work very well.

The next thing Jim knew, HF was sliding out from under the debris that covered him. "HF!" Jim called in an urgent whisper.

HF leaned over, his face close to both Murphy and Jim. "I can cover ya'll lickety split and then climb out. I'll play dead—they won't pay me no nevermind."

Jim made like he was going to reply, and Murphy reached over and covered Jim's mouth as he nodded to HF. The next thing Jim knew, leaves were flying over both of them, and the sound of light steps going up the ladder echoed in the pool. Then there was silence—a terrible, lingering silence.

Jim didn't know how long the silence lasted, but it wasn't long. Voices sounded out nearby, and some of them moved closer down the hall. He couldn't hear what they were saying, but the mood seemed jovial. At last, some of those voices became distinguishable from each other, and about the same time, Jim could hear footsteps enter the room.

They were heavy footsteps, and through the cracks of light left by the leaves and broken furniture, Jim thought he could see black boots on the side of the pool. The feet turned, and Jim thought for a moment that the person attached to them was going to leave, but they stopped and a man's voice called out, "Jackson! Come here!"

Another set of heavy steps sounded in the room, and Jim could see the toes of more boots come to a stop by the pool. A gruff voice asked, "What are you yelling about, George?"

"It's a pool," the one called George said.

"Yeah, I can see that," Jackson replied. "It ain't much use without water, though, now is it?"

"No," George said, a bit sheepishly. "But I bet it was beautiful once."

Then he added. "Hey Jackson, wouldn't it be something if we could get water up here from the river somehow and fill it up?"

"It would be something," Jackson said, not bothering to hide his exasperation. "Too bad it's impossible."

George didn't have anything to say to this, apparently, and both men were silent. Jim lay as still as he could, hoping fervently that this was the end of any interest in the pool. Then Jackson spoke again.

"Maybe we could fill it up, George."

"How?"

"Well, we could always bring the boys back here tonight after they've been drinking and fill it another way."

George laughed at Jackson's joke, and Jim felt his hope rising that the natural step after this would be an exit from the room for continued exploring. Maybe they'd go away. Maybe they wouldn't even notice HF playing dead.

"What's that?"

"What's what, Jackson?"

"Over there, at the broken window … "

Jim's heart sank as Jackson's voice trailed off. His heart thumped as he waited beneath the debris, holding onto the .22 with sweaty hands, feeling trapped and helpless. Murphy, as though sensing his mounting anxiety, grabbed his arm and clasped it hard. Jim lay still, in agony.

He heard the men walking, their footsteps echoing on the pool deck as they moved toward the windows and out of Jim's view. The footsteps stopped and Jim strained to hear anything that might indicate what was happening.

"It's a little boy," George said. "He looks dead."

Jim swallowed, and though it was cool in the room with the open window, beads of sweat rolled down his forehead. He could imagine HF sprawled on the ground, protruding out of the broken window.

"Well now," Jackson said, and then he murmured something Jim could not hear. He spoke again, this time louder. "I'm not so sure, George. I think we should take this little guy out and show Joe. Maybe we can play the bonfire game tonight."

"Oh, Jackson," George said, irrepressible joy in his voice. "Wouldn't that be something? It's been too long since we've played the bonfire game."

The men rose, and Jim both heard their footsteps and saw their feet as they left the room. The silence returned, and still Murphy clasped his arm, though some of the urgency had left his grip. Jim didn't dare move.

Where was HF, and what had he done?

# The Waiting

The next few hours were some of the longest in Jim's life. He dared not move or speak, but quiet tears slipped down his eyes as he fought with all his strength to avoid sobbing. They had taken HF with them out of the room. He hadn't seen them do it, but he knew they had.

As they waited for night and for darkness, Jim had little to occupy his mind except fear and self-recrimination. It had happened so fast, all of it, but he had let HF get up out of the leaves, cover them, and go lie by the window. Atticus had told him to take care of HF, and yet he'd let him go. He hadn't known what else to do, and he had been afraid, but he shouldn't have let him go.

And Jim knew that it might all be in vain anyway. There was no guarantee that the pack wouldn't come back and find him and Murphy. He could only imagine what had been found by them already and how strongly it suggested that people had recently been in the lodge.

The sunlight began to slip from the room, and at last it disappeared. Still Murphy didn't move or speak, and neither did he. The pack roamed the lodge, the different members moving up and down the hallway—both men and women, for now he could hear female voices, too—sometimes coming into the pool area and sometimes just going past.

Fortunately, the pool seemed never to get another look, but that didn't mean that Jim didn't feel the panic rise when the voices would come near in the hallway. The darkness deepened, and Jim's tears dried. He felt numb, lying beneath the debris, quietly panicked that HF was lost forever.

Much, much later, when it had been dark for some time and there had been no noise for hours from the hallway or anywhere else in the lodge as far as they could tell, Murphy finally started to extricate himself from the debris and the leaves. Jim followed without needing to be asked, and they climbed quietly out of the pool.

Moving toward the broken window, Jim reached forward and grabbed Murphy's sleeve.

Murphy stopped and turned, and Jim leaned in until his mouth was right by Murphy's head. "I smell smoke. Lots of it."

Murphy nodded. "Me too. They're probably using the big fireplace. C'mon."

Jim tightened his grip on Murphy's sleeve, but he couldn't think of the words. He knew they couldn't go back into the lodge, but he couldn't bear leaving HF either.

Murphy reached down and pried Jim's fingers off. His voice was soft but strong and clear. "We have to go."

They slipped out the window, and staying close to the building, moved south away from the main hall. The plentiful moonlight, which Jim had counted a blessing a few nights ago, was now a curse. He felt completely exposed as he jogged behind Murphy.

Still, if any of the men and women who'd come to the lodge were still awake, they must not have been in any position to see Murphy and Jim slipping away, for the alarm was not raised.

When they'd rounded the southern end of the building, Jim followed Murphy as he angled away up the hill toward the wood. They took a long, sweeping arc as they doubled back north through the trees, until they had reached at last the little cabin that was farthest from the lodge itself.

As soon as they were in the cabin, Jim found his voice again and plead for HF. "We can't leave him. We have to go back."

"Jim," Murphy said calmly, "we can't go back in there, not tonight."

"But who knows what they'll do to him," Jim said. "The fire… they could…"

"I know, Jim," Murphy said. "But you know there's nothing we can do about that now. We have to wait, and hope."

"Hope for what?" Jim said, anger mixed with his fear and despair. "What should we hope for? I've lost him! Atticus told me to take care of him, but I've lost him!"

"Jim, there was nothing you could do," Murphy said, trying to calm him down.

Jim plunked down in a rickety chair by a small table. He stared across the room, his eyes fixed on nothing, a vast emptiness inside him and around him. When he spoke at last, his words were numb, like the rest of him. "Atticus told me to take care of him."

Murphy squatted in front of him, putting his hands on both his shoulders and giving him a firm shake. "Jim, you can't blame yourself."

"Who should I blame?"

Murphy didn't answer that. He just squatted in front of Jim, still holding his shoulders. "Don't give up hope. We'll wait, and we'll watch."

"Wait and watch," Jim said, echoing Murphy without enthusiasm.

"Yes. We'll take turns sleeping and watching the lodge," Murphy said. "We've got a pretty good view of the main door from here, but we'll have to slip out into the woods before dawn."

"Why?"

"In case they decide to come out and explore these cabins like they explored the lodge itself—if they haven't already."

"But we'll stay close?" Jim said.

"We'll stay close," Murphy said.

They moved out just before dawn, as planned. Carefully, they made their way through the woods, not up the hill and away from the lodge, but north, along the ridge and parallel to it. Murphy thought that would be the safest move, assuming that the pack's two main choices were either to sit tight or continue on their way south, down the big road.

They found a place, far beyond the last cabin, where they still had a fairly clear view of the motorcycles parked out front. There they sat and waited.

No one stirred within the lodge, at least not that they could see. They saw nothing of the pack, and nothing of HF. The sun came up, but the air remained cold. Jim shivered, wondering where the recent warmer weather had gone.

Finally, in the early afternoon, there was some activity near the bikes. People came in and out of the lodge, but any hope that they were leaving was dashed when they never even started one, and all of them disappeared back inside.

And still, no sign of HF.

The sun went down and the moon rose, and Murphy led Jim back to the cabin. They sat in the dark, both keeping one eye on the lodge, eating their supper. Neither spoke, as a general gloom had descended over them. Jim didn't want to talk, didn't want to think, didn't want to do anything.

Jim noticed that as the evening wore on, his left ear began to hurt. In fact, it started hurting a lot, throbbing and aching. Murphy saw him wincing and covering the ear with his hand and asked to look at it.

"I don't think it's frostbite," Murphy said, shaking his head, "but I guess it could be. Either way, I'm sorry, Jim, I don't have anything to help with the pain."

Jim, like most groundlings, knew what frostbite could do, but he felt angry more than afraid. "Stupid pack," he said. "Why don't they just move on? What do they want with the lodge? There's nothing there anyone would want."

"I don't know, Jim," Murphy said. "Try to sleep. I'll take the first watch."

But as Jim lay down, his throbbing ear made sleep impossible. He couldn't lie on that side, as even the lightest pressure on his ear made the pain unbearable. And, stuck with only the other side, he couldn't shift around enough to get comfortable. As the night wore on, the throbbing continued, and finally everything became too much—losing Atticus, leaving home, the pack taking HF, his aching ear. He started suddenly to cry.

He gnashed his teeth, struggling to restrain the tears as he had in the pool, but this time they burst through his resistance, coming in quiet gasps as he lay there in the dark. Murphy slipped in from the other room and sat on the edge of the bed. He reached down and placed his big hand on Jim's forehead, like Atticus used to do when checking for signs of a fever. "It's all right, Jim," he said gently. "Hush now. Take a deep breath. We'll get him back. Just breathe."

Jim tried to take that breath, to get his tears under control. He couldn't at first, but Murphy sat with him, whispering quietly, encouraging him to try, to breathe, to relax. Soon he wasn't crying anymore, and he found that he could breathe after all.

He closed his eyes, kept focusing on his breathing, and tried to ignore his aching ear. Murphy stayed with him, and before long, he was asleep.

When he awoke the next morning, he sat up in bed and stared at the large patch of bright sunlight on the floor of the cabin. He was sure Murphy had meant to leave before dawn again, and it was obviously much later. He started out of bed, still a little shaky from having just woken up. When he stepped through the door into the main room of the cabin, Murphy signaled to him to be quiet and come to the window in the kitchen.

There he saw what looked to be the whole pack milling around their motorcycles. Soon, they started to get on the bikes, and then the quiet morning was filled with the sound of many motors starting up. It was not the distant rumbling he'd heard two days before, but a loud and thunderous sound as the engines revved louder and louder.

Jim leaned in to Murphy. "Have you seen him? Did they bring him out?"

Murphy shook his head. "I don't think so."

A few of the motorcycles started rolling. One of them pulled out into the parking lot beside the lodge and made a complete circle before coming back to a stop with the others beside the lodge. A few of the others started moving in circles and figure eights in the open space, and then the lone rider who had led the way up to the lodge in the first place, pulled out and started riding back down the private drive.

Jim knew as he watched that this must be the one they'd called Joe. He examined Joe and his bike as carefully as he could from where he was watching, and he saw nothing that looked like it could be HF. Was he still inside? And was he all right?

He could hardly wait for the pack to get back down to the main road. Eventually they did, turning left and continuing on their way south. No sooner had the sound of the motorcycles died down in the distance than he said to Murphy, "I'm going across to the lodge."

Murphy caught his arm and held fast. "You're staying here with me."

Jim looked at Murphy liked the man had punched him in the gut. "Why? I have to find him!"

"We'll go after dark."

"What?" Jim scoffed. "That's crazy. It's only midmorning. I'm not waiting all day. I have to get in there!"

Jim started to move away but Murphy held fast. "You're staying with me."

Anger boiled in Jim. Being cautious about moving out in the open was all well and good under normal circumstances, but surely Murphy wasn't going to keep him here all day just because he'd have to cross through a bit of open ground to reach the lodge?

"Look—" Jim started, but he never got any further.

"You're not going anywhere yet," Murphy said, his grip on Jim's arm tightening. "Not until we're sure they're not coming back."

"Why would they come back?" Jim protested. He jerked his arm free but didn't move from where he stood.

"What if they forgot something?" Murphy said, then shrugged, throwing his hands up. "I don't know, Jim. Why'd they come in the first place? Why'd they stay so long? How can we know? Maybe they're setting a trap. You heard them. They knew someone had been here."

"They didn't know."

"Still—"

"That's paranoid," Jim cut in, before Murphy could get going again. "We have to look for HF!"

"Jim," Murphy said. "Stop it. I know how worried you are, but he's not your brother."

"That's not the point—"

"Whatever we're going to find in there, will still be there later."

Jim crossed his arms and looked away. He knew Murphy was right. Whatever the situation was with HF, a few hours was unlikely to change it.

"Jim," Murphy said after a moment, his tone softer. "They're probably all gone, but I'd feel a whole lot better if we just waited and watched. Will you do that for me, Jim?"

Jim relented, nodding. Murphy was here, away from his family, helping him. He could wait to go back in, if that was what Murphy wanted.

"How's your ear, anyway?" Murphy asked.

"Better," Jim said, trying not to sound sulky, then turned back to the window as he settled in for the waiting.

When night came, they stole back through the woods and across to the front door. They had agreed not to use flashlights. If anyone was left behind, it would only alert them to their presence. Instead, they slipped in on tip-toes, hung close to the interior walls and let the moonlight streaming in from the western wall show them the lay of the land in the main hall.

What it showed stopped them in their tracks. Silhouetted by the faint light of the silvery moon was HF's solitary figure, hanging from one of the rafters by a rope around the neck.

He looked tiny in that enormous room, like a little child, swaying slightly in the darkness. Beneath him was the remnant of a fire that the pack had evidently built in the middle of the floor. Ash and scorch marks and the charred remains of some of the floorboards Jim had gathered lay scattered in a wide circle.

Jim approached, cautiously, half afraid of what he'd find.

"HF?" he said, whispering as loudly as he dared, still gripped by the latent fear that maybe, possibly, not all the pack was gone. "HF?"

HF's eyes flickered open. He looked down at Jim and Murphy. "I sure would appreciate a hand gettin' down. I been hanging here for two days."

"Two days!" Jim said. "They hung you up here the first night?"

"Yup. They looked me over some, then left me in a heap on the floor over yonder by the windows. I thought maybe after that they'd leave me alone, but no such luck. They built a big old fire right here in the floor, hoisted me up, and left me dangling over it. It was right unpleasant."

"I'm sure it was," Jim said. "We'll get you down."

It took a few minutes, but soon they had severed the rope and lowered HF to the floor. Jim asked the question he'd been dreading. "Has anything been permanently damaged?"

"I don't reckon so," HF said, moving his legs up and down and walking in place. "But I shut down all my systems when they took me except my auditory sensors, so I couldn't run any diagnostics."

"Sure," Jim said. "I understand."

Jim looked HF over carefully. He was built from a sturdy, durable alloy that was almost as flame retardant as it was waterproof, but that didn't mean he couldn't be damaged by prolonged exposure to flames and the heat they produced.

Soot and grime covered HF's feet and legs, but Jim couldn't see any obvious signs of permanent damage. He'd need better light and a careful look with some of Atticus's tools to be sure.

"Well," Jim said at last, "You look all right."

"I feel good too, good to be back on the ground," HF said. "I figure a little bit of cleaning should make me right as rain."

"That's good news," Murphy said, smiling and putting his hand on the robot's shoulder. "I'm grateful for what you did, HF, and I'm glad you're all right."

"Aw, shucks," HF replied, waving the comment away like he'd shoo away a fly. "It weren't nothin.' They didn't care about me none. I think it was just something for them to do."

"Maybe so," Murphy said, "but it could have been Jim and me up there with you. You might have saved our lives."

Jim shuddered. He imagined the pack finding them in the pool and dragging them in here. He pushed the images from his mind. They were too ghastly.

# Launch

A quick survey of the main hall revealed that while the logs had been rolled over against a wall, they were still there and undamaged. Jim figured that even after being trimmed down, they were just too big for the pack to burn safely. That they'd risked making a fire in the middle of the main hall on the floor at all was surprising. They could have burned down the whole lodge.

The situation with the planking Jim and HF had scavenged for flooring on the raft was less positive. Most of what he'd gathered had been burned in the bonfire. It irked Jim that he'd helped to provide the fuel for their fire, but he knew there wasn't anything he could do about it.

Murphy's tools were still in the laundry machines, and a couple of trips had them back in the main hall, laid out neatly where they had been before the pack arrived. Except for the some of the guest rooms that betrayed the obvious signs of recent use, most of the rest of the lodge looked none the worse for wear.

"Well," Murphy said. "There's too much to do to finish this thing tonight, so we might as well sleep and wait until morning to get started."

Jim did not object. When he considered that he hadn't done anything but hide and wait for the last few days, he couldn't figure out why he felt so tired, but he did. Atticus had always said that mental duress could wear a person out just as much as physical labor, and after the last few days Jim believed it.

Jim slept well, and he awoke to the sound of Murphy nailing some of the planking onto a pair of logs that he'd already tied together.

"We'll use what we have here," Murphy said when Jim asked if he should take HF and try to scavenge some more. "It won't be quite as comfortable as I'd planned, but I'll make you a square big enough to sleep on in the middle of the raft."

Murphy worked at a steady pace, and he finished all that he could do inside the lodge by late afternoon. The logs were attached in six pairs, which they would drag down to the pavilion by the river when dark came. Four of those pairs had the makeshift flooring in the middle, and when put together they would form the center of the raft. Once all the logs were down by the river, Murphy would finish attaching them, a process he thought would take a few hours, but not all night. So, if things went well, Jim and HF would get launched well before dawn.

As they sat, eating their last meal together, Jim asked Murphy a question that had been bothering him all day. "What if I miss the Vista Corp. regional hub where the Caretaker lives? How will I know?"

"You won't miss it," Murphy said between bites, sounding pretty confident of that fact.

"If I run by night, it'll be dark," Jim said. "And it isn't like I really know what I'm looking for."

Murphy nodded while he chewed. Once he had swallowed, he said, "It's hard for someone who hasn't seen the difference between a city and a town to understand just how different they really are. The scope and the size of the buildings you'll begin to see as you go south will be like nothing you've ever encountered."

"If the remains of the old city are really that big, though, how will I know where to start looking?" Murphy had meant to reassure him, but Jim felt perhaps an even deeper sense of despair. Finding the regional hub wouldn't be much consolation if he found himself confronted with a labyrinth too vast for him to navigate.

Murphy leaned forward. "Remember, Jim, the regional hub is located in a part of what used to be the city—"

"Still—" Jim started.

"Only a part," Murphy continued. "The part the river runs by. You won't need to go into the hub at all, and there's definitely no cause to go into the remains of the city itself. There'll probably be packs of feral dogs and wild animals in there, and packs of people too—and you don't want anything to do with any of them. You hear me? No matter how important this expedition is to you, no matter how curious you might be, you stay out of there. Understand?"

"I get it," Jim said, a little defensively. He'd appreciated Murphy's fatherly concern at times, but it could be a bit much. "You keep telling me what not to do and where not to go, but what am I looking for? Where am I going?"

"There's a monument, of sorts," Murphy said. "It kind of looks like the legs of a wishbone—not the whole wishbone, just the legs, but huge. They stand beside the river, gleaming and metallic, stretching up into the sky. That's what you look for."

"A monument like the legs of a wishbone?" Jim asked, trying to picture what Murphy was talking about. It didn't make any sense. "Why would someone build that?"

Murphy shrugged. "I don't know, but I saw it once, from a distance, and it is kind of impressive. Better yet, it's the very thing you need to find, and it's hard to miss."

"Why am I looking for it?"

"Because if you find that monument, you'll find the Caretaker."

"He lives in it?" Jim said, confused.

"Under it," Murphy answered. "I think there's an entrance by one of the wishbone legs to a large, underground area. That's where the Caretaker lives—at least, that's where Atticus said he used to live, but I don't think Atticus had seen or talked to the Caretaker in a long time."

"So I look for a monument that looks like the legs of a wishbone, and then I try to find a way under it?" Jim repeated, thinking this sounded too bizarre to be anything but a joke.

"Yeah," Murphy said. "That's about it."

"And if he isn't there?"

"Sorry," Murphy said, shaking his head, and Jim thought he caught a glimpse of sadness in his eyes. "I can't help you there."

Jim sat, thinking about all this, and after a moment, Murphy reached over and put his hand on Jim's shoulder. "Can I give you some advice?"

"Of course."

"I know you're doing this because Atticus told you to, and I can respect that you feel you need to ... " Murphy hesitated, and Jim could tell he was uncomfortable saying what he wanted to say.

"Just say it."

Murphy nodded, a little reluctantly. "Well, you said Atticus had been sick with fever for a long time. We don't really know that he knew what he was doing when he said these things."

"When he talked about the Caretaker, he was more clearly himself than he'd been for days," Jim said.

"Maybe so, maybe so," Murphy said, quickly conceding the point. "I guess what I want to say is, if you can't find the Caretaker, or even if you do and he can't help you with this Florence you're looking for, I think you should just come home."

Jim turned to look out the window at the tall grass waving in the wind, and beyond that at the river rolling by.

"Where's home?" Jim asked, his voice barely even a whisper. He thought of the glade by the cabin and wondered if a patch of sunlight lay upon the small dirt mound there. He wondered if he'd ever see it again.

"Home's here," Murphy said. "With us if you'd like. You don't have to stay alone in that cabin. Move in with us."

"Thanks, Mr. Murphy," Jim said, feeling himself blush a little. "I appreciate the offer, but you've got a pretty full house."

"We'll figure something out," Murphy said, withdrawing his hand. "Anyway, that's all I wanted to say. You don't have to go on a wild goose chase if this trip to the Caretaker doesn't give you the answers you're looking for."

"Thanks, Mr. Murphy," Jim said, and he felt he'd better leave it at that. He figured, having heard Mr. and Mrs. Murphy talking that night in the cabin, that he knew what Mr. Murphy was saying even if he didn't really want to come right out and say it.

Part of him wanted what Murphy was offering. In fact, that part of him didn't really want to leave at all. At the same time, another part of him told him he had to. He needed do what Atticus had asked him to do. He needed to find the Caretaker. He needed to find Florence.

It was hard work getting the raft down to the pavilion by the river, even moving it in four pieces. It made Jim a little nervous about how he'd navigate the river with it. The canoe they'd crossed the river in was light enough that one man could carry or drag it if need be, but this raft was going to be much, much heavier than that.

Murphy had cut two makeshift oars from some of the planks he'd scavenged, so he and HF could both have one, but he'd admitted they'd be of limited use when the raft was in the river's current. He'd also provided him with a sturdy branch for a pole, but this was for pushing off when they wanted to launch each night and for use when the drifted too near anything they didn't want to hit or run aground on. It wouldn't be of any use in the deep water.

Jim knew that steering and maneuvering the raft while on the river would be a challenge, and that was putting it mildly. The good news, as Murphy put it, was that the river would do the hard work. It would push and pull the raft downstream, from here to the place where the Illinois joined the Mississippi, and from there to the Vista Corp. regional hub—where hopefully the Caretaker still lived.

At last, the raft was ready, and with much work by all three of them, they got it into the water. HF crawled on and moved across to the smooth center where he sat, cross-legged, and Jim made a couple of trips back and forth across from the shore to the center, carrying their packs, his gun, and the oars.

When all that remained was the pole for pushing off, he shook Murphy's hand and thanked him for all he had done. "Please," he added. "Remember me to Mrs. Murphy, and the twins, and Sarah."

He kept his voice pretty steady when he said her name, and he was proud of himself for that.

"I will, Jim," Murphy said. "We'll all be looking forward to hearing about your adventures."

"Well, hopefully they won't be like the one we had here," Jim said. "I don't think I can handle too many more like that."

"Hopefully not," Murphy said. "Now let's get you underway."

Jim walked back to the middle and sat down, laying the pole in one of the grooves between two logs beside him. Murphy said he didn't know how strong the pole was or how much life it had in it. What's more, he'd given Jim all kinds of advice about when and how often to use it as well as several warnings about not getting it stuck in the soft mud of the river bottom. So Jim had agreed that it would be best if Murphy just launched the raft this time. He wouldn't have this kind of help later on.

Murphy waded into the water, and laboring a bit, finally got the raft dislodged. The raft drifted away slowly, but steadily, and both Jim and HF moved to the side to start working on getting it out toward the current so they could take advantage of what remained of the night.

Jim looked back at Murphy, knee-deep in the river, and waved. He wondered if Murphy would try to get his tools and head back across the river that night. He figured he probably would. His family was waiting, and ever since the episode with the pack, the lodge had lost more than a little bit of its appeal.

Murphy waved back, watching as Jim and HF drifted away. Jim turned to face the job at hand. The raft was built, he was underway, and now it was time for the river to do its work.

# The River

# South

The river flowed southward, and the raft flowed with it. It felt different from the canoe, which had rocked side to side in the current with Murphy's strong strokes, making Jim feel uneasy, like it might tip over and pitch him into the river at any moment. The raft felt more stable as it drifted steadily onward at an even if uninspired pace.

Jim had given up on trying to sleep. He was too nervous. Worried that he would sleep past dawn, he didn't want to wake up to the bright morning sun overhead. So he'd crawled over to the side of the raft and lay with his hand dipped slightly in the cold water, watching the ripples he made scatter the pale reflection of the soft moonlight.

It wasn't just the fear of oversleeping, though, that kept Jim from being able to rest. And it wasn't just the thought of being out on the open river in the bright morning sunlight that made him afraid, either. It was being out on the river at all. Jim felt naked and exposed, even under the cover of darkness. The moonlight was strong enough that he could see the trees that lined the western bank of the river and the steep hill that ran up above the road on the eastern bank. He thought any semi-alert observer must be able to see the raft and its occupants drifting lazily down the river in plain view.

Atticus had always maintained that there was a big difference between being smart and living in fear. You took reasonable precautions and avoided foolish risks, but you had to live. He had told Jim this many times, adamant that he hadn't left the hives to cower and hide, but to enjoy the world that all but the groundlings had forgotten. As far as Jim could tell, Atticus had enjoyed it. He'd loved walking through the autumn woods, skipping stones on the big river in the moonlight, planting seed in the spring and smelling the freshly turned earth. These and more were all things he'd taken time to appreciate.

Still, the line between being smart and living in fear had always seemed pretty fine to Jim. Fear was a rational response to danger. Fear kept you alive, and staying alive was pretty important to all the things Atticus had taught Jim to love. Consequently, staying alive had always seemed pretty important to Jim; it tended to trump all the rest of Jim's inclinations.

Here he was, floating in the middle of the river, out in the wide open, where anyone with eyes to see could spot him, completely unsure of whether he was being smart or living in fear. He tried to think like Atticus, like an engineer, calculating the relative risks of his various options so he could take some comfort in the fact he was pursuing a course of action that was safer than his other options for achieving the same goal. But if truth be told, he found little comfort in that knowledge. He didn't like being out here, floating slowly in the great wide open. What he wanted was to be inside his cabin, preferably by a nice warm fire.

Jim rolled over onto his back, ignoring the uneven surface beneath him as he placed his hands underneath his head and stared up at the sky. He understood better now why Murphy had wanted to cover the whole raft with those floorboards, but he figured he could endure this well enough for the few nights it would take to reach the Caretaker.

One thing Jim did like about being out in the open was the clear view he had of the sky. The whole expanse, though dominated by the partial moon, was filled from north to south and east to west with a million stars. Whether large or small, bright or faint, Jim wondered about all of them. How far away were they? How old were they? How many planets surrounded each one? What were they saying?

Atticus said every star whispered something a little different about the majesty of the universe, but it was a message only the groundlings could hear; the groundlings, after all, were the only ones listening. Jim didn't know what that meant, exactly, but he did like looking at the stars, and listening. He hoped he would learn to hear them one day, like Atticus.

"Jim?" HF called from the center of the raft. "I think we might ought to think about headin' ashore."

Jim sat up and looked over at HF, sitting in the middle of the raft. He was looking east, where the horizon was largely blocked by the hill that ran steeply up just beyond the big road. As Jim peered up at the place where the crest of the hill met the night sky, he thought he could just see the faintest hint of morning there.

"All right, HF," Jim said, crawling back to the middle of the raft to grab one of the makeshift paddles. "I guess we should start heading in."

"I s'pose so, Jim," HF said, taking up a paddle too. "How ya reckon we get this thing ashore?"

Jim followed HF's gaze over toward the eastern shore. For the first time since the launch, he thought about the fact that he didn't have to put in on that side if he didn't want to, and he didn't. The road the pack was traveling on was there, which meant they might be, too. It occurred to him that if the pack lingered some other place the way they had lingered at the lodge, he might actually overtake them.

Even beyond that, he hadn't seen anything yet that looked like the Illinois merging with the Mississippi. He figured the western shore was still part of the peninsula, which felt both familiar and safe, even if in reality, he had no idea if it was either. Both these factors made him want to avoid the eastern shore and put in on the western side, but a fair appraisal of the situation said they were far closer to the eastern shore and that getting across the current to the western side might be quite a chore.

The fact that Murphy had also said the regional hub for Vista Corp would be on the western side wasn't a big deal—he had plenty of time to navigate across the next night—but he was angry at himself for not considering this sooner. Instead of lazing about, he could have been working to get through the current and over to the western side—away from the road and away from the pack. Now, he might not have a choice.

Jim turned to HF. "You paddle and I'll man the sweep," he said. "Let's see if we can get the raft through the current toward the western shore." He wasn't willing to give up yet, without even trying. The light in the east seemed awfully faint.

HF turned to look across the river toward the west, as though he hadn't even considered this possibility. He looked from the river to Jim and said, "That seems like a powerful long way, Jim."

"I know, HF," Jim said. "Let's just try. We'll have to cross through the current to the far side sooner or later."

"All right," HF said. "I'm game if you are. Let's give it a shot."

And they did. Jim directed HF on how to paddle, while laboring pretty hard himself, but he wasn't very skilled with the sweep, and one robot with one paddle was hardly a match for the current of the Mississippi River. After they'd been at it for quite a while, Jim stopped to take stock of how far they'd gotten and was more than a little discouraged. Perhaps the river had widened, but the western shore seemed as far away as it had been when they started. Even more discouraging was the fact that the faint morning light now appeared markedly less faint.

"It's no good, HF," Jim said as he caught his breath. "We need to head to the eastern shore. We'll try to get across tonight, when we have more time and energy."

"That's probably wise," HF said, following Jim as they repositioned themselves to steer the raft in a new direction. Without the current to fight, they made much better progress and soon were quite close to the eastern shore.

Jim studied it appraisingly, and he was a little surprised to note that the road, which had followed the river closely since the lodge, turned inland here, as did the hill beyond it. Between the road and the river, there were several buildings along the riverfront. Some looked like houses, others like shops, but all of them made Jim nervous.

As they drew near the shore, Jim turned to HF. "What do you think, HF? Look like a place where that pack might hole up for a night or two?"

"I sure hope not, Jim," HF said. "I don't want to run into those fellers again."

"Me neither," Jim said.

He let the raft drift downstream beside the shore. This far from the main current, it felt as if they were crawling. Any thoughts Jim had of bypassing this cluster of buildings and looking for a less conspicuous landing spot disappeared as he contemplated the bend in the river ahead and the steady presence there of buildings just like these. He had no wish to drift slowly past all of them in the steadily increasing light of day. It was time to go ashore.

Murphy had driven small metal rings into each corner of the raft so Jim would be able to secure it each time they landed, but it took him a few minutes to find a suitable tree close enough to the shore for his rope to reach. Once the raft was secure, he crept with HF up from the river to scope out the nearest building, a small blue house.

There was no sign of habitation, nor were there signs at any of the other buildings nearby, all of them houses of a similar size and shape. Jim and HF approached the blue house carefully and circled around it with caution. The front door faced the direction of the main road, though there were several smaller streets between this house and it. A smaller back door opened from the house onto a deck that overlooked the river, and Jim thought he'd try his luck there.

A rickety screen door hung by a hinge, and even though Jim tried to open it gently, no sooner had he tugged on it at all than it broke loose and fell clattering onto the deck. Jim froze, and he and HF looked around, trying to see if the sudden noise had drawn any noticeable attention. Jim didn't linger. The door handle for the wooden door turned pretty easily, but the door stuck. He pushed it open forcefully, and he and HF disappeared inside.

The room they were in was westward-facing and pretty dark, so they felt their way carefully through the gloom until they found a hallway, which they followed to the front of the house. Jim knelt by one of the front windows and parted the curtains to peer out in the direction of the streets and the other houses. If his arrival and entrance here had been seen or heard by anyone in any one of them, he saw no sign of it. Nothing stirred anywhere that he could see. Eventually, he let the musty curtains fall, and he switched on his flashlight to explore the house.

The rodent droppings and other evidences of small animal habitation were comforting. They were recent enough to sufficiently reassure Jim that no human had been here in some time. He didn't think any of these creatures would bother him, and since he only meant to pass the daylight hours here, he figured he could stand them if they could stand him.

He settled on a small bedroom on the second story that overlooked the river at the back as the room where he planned to sleep. The smell wasn't so bad there, and he liked the view. HF agreed to sit by a window in what had clearly been the master bedroom at the front of the house and keep an eye on things.

Just as HF was leaving to take up his post, Jim blurted out the question that had been on his mind the last few days. "HF, why did you get out of the pool? We could have all three hidden there."

HF stopped at the door, turned around and stared at Jim. For a moment, Jim wondered if the robot had understood the question, coming like that out of the blue. When he spoke, though, Jim knew he'd followed his thinking just fine. "Atticus told me to help you, to take care of you."

"He told us to take care of each other," Jim corrected him. "I couldn't protect you once you climbed out of the pool."

"I don't mean no offense now, Jim," HF said, "but I don't reckon you could have protected me if I'd stayed in the pool with you, not if them fellers had found us all hidin' down there together."

"Maybe not," Jim admitted. "But I was still worried about you."

"I was worried about me, too," HF said, "but it sure 'nough seemed like the right thing to do. Even though they strung me up, and I sure didn't like that none, I figure it turned out all right in the end."

"True," Jim said, "but I want you to promise me you'll be careful from here on out. I don't know how hard it'll be to find the Caretaker, or where this will go from there. I may just need your help."

"Seems fair," HF said. "I won't do nothin' foolish, if you won't."

"Deal," Jim said. The robot walked away, and Jim crawled into bed. It was reassuring to know HF was out there keeping watch, and he didn't like to think of what this journey would be like if he were on his own.

# The Griffin

The rolling boom of thunder woke Jim. He sat up, a bit disoriented in the half-light of the strange room. His first thought was that it must be almost sundown, as the light coming in through the window was faint and pale. He felt a sudden panic that he wasn't down by the river, ready to launch, but as the patter of raindrops on the roof grew steadily louder until they beat furiously against the house, he realized the gloom was due to the storm, not the hour.

He got up and walked to the window, yawning. The rain was pouring down, and he couldn't see very far in any direction. The river looked choppy and turbulent. He didn't mind getting wet, and his fleece would keep him relatively warm and dry above the waist, but he didn't like the thought of the raft swirling rapidly around and bobbing up and down all night.

He didn't really want the rain to stop, though. Most hunters, used to the comfort of the hives, didn't like to get wet, and the rain limited the visibility for the few that would persevere despite it. With any luck, the really heavy rain would pass, and perhaps a slower, steady rain would keep them company tonight. Either way, if it kept raining, maybe Jim would feel less exposed on the river.

HF was sitting on a chair in front of the big windows in the main bedroom, gazing out through the rain at the houses that lined the streets. He didn't turn around when Jim entered, but he must have heard him come in. "Howdy, Jim. Get some rest?"

"Yeah, I did, thanks." Jim said, walking up to look out the window too. The rain was blowing down the street in sheets, almost in waves. "Nothing stirring?"

"Not that I can see," HF said. "Been mighty dull. Just like we like it, right Jim?"

Jim looked down at the robot, who was now looking up at him with something very like a grin on his usually inexpressive face. "That's right, HF. We like it dull."

"I hope you tied the raft good," HF said.

"Don't worry," Jim said. "Atticus taught me how to tie a pretty mean knot."

Jim yawned again. "Excuse me, HF, I guess I'm still waking up."

"That's all right, Jim."

"How long until dark, do you think?"

"Oh," HF said, scratching his head. "I reckon it's still mid-afternoon. Probably several hours."

Jim knew HF didn't have to think to answer, that the gesture and the pause were just part of Atticus' programming to help make the robot look and feel more life-like, but he still found himself startled from time to time by how convincing it was. He could almost forget that under HF's synthetic skin was circuitry, not sinew.

"Well," Jim said, as HF stared at him, unblinking. "How about we go have a look around out there?"

"Out there?" HF said, glancing outside. "That rain's comin' down something terrible."

"Yeah it is," Jim said. "Still, I'd like to have a look through some of these houses."

"Why, Jim?" HF said. "Why not lay low until dark, like we planned?"

"Well, I don't think we need to worry about the pack, HF," Jim said. "Now that I've had some sleep and can think straight, I don't think there's much chance that a few hours on a raft could possibly have made up the head start they had on us."

"I still don't see no sense in it," HF said.

"Look," Jim said. "If I'm really careful, I probably have enough biscuits to keep me going another day or two—maybe. But I'm sick of biscuits, and I can't hunt while I'm on the raft, now can I?"

HF stared out the window. "You aim to hunt vermin in them houses, Jim?"

"No," Jim said, "Though that's not a bad idea. I'll keep my .22 handy. I'm hoping that I might be able to find some fishing gear, or something I could use as fishing gear, anyway."

"Fishing," HF said, looking back at Jim. "I hadn't thought of that."

"Yeah," Jim said. "Me neither, not until I looked out over the river just now and thought of all the times Atticus took me out to fish in the rain when he wasn't worried about hunters. Not too clever for us to set out on the river and not consider fishing sooner, eh?"

"I don't reckon so," HF said, "but we've had a lot on our minds since Atticus died."

It was the first time HF had mentioned Atticus' death since leaving the cabin, and Jim thought maybe he could hear a bit of sadness in his voice. "It's all right to miss him, HF. It's part of remembering."

"I know, Jim," HF said, and whatever Jim thought he'd heard in the robot's voice was gone now. "Well, if we're going out there, we might as well get a move on."

Jim decided to work down the row of houses closest to the river first, though he admitted to himself that the proximity to the water didn't mean they were any more likely to have fishing gear. Still, he wanted to be methodical so he didn't get confused about which houses he'd looked in already, and going that way was as easy as any other.

The next house down seemed a lot darker to Jim. Maybe there were fewer windows, or smaller. Maybe the curtains were thicker or the windowpanes more cloudy. Whatever it was, he didn't like being in that house at all. He made quick work of it, moving on to the garage after a cursory look through the house. There were scattered tools and perhaps a few odds and ends that could be useful, but he knew he needed to travel light. He'd make a mental note of things he could come back for if he didn't find the fishing gear, but he wasn't ready to start toting around every object that looked somewhat helpful—not just yet.

About five houses down, he found a spool of wire in the basement, and he decided to cut a length of that and take it with him. If he didn't find the real thing, he could always make a hook with some scrap metal and attach it to the wire. It wouldn't be ideal, but it might work if nothing better presented itself. He played out the wire and cut off a good long piece, then after winding it around his fist, he slipped it off and shoved it in his pocket.

About ten houses down, Jim crossed over to work back up the row of houses on the other side. There were more houses along the riverfront, further downstream, but they lay beyond a big open stretch of ground that might have been some kind of park at one time. An open building lay out in the middle of it, but through the heavy rain, Jim couldn't make it out very well. He didn't see any point in going further that way, as there were three or four streets right here with rows of houses on either side—more than enough to keep him busy looking until dark, and each as likely or unlikely as the next to have what he was looking for.

The houses on the other side of the street offered some interesting odds and ends, but no usable fishing rod. He did find one with a broken reel and no line, but he decided it didn't get him much closer to actual fishing than his length of wire. He had by now, though, scavenged three or four pieces of scrap metal that might be shaped into reasonable hooks, though each of them would need some work. Jim figured he'd have plenty of time on the raft to fool with that.

Coming out of the last house on that side of the street, Jim led HF around the outside, past the back yards of both the house he'd just been through and the house behind it on the next street over. The rain had slowed down a fair bit now, so that it fell steadily, but not nearly so thick and heavy has it had been.

"Rain's letting up," Jim said, pausing to look up at the sky before turning in to start work down the next row of houses. "Hopefully it won't quit altogether. I'd like the cloud cover tonight."

HF stopped with Jim, but he didn't answer. Jim looked at HF, but he was staring back upstream and inland, at a place where what had been a hill for most of the trip downriver looked to be something of a sheer cliff as it cut inland. "What is it, HF? What do you see?"

"Over yonder," HF said, still staring at the cliff. "Above the cave at the base of that there cliff. Do you see something?"

Jim squinted as he peered through the rain. He hadn't even noticed the cave at first, but now that HF mentioned it, he could see the dark opening that stretched out for a fair distance at the bottom. "What am I looking for?"

"It looks like somebody painted some kind of critter up there," HF said. "It's mighty faded, but he still looks pretty fearsome."

Jim took a couple steps forward, almost involuntarily, though he knew a few feet wouldn't make much difference at this distance. As he stared, though, he started to think he could see what HF was talking about. Dark lines and patches he'd taken for cracks or protruding rocks in the cliff face were actually painted lines. He could see now that they weren't all the same color, though the weathering had made them more alike over time. He studied the lines, and as he did, the shape that emerged was fearsome indeed.

The large body of the creature was ambiguous at best, but whatever it was, it certainly didn't match the four feet underneath it, which looked a lot like claws you'd find on a bird. Though the body above the claws wasn't bird-like, something like a great wing or wings were lifted above it, and a design had been painted on the wing, though it was all but lost now.

The head was turned to face outward, even though the rest of the thing was in profile view. The face was horrible, Jim thought, especially the eyes. Despite how faded the rest of it was, the longer Jim looked at those eyes, the more piercing they appeared. They were a wicked shade of red, still fairly vivid after all this time. Jim had the eerie thought for a second that maybe the thing could really see him.

"It looks like it might be a griffin," Jim said, making himself look away as he turned back to HF. "I remember Atticus telling me about them when I was little."

"Well I don't want to run into no griffins in real life," HF said, matter-of-factly.

"Don't worry," Jim said, glad of the robot's ignorance. It helped snap him out of the spell the painted creature had cast upon him. "They're not real. They're myths."

"Why'd somebody paint one up there?" HF asked. "I don't reckon I'd like that thing lookin' over my house."

"Me neither," Jim said, and then he shrugged. "It creeps me out. How about we leave it be and keep looking?"

"All right," HF said, turning toward the front door of the nearby house.

Jim followed behind him, but he paused on the top step heading up onto the front porch of the house and took one more look at the painted monstrosity on the cliff. He was drawn almost irresistibly to those bright, terrible eyes, and he thought of Atticus, telling him stories of the world before the hives. Atticus always said it had been a beautiful world, but some of the things he'd told him about it made Jim wonder. So did this creature, perched up there, looking down over the empty houses stretched out before it. Jim turned his back on it, all too aware that now he knew it was there, he wouldn't be able to get rid of the feeling he was being watched.

He turned and went into the house.

# Dogs

Jim stepped through the door. The smell of something stronger than the usual assortment of small animal droppings he had encountered so far greeted him, something beyond the musty vestiges of decay that often plagued the long empty dwellings of the past.

He stepped back to the threshold, hesitating, almost reluctant to go back in. His instincts told him to move on, not even to bother looking here. Whatever the source of this odor was, he didn't want to find it. And yet, as he watched HF move through the front room and down the dim hallway toward what looked to be the kitchen in the back of the house, he thought that maybe he was overreacting.

On the one hand, he realized that HF's apparent nonchalance as he walked through the house shouldn't influence him very much. After all, the robot couldn't smell—not really. Excellent smoke detection capability wasn't the same thing as olfactory sense. His visual, audio and tactile sensors were so good, it was easy for Jim to forget that HF had no idea how the world should taste or smell. And, lacking that, he had no ability to recognize when an odor was sending out a clear and pungent warning.

On the other hand, the sight of HF strolling down the hall, small and unconcerned, couldn't help but make Jim think that thoughts of danger were unfounded. Most likely, something larger than the usual assortment of rodents and vermin had crawled in here to die recently, and Jim had just happened upon the house at the wrong time.

What's more, knowing how life often worked out, Jim wondered if maybe this might be the very house that yielded a working rod and reel. Atticus had often said that in life, the good and the bad seemed frequently to come together. If that was true, then this house, which smelled awful, must have something wonderful somewhere inside to go with it.

Jim stepped back through the open door. He was prepared for it this time, so the smell didn't hit him as hard. Still, the rank smell was enough that Jim was determined to make this quick. He moved down the hallway, past an old wooden chair so small that it must have been made for a toddler, and caught up to HF as he moved into the kitchen at the back of the house.

The kitchen was small and surprisingly cheery. Bright yellow curtains with a faded pattern of curling green lines hung on the sides of the big window over the sink. These and the carefully stenciled flowers that circled the room just below the ceiling provided color, and the slowing of the rain provided a little more light than they'd had so far in any of the other houses. The room was cozy and neat, an odd juxtaposition to the smell that was even stronger here than it had been out front.

Jim glanced around the kitchen, half expecting to find something rancid lying on the table or countertops. He didn't see any obvious source for the smell, and confronted with turning left to go through into the dining room or right to go to the garage, he chose right. The garage was more likely to have fishing gear, and he didn't want to linger.

There was no door in the doorway to the garage, and Jim wondered what had happened to it. He didn't wonder for long, though. The garage was full of various items of all sizes and shapes that would take some time to explore. Though there were some nails that might have had fishhook potential, they didn't look any better than what he already had. Most of the rest of what he found was junk, and after spending a lot more time than he would have liked, he gave up, ignoring a handful of old boxes in the corner that seemed entirely too small to conceal what he was after. He sighed, disappointed. He would check the closets in the house and then be on his way.

As soon as he and HF entered the kitchen again, however, the robot reached over and grabbed his arm. They stopped in their tracks, and HF made a gesture for Jim to be quiet and pointed to his ears to signal that he should listen. Jim did just that, and a moment later he heard a howling on the wind outside. He looked inquiringly at HF, as though to ask if that was what he'd meant for Jim to hear. HF shook his head.

Then Jim heard it. It was a kind of snort, followed by a chewing sound. Jaws working. Teeth gnawing. A mouth smacking.

They weren't alone.

Jim started forward, tiptoeing as quietly as he could across the kitchen floor. He looked down the hall that led back toward the front door, which Jim could see was still standing wide open. Another sound like a snort, and he froze where he stood, glancing sideways into the dining room.

At first he didn't see anything but a large wooden table and china cabinet along the near wall, but then he noticed in the far corner, a body half obscured from his view. Leaning forward, he could see from the lower half of the torso down to the feet, but the rest was out of view. The part he could see was wearing clothes that had been ripped and torn by various animals.

The head and shoulders of a large, wet, black and brown dog popped up and into view. The dog wasn't looking his way, but Jim could see his jaws working as he chewed whatever part of the decomposing mess he had just ripped free. Jim was glad the head and shoulders of the dead man or woman were hidden from his view. The part that he could see was disgusting enough.

In fact, the combination of seeing the dog chewing merrily away, hearing the sounds that went with it, and smelling the foul, rancid odor of the badly decomposed body made Jim gag. He tried to stifle it but failed, and the dog turned, looking up and over the table at the door. For a brief moment, their eyes locked and neither moved. Then Jim broke for it, racing down the hall toward the open door, followed closely by HF. The dog barked as it leapt across the room to come after.

The hall felt much longer as he ran down it than he remembered it being on his way in. Behind him, he heard dog paws scrabbling furiously on the tiled kitchen floor, but Jim didn't dare turn to see if the dog had slipped. He dodged the little wooden chair as he passed out of the hallway into the large, open front room.

"Jim!" came the desperate plea from HF behind him, but before he could turn to see what was going on, he felt the robot's arms and head crash into his own legs, sending him sprawling.

He was up again in a flash and turning as he rose. The dog had evidently leapt for HF and hit him hard enough to send him flying into Jim. Now the brute had his forelegs on top of HF, his awful teeth barred as he growled over the robot's terrified face. If he tried biting HF, he'd get a shock—literally, depending on where he chose to bite—but it might also cause damage that was beyond Jim's ability to repair.

Jim couldn't let that happen.

He saw the little chair in the hall, just behind where the dog had pounced on HF. With courage he didn't know he had, he sprinted past them toward it. The dog, momentarily distracted by Jim's surprising move as he passed by so close, turned its ugly head and snapped at him. Perhaps it was sending a defensive warning to Jim to stay away, or perhaps it was signaling its disappointment that part of its quarry was getting away. Whatever the dog was thinking, it looked back to HF when Jim was past, but before it could bite down on the robot, Jim snatched up the little wooden chair and slammed it down with a thud on the dog's spine and head.

The little wooden chair broke into several pieces, and the dog yelped as it scrambled forward to get off the robot, turn and defend itself. Jim stepped forward beside HF and took the bigger of the two pieces of wood that he now held and slammed it down on the dog again as it turned. The wood was solid and thudded solidly on the dog's head, right above its dark, staring eyes.

As the dog staggered back, Jim reached down and helped HF up. "We have to get out of here."

HF sprang up without delay. "You don't need to tell me twice!"

The dog was now between them and the door, and Jim advanced toward it, waving what remained of the chair threateningly. The beast growled as it backed up slowly, wary but angry. Jim knew a feral dog might stoop to eat dead meat, but that didn't mean it wouldn't rather have its dinner fresh whenever possible.

Then Jim saw something moving in the distance outside. He glanced over the dog and out the door and saw another dog—every bit as large as this one—running across the lawn of the house directly across the street. He thought of the howl he'd heard a moment ago in the kitchen and wondered if there was a whole pack on its way, and if so, how long before every one of them came pouring through that open door.

He grabbed HF and physically manhandled him, pulling him across the floor and over to the foot of the stairs that went up from the front room to the second floor. "Get up there, now!"

HF didn't argue, and Jim could hear his feet pounding up the stairs as he covered their retreat, taking frequent, vicious swipes in the direction of the dog who was now looking over Jim's head and watching HF's progress up the stairs.

Jim dashed forward, surprising the dog with his aggression and managing to strike it again. This blow seemed less effective, and as he turned to head up after HF, the last thing he saw was the second dog jumping up onto the porch.

He took the steps two at a time, knowing that both dogs would be right behind. HF had stopped at the top, unsure where to go next. Jim grabbed and pulled him along behind as he sprinted down the short hall to the main bedroom in the front. Thrusting HF through the door first, he turned once inside to close and latch the door.

The dogs were already in the hall, coming fast and barking angrily. He grabbed the door and threw his whole weight behind it as he tried to slam it closed. One of the dogs, the new one Jim thought, leapt into the air to get through the doorway before the door closed, and Jim braced for a collision.

Door struck dog, and the dog won, sort of. Jim was thrown back, but the dog was stunned too, falling to the ground, half in the room and half out. HF, though, appeared immediately over the dog's body, a glass lamp held high, and he brought it down on the animal with a crash. The glass shattered all over the floor, and Jim kicked the door that had bounced back toward him off the animal with his legs so that it sandwiched the dog between the solid wood door and the doorjamb.

The head of the second dog appeared over the body of the first, snapping and snarling through the small gap that remained. HF didn't hesitate to take one of the bigger pieces of glass and stab downward, driving the glass fragment into the creature's snout. It snarled and yelped and backed away. Jim kicked the door again, sliding forward to get more leverage and power, and he heard the ribs of the dog in the doorway crack. Still he kicked, as fast and as hard as he could.

"Jim," HF said, reaching a hand down and placing it on Jim's shoulder.

Jim hesitated, and HF shoved the dog out the door. The creature seemed more than a little eager to get out of its way, so it didn't protest but slid awkwardly back into the hall. HF shut and latched the door.

"Come on," Jim said, rising to his feet and unshouldering his .22. He walked over to the front windows and threw one open, kicking out the screen. "There might be more coming."

He stepped out onto the roof over the front porch. The shingles were wet and slippery, and he almost fell. He helped HF out into the rain, and then took a quick look up and down the street. He didn't see more dogs, but he knew that didn't mean they weren't out there. They'd just have to risk it.

He sat down and half slid, half scooted down to the corner of the porch where he dropped a bit less gracefully than he'd hoped into an overgrown bush below. HF tumbled down too, just missing him, and soon they both rolled out of the bush and onto the soggy front lawn.

Without hesitation or conversation, Jim was up and running through the steady rain, clasping his gun tightly, heading back toward the little blue house where their day had begun.

# Providence

As soon as they were safely inside, Jim closed and locked the door. He moved straight down the hall to the back door in the kitchen and checked and double-checked both the lock in the doorknob and the deadbolt. Once both doors were secure, he moved systematically around the entire first floor, checking all the windows.

With each one, he made sure the window was latched, yanked the curtains shut, and then hovered beside them, peeking through and watching for movement anywhere outside. He'd hover, peer out, and once he was reasonably confident that no threat was imminent, move on to the next one and repeat the process.

Once a complete circuit of the house had been made—HF trailing silently along as he went—Jim walked straight back to the front room. He stood before the front windows for a moment, then grabbed a hold of the large armchair sitting there and pushed it to the side. As he did, an idea dawned on him, and he kept pushing until the chair was sitting up against the front door. He observed his impromptu barricade with satisfaction for a moment and then slid over to the window, knelt down on the floor, and took to once more peering out through the side of the curtain at the street.

"I should have known," Jim said bitterly, half out loud. "I did know. I knew, and I went in anyway."

"Jim?" HF said cautiously from behind him.

"What?" Jim said.

"Ain't we overreacting a little bit?" HF said, recoiling a bit. "They're dogs, not people."

"Dogs that almost tore us up and ate us for dinner," Jim said, turning from the front window to glare at HF as he spoke.

"True," HF said. "I got me a closer look at dog teeth today than I ever wanted, and no mistake. But still, they ain't gonna bust down no doors or break through no windows."

"Well," Jim said, "they got into the other house, didn't they?"

"Yeah," HF said, sounding a little confused, "but the door was open."

Jim thought of the door he had left open because the stench was so thick that he thought it might help air the place out. It hadn't occurred to him that this was the explanation. In the rush and confusion of the episode, he had just assumed that the dog had been somewhere else in the house when they had entered, perhaps even under the table and preoccupied with his food even then. It hadn't occurred to him until just now that it might have been he who let the creature in.

No, not might have. It had been him. He saw that now. He had left the door open, and the dog—already somewhere nearby, no doubt—had smelled the dead body and come for food. All the while, he had been in the next room, sifting through useless junk, oblivious.

He stared out the window, a sinking feeling in his gut. He had taken them into the house, opened the door to let the scent of meat drift like a beacon throughout the whole neighborhood, and waited long enough for the nearest predators to come and feed.

"I'm such an idiot," he whispered, still gazing out at the empty street.

"Come on now," HF said. "There ain't no cause to be so hard on yourself. You couldn't have known there was a pack of wild dogs nearby."

"Maybe not," Jim said, "but I could smell that dead body as soon as we opened the door. I knew we should move on, but I went in and left the door open. I almost got you ripped to pieces and me killed."

"Well, maybe so, but it all worked out all right, didn't it?"

"Barely," Jim said, keeping his back to HF. "Carelessness like that is inexcusable. I should have known better. Atticus taught me better."

"Well I couldn't smell nothin'," HF said, and it took Jim a moment before he realized the robot had made a joke. He turned and looked at HF, who'd kept a pretty straight look on his face, but Jim thought he could see the start of a smirk curling up at the corners of his mouth.

"I appreciate what you're trying to do," Jim said, still downhearted, "but I messed up, HF. It could have been really, really ugly in there."

"Could'a been, but it wasn't. Give yourself a break."

Jim didn't answer. Instead he turned back to the window and looked out. Across the way, between two of the houses across the street, he thought he saw a dark shape sniffing around the bushes. He watched but couldn't ever make anything out for sure.

"You know, Jim," HF said after a moment. "We might'a gotten lucky in there."

"I know we got lucky," Jim said. "The dog could have gotten me down first, or there could have been more than one right from the beginning, or any of a number of other things could have gone wrong."

"No, that's not what I mean," HF said, shaking his head as though Jim had totally missed the point. "I mean that if that pack was roaming the area, we probably would'a bumped into them sooner or later no matter what you did or didn't do, and it might just have been a stroke of powerful good luck that it happened there."

"Why?" Jim said. "I mean, I see your point that we might have had to deal with them eventually, but why were we lucky it was there?"

"Well, it sure looks to me like that dead body came in mighty handy," HF said. "That first dog must not have smelled us when he came in, no doubt because it smelled the dead feller instead. Why else would that critter have left us alone?"

Jim thought about this for a moment. He'd recognized the fact himself, just a little while ago, that even feral dogs preferred fresh meat. So why had the creature turned into the dining room and started working on the corpse when Jim had been only a short distance away, in the garage, with nowhere to run?

He thought of his close proximity, of the fact that they must have made at least some noise while they were searching the garage, and of the fact that the dog had been so preoccupied he'd taken no notice of it. Either that, or he'd only just entered the house after Jim had given up rummaging but before he exited the garage.

That had to be it. The dog had come in too late to hear Jim and HF looking through boxes in the garage but too soon to see them returning to the kitchen. In that one, precise, single moment, the conditions had been just right for the dog to miss their presence and turn away from them to the dead body. A ripple ran down Jim's spine, and he suddenly felt very aware that they hadn't just been lucky, they had been so lucky it was absurd. Just a second, either way, and they might not have made it out of that house of death.

Jim nodded, looking up from where he knelt by the window at HF. "I think you're right, HF. We did get lucky."

"Then you can't be mad anymore, Jim," HF said matter-of-factly. "When you've just been that lucky, all you can do is be thankful."

Jim smiled at HF and nodded. "You're right."

A moment later he added. "Atticus wouldn't have called it luck, though. He'd have called it 'Providence.'"

"Well, you can call it whatever you like," HF answered, "I'm just awful grateful we made it back here in one piece."

"Me too," Jim said. He ran his fingers slowly through his curly hair. Suddenly it was Atticus, not the dogs that was on his mind. "I thought he was wrong, HF. I doubted him."

HF just stared back. "I'm sorry, Jim. I don't know what you're talkin' about."

"Atticus," Jim said, clarifying. "He used to say that in life, the good and the bad often come together—that's how I justified going into that stinky house in the first place. I thought a place that smelled that bad might just be the place we found something good."

"You mean the fishing gear," HF said, catching on.

"That's right," Jim said. "And after that dog attack, I just figured he'd been wrong. But he wasn't wrong. We did find something good there—Providence."

"Yep," HF said, agreeably. "But even if we hadn't found any of this here Providence, that wouldn't have meant he was wrong."

"No?"

"Heck no," HF said, thumping his fist into his open palm. "You said yourself that good and bad often come together, but often ain't always, Jim."

"No," Jim said, thinking about it. "That's true. Often ain't always. I'm sure there are plenty of time when bad just comes with bad."

"You can believe it does," HF said emphatically.

Jim laughed, rose, and walked from the window. He stood in front of HF and put his hands on the robot's shoulders. "I'm glad you're with me on this trip, HF."

"Where else would I be, Jim?" HF said, looking genuinely confused.

"Nowhere," Jim said. "Never mind."

"Well," HF said after a moment of slightly awkward silence. "What are we gonna do now? Just hang out until dark?"

"I suppose so," Jim said, looking around at the front room with very different eyes, now that he was calmer. "You know, we didn't actually check this house for fishing gear."

"We had a good look around when we first got here," HF said. "Didn't see much of interest then."

"True, but I wasn't looking for a rod then. I wasn't very careful. How about we take a look?"

"I'm almost afraid to, Jim." HF said. "If we find a fishin' rod here, now, after all that, I think I'll … well, I just don't know what I'll do."

Jim laughed. "We'll be grateful for our good fortune, right HF?"

"I reckon," HF said, shrugging his little shoulders. "Let's take a look then."

A more careful examination of the garage and the ground floor closets yielded lots of junk, dust and spider webs, but no fishing gear. Jim trooped dutifully upstairs, determined to leave no stone unturned. He checked in closets and under beds, and he was just about to call it quits, when he noticed the cord hanging from the cut-out in the ceiling. He gave it a tug and lowered the folding ladder he found attached to it. With his flashlight on, he climbed up into the dark attic.

HF remained below, not so eager to go exploring in the dark. A moment later, he heard an exclamation from Jim. He waited, peering up, and just a short time later, saw Jim's head pop down through the opening.

"Well," Jim said, gazing down, half upside down himself, "You'll never guess what I found up here."

As he spoke, he lowered a long, slightly rusty, but otherwise entirely intact, fishing rod.

HF shook his head. "You don't say, Jim. Would Atticus have called this Providence?"

"Probably."

"Well, I think I like it then," HF said. "I hope we get some more."

# The Western Bank

Jim waded out into the river until the water was up to his thighs. It was cold, like the rain, but he didn't mind. He was just glad to be leaving. He climbed up onto the raft, and as they drifted slowly away from shore, he hesitated on the edge, looking back.

It wasn't exactly pitch black, but it was pretty dark. The houses where he'd spent his afternoon were mere outlines, as was the hill, the ridge and the cliff with the faded griffin in the distance. He couldn't make it out anymore, the light was too dim, but he knew it was up there, keeping silent watch over a world that wasn't as empty as it seemed. Jim could still picture those vivid, fierce, red eyes, and he wouldn't soon forget them.

Jim crawled across the raft to its smooth center, where HF was already sitting cross-legged under the tarp. The rain was still steady, but it wasn't nearly as heavy as it had been. The synthetic fibers of his fleece were waterproof, but the fleece couldn't keep his whole body dry like the tarp could, so he crawled under with HF.

"It ain't exactly cozy, Jim," HF said as Jim pulled the tarp up over his head too. "But at least it's a bit warmer tonight. That rain could make for a cold, miserable night otherwise."

"Yeah," Jim said, wondering for a moment if cold and wet felt any more miserable to HF than warm and dry, or if the robot had said that just for his sake. "It's not too bad, though. I'm just glad for the cloud cover."

"Yep," HF said. "We sure could use an uneventful night, couldn't we?"

"Sure could," Jim agreed. He gazed out over the dark water, which thankfully, wasn't nearly as choppy or turbulent as it could have been after all that rain. He could just barely make out the western shore, and he thought of his frustration at having to put in on the eastern side that morning. "We could use an uneventful night, HF, but I'm afraid we have some work to do."

"Work?" HF said. "You fixin' to do some night fishin'?"

"That's not a bad idea," Jim said, "but I meant that we should work on getting through to the far side of the current, so we're nearer to the other side."

"Well, I'm game," HF replied simply. "When do you want to get started?"

"Might as well do it now," Jim said, sighing. He'd had a few hours of sleep early that morning, but he was tired. He wasn't looking forward to fighting the current again, but he didn't dare sleep first, lest he wake up and find himself in the same position he'd been in last night, with too far to go before daylight and too little time to get there.

He slipped out from under the tarp, and moved to the back of the raft where the sweep pivoted on the oar bench. HF took up a paddle, and before long, they were both working hard, trying to steer the big, heavy raft across the current. It was slow going at first, but their persistence paid off, and Jim could tell they were moving steadily, not just downriver, but cross-current too.

"Keep going, HF," Jim called out, as much to encourage himself to keep going as to encourage the robot. His arms were tired, and his hands were so sore that he was struggling to maintain his grip on the long oar. He clung to it, though, with all the strength he had, realizing that if he let it go and the river took it away, there'd be trouble ahead.

Jim didn't know how long this went on, but when he finally let the oar-sweep drift, his fingers trembling from fatigue as they let go, he knew they'd be all right. They were through to the far side of the current. The raft was sweeping along there, at a good steady clip, and unless they somehow drifted back eastward while he slept, getting out of the current and putting in on the western side of the river wouldn't be very hard.

Jim yawned and stretched his cramped arms. He needed sleep. He was worn out, both mind and body. He crawled back to the tarp, eager to stretch out and close his eyes. "HF, you'll need to keep watch on the western shore for me."

"All right, Jim," HF said. "I'll keep watch. What am I watchin' for?"

"The big monument Mr. Murphy told us about. The one like a wishbone standing, remember?"

"There's a monument like a standing wishbone?" HF asked, looking at Jim like he was crazy.

Jim yawned again. "Yes, HF, there is, and no, I don't know why. Just keep your eyes open, and if you see any sign of it, wake me up."

"All right, Jim. I will."

"In fact, if you see anything suspicious, anything at all, wake me up then, too."

"I will," HF reassured him. "Don't you worry about me none. I'll keep my eyes open, and if I see anything like what you're lookin' for, or anything worrisome, I'll get you up."

Jim nodded, slid under the tarp and lay down. The floorboards were hard and not nearly so comfortable as the bed he'd slept in that morning, but he was tired enough that it didn't really matter. He closed his eyes and lay listening to the gentle, rhythmic patter of the raindrops on the tarp. Before long, he'd slipped off to sleep.

When he woke, some time later, he found that he'd thrown the tarp off in his sleep, though not entirely. It was tangled around his legs. He untangled it, but since the rain had stopped, he didn't pull it back up over him.

The moon broke through the clouds and pale light reflected off the river. Jim looked up, not entirely disappointed to see it, even if it meant they were losing some of their cover. Before long, another bank of clouds moved in front of it, and the glimmer of light it had given was gone as quickly as it had come.

Jim crawled over to where HF was sitting on the side of the raft that faced the western shore. He knew that between the sounds he made crawling and the slight up and down bobbing of the raft that he caused as he moved, the robot would know he was coming, but still HF sat, eyes straight ahead, focused on what he'd been told to watch.

"Any sign of that monument, HF?"

"Nope," HF said. "Unless this here monument is really small. If so, then maybe I missed it."

"No," Jim said. "I had the impression it's really pretty big. I think Mr. Murphy said he'd seen it once himself, from a fair distance away."

"Then we haven't passed it yet, Jim," HF said. "I woulda noticed somethin' like that."

"I think so too," Jim said. "Thanks for keeping watch. I really needed some sleep."

"Yup," HF said. "That's fine, Jim. I like to be useful. Besides, I could tell you was licked."

"I was licked, that's for sure," Jim laughed. Just then, the moon broke through again, and Jim studied it and the sky. He wished he could read the sky better, but he couldn't tell what time it was. "HF, how long was I asleep?"

"You slept a good while, Jim. Several hours I'd expect."

"So how long until first light?"

"A few more hours still, I reckon."

They floated on through the night, and as they did, Jim scanned the western shore. He alternated between examining the shore before him and looking as far ahead as he could make out. He strained to see through the darkness but couldn't make out anything that looked like the monument looming in the distance. He could see, though, an increased frequency of buildings on both sides of the river, as well as some other signs of what had once been a denser population down here, like the large, faded signs he saw, posted here and there a little ways back from the river.

He'd never seen so many buildings so close together. And, while they fascinated him, they also made him uncomfortable. Perhaps lost in the immediacy of the dog attack the previous day, was the fact that the dead body meant someone had died or been killed in that house not all that long ago. Jim hadn't had a good look, so he had no idea how the person had died, but like the pack that had come to the lodge, it reminded him that he wasn't the only one moving through the great wide world, trying to keep a low profile. More buildings meant more chances to encounter one or more of these others.

And of course, he thought, trying to calm himself, more buildings might also decrease the odds that he'd accidently stumble on and disturb someone where they were hiding out. There were so many places on both sides of the river down here where a traveler could hole up for the day—or the night he supposed, as the pack had appeared comfortable traveling in the plain daylight—that he was probably safe picking just about any place that he liked the look of.

"I'm going to get my paddle and start steering us ashore," Jim said to HF after a while. "I want to give us plenty of time to find a good place to leave the raft and get inside before dawn."

"I'll help," HF said, turning from the shore finally to follow Jim over to the paddles.

Jim picked his up and gripped it tenderly. He could feel the blisters that were forming on his hands. With any luck, they'd harden soon and become calluses, and then maybe it wouldn't hurt so much to use the paddle.

They hadn't drifted eastward while he slept. If anything, they'd been pushed by the current closer to the western shore. It was fairly easy work getting in close, where Jim could see both the terrain on the riverbank and the buildings set back from it pretty well. It took a little while before he saw a place he liked the look of, but he did—a nice little alcove of sorts to put into, with a small house not far away. He steered them in close.

Tying up and getting settled in the house was uneventful. He ate what was left of the food he'd brought with him. He'd have to start fishing the next night, but he didn't mind that. It would be easier than fighting through the current like they'd done this time.

Besides, with any luck, they'd find this wishbone thing the next time out, as Murphy had thought it would only take a few nights to get there. That also meant that with any luck, they'd find the Caretaker tomorrow too.

After that, well, Jim guessed he would find out what came next soon enough.

# Monument

Jim paddled the raft out from shore. He'd slept pretty well—most of the afternoon, in fact. There had been relatively little time to kill before it was dusk and time to head back down to the raft. He was growing more accustomed to life on the water, and with the empty unfamiliarity of the houses they occupied each day not especially inviting, the raft was starting to feel like home. He paddled with a steady, firm stroke, his hands no longer raw and sore from the previous evening's exertion.

"It's a fine night, isn't it HF?" Jim called to the robot, sitting behind him and paddling right along too, matching him stroke for stroke.

"Yep," HF replied. "I reckon it's a fine night, all right, but it's plenty clear, too. No cloud cover tonight."

Jim peered up at the bright moon on the horizon, shining in the clear night sky. Ordinarily, he'd have felt nervous, out in the open on a night like tonight, especially as they were floating through a landscape increasingly dominated by empty buildings that could be hiding just about anything. Somehow, tonight—for whatever reason—he couldn't be worried.

The world was beautiful. Near misses with the pack at the lodge and the dogs after that had him thinking that maybe he was riding some kind of destiny. Maybe this "Providence" that Atticus used to talk about was watching over him while he went on his father's quest. Maybe he was safe as long as he was searching for the Caretaker and trying to solve the riddle of "Florence."

But what about after he found the Caretaker? And after he solved the riddle? Would this destiny or Providence or whatever it was, still watch over him?

He couldn't worry about that now. He didn't want to worry about it at all. He'd spent too much of his life worrying. The pack and the dogs hadn't gotten him, but it wasn't worry that had saved him. He'd been as careful as he knew how to be—or near enough, anyway—and danger had still found him. In the end, you couldn't be reckless, risking yourself unnecessarily, but you couldn't spend life huddled up in the dark either.

If you were going to do that, Jim thought, you might as well just go live in a hive and have done; there wasn't much point living out in nature if you didn't ever enjoy it.

Jim put down the paddle, and HF put his down too. They were on the outer edge of the main current, and he didn't want to get any further in or move any faster. It was time to try some night fishing. As for making progress, well, he trusted Murphy's estimate of the distance and felt sure they'd find this monument tonight.

He grabbed the rod and reel he'd salvaged and examined the hook. Seeing the dead squirrel under the porch of the house he'd slept in that day had been a stroke of good fortune. He'd found several maggots inside it, a few of them quite juicy and substantial, at least as far as maggots go. He fished around in the pocket of his fleece for the biggest of these, a plump little creature, and found that as large as it had looked inside the squirrel, it was still pretty small relative to the hook.

Still, he fiddled around until he had it on there pretty good, and then he cast softly into the cold river. He played the line out a bit and tried to make himself comfortable.

The raft drifted on through the crisp, clear night, and Jim held the rod, watching the shore at times, but mostly watching the water, waiting for any signs of life below. Once, he thought he felt some tension in the line, but whatever it was, it stopped almost as soon as it started, and reeling the hook in to take a look didn't reveal anything but a limp maggot.

He cast the line back out, and for the first time in a while, looked up to examine the shoreline. He was stunned by what he saw. He thought the buildings crowding the land on either side of the river had been large and plentiful before, but that had been nothing. The size of the structures here and the density—so many, all so close to each other—was like nothing he'd ever seen.

"Jim?" HF called softly from the center of the raft. "Take a gander up ahead."

Jim turned to scan the shore ahead, and scarcely had he done so when he caught sight of it. The standing wishbone that Murphy had spoken of loomed in the distance, and it was much, much bigger than Jim had imagined it would be.

It rose, like the legs of the Colossus, straddling the earth beside the river. Bright moonlight reflected off it, and Jim could see the gleam, even at this distance. He had no idea how far away it was, though it looked a long way off still. He knew, at least, that they would be there before dawn.

He was struck once more by the question he'd had when Murphy first told him of the monument: who had built this thing and why had they done it? What purpose did it serve? He didn't know if it was solid or hollow, but if there was space inside the giant, curved legs, what function could it serve?

He didn't understand why someone had chosen to paint that griffin on the cliff, either, but it made more sense than this. The griffin was ugly and creepy and not at all the kind of thing he'd want to look out his front window and see looming in the distance, but it was identifiable as a griffin, at least. This wasn't identifiable as anything he could think of but the wishbone to which Murphy had compared it, and he doubted very much that the people who built it had meant to memorialize a wishbone.

Still, as he looked up at its gleaming splendor in the distance, he had to admit it was impressive. Maybe that was it. Maybe the people who built it had only meant to make something interesting, something different, something impressive. He liked that idea, though it was still hard to fathom going quite to those lengths in order to make something that had no larger purpose than decorating the river.

Jim took the raft in close to the shore, beside the monument, which from close by was so tall that Jim had to crane his neck upward to see the top. The legs were massive, thick structures, as big across at their base as their cabin on the island. Bigger, perhaps. Jim smiled as he thought of Murphy trying to reassure him that he needn't worry—he wouldn't miss the monument.

Unfortunately, no great place to hide the raft presented itself. Much of the land beside the river was covered with concrete, but evenly spaced along the shore, at least, beside the raised plateau where the monument stood, there were several thick wooden posts, each only a few feet tall. Jim thought maybe they'd been put here for boats to tie up, once upon a time. Without a better option, he decided he might as well put in here and put one of them to its intended use.

As he went ashore, pack over his shoulder and .22 in hand, he was struck by the large, open space and by how much of it was covered with concrete. Steps were carved into the hill that went up from the river to the plateau below the monument, and Jim climbed them steadily, scanning the horizon as efficiently as possible. He wasn't used to being so exposed, even at night.

At the top, he gazed at the vast, empty, concrete expanse below the monument and the fields of tall, wild grass beyond it. With scores of immense buildings forming a striking skyline beyond that wide-open space before him, he was all the more impressed by how much land lay essentially unused here by the river. The further south he'd come, the buildings had grown gradually bigger and increasingly close together, but not here. It was as though the monument's builders had made some everlasting decree that nothing would ever be built to block the view of their strange but fascinating creation, and perhaps they had.

Jim stood on the concrete plateau and surveyed the great buildings in the distance. He understood why Murphy had assured him that he'd know the city when he saw it. He'd had no concept of its magnitude, that the difference between a town and a city could be so vast. Gazing at it filled him with wonder.

"Jim?"

Jim turned from the city to look at HF.

"Maybe we should get out of the open. I think we'll find the old feller who lives here below ground. Over there."

Jim frowned, puzzled, and looked in the direction the robot was pointing. Over by the leg, stairs went down, and down below ground there appeared to be some kind of trench or tunnel, but from where Jim was standing, he couldn't see where it led, though perhaps there were doors to someplace else down there. He looked back at HF. "Why do you think we'll find him there?"

"Well," HF said, as though the answer should be obvious, "that's where he was the last time."

"Last time?" Jim said, surprise and anger vying for control. "What do you mean, HF? Have you been here before?"

"Course I have, Jim," HF said, also sounding surprised. "With Atticus, when we come upriver the first time."

"With Atticus," Jim said, almost under his breath, staring at HF. "You've been here and ... didn't it occur to you before now that it might have been helpful for me to know that?"

"No," HF said. "Why are you gettin' all worked up?"

"Why am I worked up?" Jim said, roughly. "If I'd known you'd been here, I could have asked you questions about it. I'd have known you'd recognize this place when you saw it. Why didn't you tell me?"

"You didn't ask," HF said.

"I didn't ... " Jim stared, flabbergasted. "And when I told you we were looking for a monument that looked like a big wishbone? It didn't occur to you then that maybe telling me about your previous trip to a monument that looked like a big wishbone might be a good idea?"

"Well," HF said, "Atticus never it described it like that, and I didn't know you meant this place until we got here."

Jim swallowed and clenched his teeth. He tried to think of Atticus, who'd always controlled his irritation and his anger. To do that, Jim had to look away. The sight of HF's bewildered face made him seethe. He couldn't understand why the robot hadn't mentioned his familiarity with the monument, but he didn't really want to waste any more time talking about it.

"Come on," Jim said brusquely, and he stalked off toward the steps that led down to dark tunnel below.

He was glad the tunnel was open at the top and that some of the moonlight reached its bottom, so it wasn't completely dark. Up ahead, he saw several large doors that looked to be metal and black glass, and he approached them cautiously. As he leaned in to listen against one, he heard a loud bark and stumbled back, images of wild dogs running through his head. He lost his balance and fell hard backward, onto the concrete.

As he hit the ground, badly scraping the hand he put out to break his fall, he heard a voice call out from the other side of the door. "Shep, be quiet!"

One of the doors opened, and Jim scrambled to point the .22 at it with his uninjured hand.

# Disconnect

"Why don't you lower that gun," the voice said from inside. The door remained partially open. "Then I'll come outside."

"Who are you?" Jim asked, lowering the gun at first before changing his mind and lifting the barrel back up.

"My guess is I'm who you're looking for," the voice said, still behind the dark glass. "You did come looking for someone, didn't you?"

"You're the Caretaker?"

"Some call me that," the voice replied, "though it's been a while since any have."

Jim lowered the gun now and started to pick himself up. The door opened a little further, and a massive bundle of fur that Jim took to be Shep bounded out and almost knocked HF over with its enthusiasm.

"Shep, get down!" The owner of the voice stepped through the door now, and Jim saw in the dim light a small man, perhaps five and half feet tall, and very thin, though not exactly frail. He was bald, and the moonlight gleamed on his shiny head like it did on the monument.

The dog obeyed and settled down, though Jim could see that it didn't want to. HF, who had stepped back to avoid being knocked over, went over to Shep and stroked the thick hair on the dog's large head. "Well, no one can say you ain't a friendly feller."

"He is that," the Caretaker said, walking past the dog to the place where Jim now stood, examining his scraped and stinging hand for the first time. There was more blood than he'd expected.

"Can I see that?" the Caretaker asked. Jim extended his hand and he added, "Sorry I scared you."

"It was the dog, actually," Jim said, not wanting the man to think he fell over every time he heard a voice or saw a door open.

"Don't like dogs?"

"Like 'em just fine, most of the time," Jim said. "But a few nights ago I had a run-in with a few wild ones. On edge, I guess."

"Ah," said the Caretaker. "I see. Shep was just trying to be friendly, you know. He saw you through the doors and barked."

"He saw me through the doors?" Jim said, glancing over at them again.

"The glass is opaque on this side, translucent on the other. Handy when you want to see what's outside without being seen yourself."

"I guess so," Jim said.

"Come on," the Caretaker said, turning to head back inside. "Let's go in. Wherever you've come from, and whatever you've come to see me for, there's no point lingering out here."

The Caretaker held the door opened and whistled, and Shep bounded back inside. Jim and HF followed the dog in, and Jim let Shep have a good sniff and lick of his uninjured hand while they waited for the Caretaker to follow them in.

Jim heard the door shut and latch, and without saying a word, the Caretaker walked past them and into what appeared to be a vast underground room. As the Caretaker walked, lights sensed his motion and flickered on above, so he was always surrounded by the glow of soft light. Behind them, by the doors, the light that had welcomed them switched off as they moved away.

Jim surveyed the enormous room with wonder. Jim had never seen anything quite that large. Lots of machines lined the walls, or maybe it was only one really big one, but there were lots of monitors and lights and who knows what else. Jim didn't understand what any of it was, but he could hear the quiet whirr of something, perhaps a fan or fans, clicking on and off, along with several other distant sounds, some coming from the dark places beyond what was currently lit for him to see.

The Caretaker paid no attention to any of this but walked more or less straight through the empty center of the great room with Shep at his side. Jim trailed, mesmerized by what he was seeing all around him, but when he saw the Caretaker turn and approach the wall off to the side, he hurried to catch up.

A door opened into a much smaller room, set up with a sofa and chair on the right and a small wooden table on the left. A small alcove just beyond the table and chair was set up as a kitchen, and it was at the entrance to this alcove that the Caretaker finally turned and surveyed Jim. "Come over to the sink, and let's wash that hand."

Jim walked over to the faucet, and when the Caretaker turned the handle, water came gushing out. There'd been a faucet much like this in the cabin, but turning the handle hadn't ever made water come out. Atticus said the well that supplied the cabin had long been dry. Jim thought of the vast space through which he'd just walked and of the massive city nearby and wondered how many wells it had taken to supply it all with water, and how many of them still had water if this faucet worked so well.

The water flowing from the faucet was warm and felt good on his hand, and once the blood was washed off, the Caretaker grabbed a soft cloth and wrapped it gently. "There," he said at last. "It's really just a bad scrape, but that should keep it clean until it scabs over."

"Thanks," Jim said, regarding the Caretaker more carefully now. He had a serious face, but not unkind. Outside, Jim had thought him dressed in black, but in the light he saw that wasn't the case. His crisp, neat shirt and pants were a dark blue. On the shirt, over the man's left breast, there was a gold insignia of the letters 'V' and 'C' overlaid in large block letters. Jim had never seen the mark before, but he didn't need to be told it must stand for Vista Corp.

"Hungry?" the Caretaker asked.

"A little," Jim lied. He was famished.

"I bet," the man said, turning back into the kitchen. He took a plate from his cupboard and opened the refrigerator, reappearing a moment later with the plate covered with meat and cheese and several slices of bread. Jim couldn't believe his eyes, and the growl that burst from his stomach echoed in the room.

"Sit. Eat." the man said, handing him the plate and indicating toward the table with a smirk on his face. "Before you keel over."

Jim took the plate and set it carefully down on the table as he took a seat himself. He picked up some of the meat and stuffed it in his mouth before it occurred to him that it would have been more polite to say thanks first. He tried to say it now, but his jaws seemed reluctant to stop chewing long enough for his words to be intelligible. The Caretaker smiled and said, "Never mind all that. There will be plenty of time for words later."

Jim didn't try to speak again until he'd finished every crumb off the entire plate and washed it down with a glass of cold water that had come from the same faucet. The Caretaker, who had taken the only other seat at the wooden table, had turned his attention to HF. The robot was sitting on the chair on the other side of the room, looking at Shep, who was lying next to him on the sofa, panting rhythmically.

"You're robotic friend looks quite familiar," the Caretaker said at last, though without turning to look at Jim. "I believe we've met before."

"You have," Jim said, impressed by the man's memory. "He came here many years ago with my father."

"And with you," the Caretaker added, looking from the robot to Jim at last. "Unless I'm very much mistaken, you're Atticus' boy."

"I am," Jim said.

"And your father?" the Caretaker said. "He didn't come with you?"

"No," Jim said, the image of Atticus, lying in the cabin, the candle burning on his chest suddenly appearing before him. "He's dead."

The Caretaker nodded thoughtfully, as though he'd half expected to hear that answer. "I'm sorry, son. Atticus was my friend."

"I think that's why he sent me to you," Jim said.

"He sent you here?"

"Yes. He was sick for many days, feverish and confused, but on the day he died, he seemed to come out of it briefly. He told me to find Florence and to go to the Caretaker. I didn't know where Florence was—and still don't—but a neighbor told me I might be able to find you here."

"Ah," the Caretaker said, but with a slightly distracted air, as though Jim's words had jogged a distant memory. "I see."

Jim wasn't sure what else the Caretaker might need to know, so he kept on explaining. "Murphy, my neighbor, built me a raft, and I came downriver looking for you, hoping you could tell me where to find Florence. Murphy hadn't ever heard of the place."

"I'm not surprised," the Caretaker said, lifting his hand to stroke his chin. "Florence isn't a place. It's a person"

"It is?" Jim asked, the slight embarrassment he felt for not having known that, eclipsed by his joy that the Caretaker clearly knew precisely what Atticus had been talking about. Whatever came next, his journey had not been in vain.

"As I recall," the Caretaker said, "your mother had an older sister named Florence, though I believe Atticus generally referred to her as 'Flor.'"

"My mother's sister," Jim repeated, feeling a little dazed. "I have an aunt named Flor."

"You do," the Caretaker said, his eyebrows rising slightly as he watched Jim's response. "Atticus never told you?"

"No," Jim said, not sure what else to say. Atticus hadn't liked to talk about Jim's mother. He always said it was too hard, and Jim had tried to respect that, even if he didn't like it. But how could he have not known his mother had a sister? How could Atticus have never mentioned that? It stung. It felt like betrayal.

"I liked Aunt Flor," HF sung out cheerfully, blissfully unaware of the mixed emotions raging inside Jim. "She always treated me fair. She was a real nice lady."

Jim pushed back his chair and leapt to his feet, rounding on HF savagely. "You've got to be kidding me!" Jim fairly spat out the words in an angry shout. "You knew I had an Aunt named Florence?"

"Easy son—"

"Sure I did," HF said, looking at Jim with wide-eyed wonder. "Whatcha getting all mad and hollering for? You're jumpier than a bullfrog these days, Jim."

"Why am I mad? I'll tell you why I'm mad. You knew I was looking for a monument that looks like a wishbone standing, and you never mentioned the fact that you'd been there. You knew Atticus told me to find Florence, and you never mentioned that I have an aunt by that name."

Jim stood, glaring at HF, and the Caretaker moved softly up beside him. "I realize—" he started to say, but Jim ignored him and kept on shouting.

"You want to know why I'm shouting? I'll tell you why. It's because I'm stuck with the world's dumbest robot, who only tells me what I most need to know after I already know it."

HF stared at Jim, open-mouthed. Suddenly, the room was very quiet, and at last, HF said softly. "I'm sorry, Jim. I didn't mean to let you down. I guess I ain't so useful after all."

Jim felt a pang of shame, but he pushed it away. He'd spoken the truth. The robot was useless.

"Can I have a word?" the Caretaker asked.

Jim saw the man pointing to the large room beyond the door. "Sure," he said, a little sulkily, and followed him outside.

The Caretaker took him out, a short distance away, then stopped and turned to face him. "I can see you're frustrated, but it's not the robot you're angry at. Not really."

"No?" Jim said, brusquely.

"No, Jim. It's Atticus," the Caretaker said. "And I don't blame you, he should have told you about your aunt."

"He didn't like to talk about my mother," Jim said, trying to defend his father, though his words rang hollow.

"He was always a private man," the Caretaker conceded graciously. "Still, we both know you had a right to know about Florence before now."

"That's right," Jim said. "And that's why I'm angry at HF. He could have told me."

The Caretaker studied Jim carefully, and Jim squirmed a little under the intensity of the scrutiny. "You don't know, do you?"

"Know what?" Jim said.

"About the robot. About what Atticus did."

"What do you mean?" Jim said, annoyed at the inference that there might be more that Atticus had kept from him.

The Caretaker sighed, then led Jim further away from the door, as though to make doubly sure that they couldn't be overheard there. "Atticus was obsessed with making a robot that would look and sound like he thought Huck Finn would look and sound."

"Yeah, I know."

"He designed and built several until he got one that looked right," the Caretaker continued patiently.

"I know, and sounded right," Jim said. "Good old HF-17—it took that many tries for Atticus to make an HF that finally sounded close enough to what he imagined Huck Finn would sound like.

"True," the Caretaker said. "Atticus did tinker with their voices and vocabulary until he thought he had one that sounded right. But, even then, he wasn't satisfied."

"Why not?" Jim asked, his curiosity getting the better of his petulance.

"He was too smart. It didn't matter that he looked like a kid and sounded like your father's vision of one of his favorite fictional characters, he still observed everything, remembered everything and made connections between these things just like the top of the line robot that he was.

"Your father only designed and built the best. All the mannerism and affectation in the world couldn't cover up the fact he was a robot with flawless programming and incredible processing speed. He might look like Huck and sound like Huck, but he betrayed all the time that he couldn't possibly be Huck, and Atticus hated that."

"So what did he do?"

"I'm not a robotics engineer, so I couldn't say exactly, but he basically went in and sabotaged the robot's ability to process information. Whether he disconnected things that should have been connected or reprogrammed him or what, I couldn't say, but the robot lost the ability to put two and two together and get four. Maybe not entirely, but pretty close."

Jim looked back at the door, imagined HF sitting by Shep, still smarting from the tongue-lashing he'd given him. There had always been something odd, something not quite right about HF, about what he did and didn't seem to understand. He had always known that, even if he hadn't known why.

A half a dozen memories of HF's surprising ignorance flashed through his mind, none more recent or more vivid than the robot's apparent inability to understand that Atticus was dead and what that entailed. He had gotten angry then, too, but now he realized that HF couldn't help it. He was exactly what Atticus had made him to be—an ignorant child.

"He still sees what a robot would see," the Caretaker explained, "still stores information a robot would store, still remembers what a robot would remember, but he lacks the ability to sort and sift and combine that information in a way that would approximate higher order human thinking. He probably knows a lot more stuff you'd like to know, Jim, but it never occurs to him to tell you.

"It can't."

# Daylight

Jim lay awake on the Caretaker's sofa, staring through the darkness at the ceiling he could not see. The darkness felt so complete that Jim thought it might swallow him, and he almost wished it would. The silence wasn't nearly as complete as the darkness. The sound of whirring he had heard on the way in continued unabated from the cavernous room beyond the nearby door. And now that he was listening more carefully, he could hear the stillness of the night punctuated by the occasional click as well, a sound as inscrutable to him as the periodic whirring.

The Caretaker was in the small bedroom that lay beside the alcove kitchen, and Shep was in there with him—at least at the moment. The dog had been out a few times to check on Jim and HF, who sat motionless at the small wooden table. Jim did not want to encourage the visits—just in case he actually managed to fall asleep at some point—so he had so far ignored the occasional sound of padding feet and panting when it came near.

He was heartily ashamed of his earlier outburst and had apologized to HF, not that it had made any difference. The robot had waved the episode off like it was already forgotten, or like it had been nothing to begin with, and that hadn't helped. It just left Jim to wonder if HF was capable of connecting the apology with the offense. Maybe the robot couldn't really grasp the reason for Jim's contrition.

A host of memories had come unbidden as he lay there. Memories of occasions over the years when he'd made fun of HF for his failure to understand things Jim thought he should understand. Things he would have understood save for Atticus' alterations to his circuitry. All those times he'd mocked HF, it had never occurred to him to attribute the robot's deficiencies to its maker.

Now that he knew, he wasn't sure what to think. Atticus had made the robot to be his companion, so he guessed Atticus had a right to make it in whatever manner he saw fit. Even so, it felt somehow cruel to deprive the robot of a better understanding of itself and its world. And yet, even as he thought that, Jim knew he was treating HF like a human being, and he wasn't. It wasn't. It was a machine, and like other machines, it had been made for the pleasure and convenience of man.

But, even if that was so, why hadn't Atticus' told him? And why hadn't Atticus told him about his Aunt? The Caretaker had been right. The anger directed toward HF was really anger at Atticus. He wished Atticus were there so he could take him to task. He wanted to believe there was a good reason for his father's silence, but even if there were, he'd never know it now.

There, in the darkness, the anger dissipated, replaced by sadness. He had found the Caretaker, found the answer to the riddle of Florence, and yet there was no joy. Not tonight anyway. Maybe tomorrow, by the light of a new day, his spirits would revive. Tonight, there was only darkness and melancholy and the strong and persistent desire in his heart to be back at the cabin in his own bed with Atticus sleeping soundly across the room.

Just like things had always been, before the fever.

A hand shook Jim gently, and he realized with a start that he must have fallen asleep after all, sometime during his mournful vigil. He opened his eyes and looked up at the Caretaker, who stood beside the sofa, Shep panting beside him.

"Come," the Caretaker said softly. "You should see the city at dawn."

HF didn't stir as Jim rose quietly and followed them out. They retraced their steps of the previous evening, only when they approached the doors through which Shep had seen Jim and HF, Jim could see the early rays of morning shining through. The Caretaker pushed the door open and strode out, followed closely by the dog.

Jim followed them, not wanting either to be left behind or be thought a coward, but as they climbed the stairs out of the trench, returning to the vast concrete plateau on which the monument rested, he felt increasingly exposed and afraid. His eyes were drawn skyward, but not to examine the monument.

"Don't worry," the Caretaker said. "You're safe from them here."

Jim looked at him. "How?"

The Caretaker motioned to the monument and the area around it. "This is the entrance to the regional hub for the Vista Corporation. No hunter would come here. On the outskirts of the city, north or west or south, maybe, but not here. Not near the river, and not near the monument. They know this is forbidden."

"I thought hunting for groundlings was always forbidden," Jim said, scorn in his voice.

"It is," the Caretaker said, ignoring Jim's tone.

"Then why should I believe I'm safe, simply because it's 'forbidden?'"

"Because that's what I'm telling you," the Caretaker said. "There are rules they disregard, but there are also rules they don't."

"I guess it's good to know that something restrains them," Jim said, knowing he probably still sounded rude, but not caring much. He'd spent enough of his life hiding from the light of day for fear of hunters, that he didn't feel a need to hide his contempt for them.

"Look," the Caretaker said, directing his attention to the city skyline in the distance. "This is what I brought you here to see."

Jim turned to look then, and he almost gasped at the beauty of what he saw. The tall, majestic structures of these unusually large and magnificent buildings glinted in the morning sun that rose behind him in the east. He could see that some of them were damaged, and all of them showed signs of neglect, but there was enough of their original splendor that he caught a glimpse in his mind's eye of what this place must have looked like in the days long ago when people had lived here and the city had been alive.

As Jim stood and stared at them, feasting his eyes on their glory, he said to the Caretaker. "Why did people abandon such great cities as this to move to the hives?"

The Caretaker chuckled, and Jim turned to face him, wondering what had prompted the laughter. "Why am I not surprised you don't know that story?"

Jim felt his face redden with embarrassment. Here was yet another thing Atticus hadn't told him. Did he even know anything, or had Atticus systematically kept him from knowing more than a child would know? Maybe he was the living version of the HF experiment.

The Caretaker observed his reaction, seemed to realize that he'd implied more than he meant to, and stepped over, putting a firm but kindly hand on his shoulder. "I'm sorry, my boy, I didn't mean any offense. Atticus had a deep and abiding hatred of the hives, is all, and I just meant to say I'm not surprised he didn't talk about them, let alone explain their history."

Jim nodded, acknowledging the Caretaker's words, hoping that his visible embarrassment had faded. He had no reason to doubt the Caretaker, but it was too late to hide his obvious doubts about this father. The seed of the idea that Atticus had meant to keep him unnaturally young, like HF, was hard for him to disregard once planted.

The Caretaker hastened on. "It's the kind of thing I've always been interested in, myself. History, and all that. Your father never cared much for it. In many ways, he was a typical robotics engineer, his head full of diagrams and schematics. In other ways, of course, he wasn't.

"He liked stories from the old world, because they showed man living on the land, not in the sky. Still, he didn't really care about the particulars of what had transpired to reshape the world and why."

"Would you tell me?" Jim asked, now looking at the sunlit skyline again. "I'd like to know."

"Sure," the Caretaker said. "I don't see why not. I can, though, do even better than tell you about the hives."

"What do you mean?" Jim said, turning back to face him, a pulse of wonder and excitement rising within.

"I visit the hive a few hours northeast of here by hovercraft every month to see my doctor and get supplies, and it just so happens I'm supposed to go today. I was thinking of rescheduling, but why don't you come?"

Jim swallowed, a shiver running down his spine. He blinked as he stared at the Caretaker. The man looked perfectly serious. He meant it. He was offering Jim a chance not only to see a hive, but to go inside one.

"You go to a hive? Every month?" It was all Jim managed to get out.

"Sure," the Caretaker said. "I do work for Vista Corp, and even though I like living on the ground, like you, I also like taking advantage of what a hive can offer when it comes to food and medical care, among other things."

Jim turned back to the skyline in the distance, but it wasn't those shining towers that occupied his thoughts now. He had often wondered what it would be like in a world where food didn't have to be hunted or grown. Where automated transports brought food in abundance. Where comforts like Jim had never experienced were available to all. Now he could go and see for himself.

But then his heart sank. He couldn't. He knew that without needing to entertain the notion any further. Atticus hated the hives, hated the hunters, hated the whole world he'd left behind. He would never have wanted Jim to go there.

"I can't," Jim said, forlorn. "Atticus wouldn't want me to. He'd never have allowed it."

"Well, he wouldn't have liked it, probably," the Caretaker said. "But Atticus isn't here, Jim. He wouldn't have liked you showing interest in the hives at all, but you have, and that's both understandable and reasonable, I think."

"That's different," Jim said, protesting. "Learning about them and visiting one are two different things."

"That's true, but you're just as free to do the one as the other. Your father grew up in a hive, so his opinion was based on his experience. I don't doubt that he wouldn't like the thought of you going, but at the same time, I find it hard to believe that he wouldn't want you to form your own opinions, based on your own experiences."

Jim stared at the city in the distance. From the moment Atticus had died, he had thought of nothing other than doing what Atticus had told him to do—going to the Caretaker, finding Florence. It was dawning on him, at that moment, that sometime, perhaps soon, he would be finished with that task. What then? He had a life to live, and Atticus wasn't there to give him any more guidance about how to live it.

He had to make his own choices now, and take responsibility for them.

"Let's go back inside," the Caretaker said. "Get some breakfast. I won't leave for another hour. You can tell me anytime up until the moment I leave whether or not you want to come.

"It's up to you."

# Flight

Jim had never seen a hovercraft up close before. The Caretaker's was sleek and silver, the top half almost entirely transparent so the pilot could see outside in any direction. At a voice command from the Caretaker, a slender section of the hovercraft on one side folded down into a narrow stair, which rested firmly on the ground.

The Caretaker carried a small bag up those stairs, and Jim watched from the ground as he stepped inside and momentarily disappeared. HF stood silently beside him, and Shep lay contentedly at his feet. A moment later the Caretaker's head popped up in the opening again, and he said, "I have my own private hangar you know. Bought a new place a few years ago, just for that reason."

Jim didn't know what a hangar was, so he just said, "Yeah?"

"Yeah, so you wouldn't have to go anywhere in the hive you didn't want to go. You could see the hive as we fly in, stay at my place while I do what I need to, and then fly back with me. Easy, and absolutely no need to venture around inside if you decide you don't want to."

"What's your real name?" Jim blurted out, searching for something else to talk about and finding only that. He cringed a bit at the directness of the question, but he was feeling drawn to the hive and hoped that changing the subject might stiffen his resolve.

The Caretaker leaned in the opening to the hovercraft and said, "My real name is Daniel Robinson, but almost all my friends call me Doc."

"Why?"

"Cause I'm a Doctor."

"You are?" Jim said, looking at him curiously.

"I am, just not the kind you're thinking of."

Jim frowned, not sure what he meant. "What other kind is there?"

"I went to school for a very long time, and part of my reward for studying so hard, was that I earned the title of 'doctor.' Your father was a doctor, too. Did you know that?"

Jim shook his head, no longer surprised that there were things like this that he didn't know about Atticus. "So he went to school for a long time too?"

"I didn't know him then," the Caretaker said, "but he sure did. He was a really, really good robotics engineer, Jim. That kind of mastery doesn't come easily."

"How'd you become known as 'the Caretaker?'" Jim asked, once again reaching for a way to change the subject.

"Ah, well, that's a bit of a story, and I need to be getting on my way. How about you come along and I'll tell you?"

Jim took a deep breath and braced himself, but he knew his resistance had slipped away. Here was his chance to see a hive in safety, to actually fly into one with somebody who knew where to go and what to do. As a groundling, he might never get another chance like this.

He nodded.

"Good," the Caretaker said. "That's settled then. HF could squeeze in too if you'd like to bring him along, but he'll be just fine here with Shep if you decide not to."

Jim turned to HF. "What do you think, HF? Want to come see a hive with me?"

"I don't know, Jim," HF said uncertainly. "Atticus never had nothing good to say about the hives. You sure about this?"

"The Caretaker knows where he's going and what he's doing, HF," Jim said. "But if you'd rather not come, that's fine."

"I'll stay with Shep," HF said. "He'll be awful lonesome if we all go."

"That's very thoughtful of you, HF," the Caretaker said warmly. He turned to Jim, "Well, unless there's something you need to go and get, why don't you come on up? We might as well be on our way."

Flying wasn't nearly as scary as Jim had thought it would be. He felt a little sick at his stomach as the hovercraft rose up into the air, but now that it was flying in a more or less straight line, he didn't feel sick anymore. He knew they were going very fast, and it was a strange sensation, but he was too curious about the world they were flying over to dwell on that for long.

The Caretaker pointed out all kinds of interesting things, including the automated supply trains heading northeast across the open land. They were headed to the hive from the regional hub, he said, carrying the food that fed the millions who lived there. Not far from the lines headed north were the lines headed south, full of empty trains heading back for more. They were both part of an essentially continuous process that ran night and day, every day of the year.

"Doc?" Jim said, as they left the trains behind, then Jim hesitated and turned to see if the Caretaker had reacted. "Do you mind if I call you that?"

"Go ahead," the Caretaker said, smiling just a little bit. "I said that's what my friends call me. Call me 'Doc,' or 'Doc Robinson' even—both are easier and more personable than 'the Caretaker.'"

"All right," Jim said, settling into the small but comfortable chair beside the Caretaker. "Where'd that name come from?"

"It was nearly 40 years ago. I'd only just started at my station, when the sensors picked up movement up above, under the monument—that's how I knew you were coming, by the way," the Caretaker added, turning to look at Jim. "There are motion sensors that tell me whenever anything comes ashore near the monument, or when anything crosses the empty ground from the old city, too."

Jim nodded. He'd wondered how the Caretaker had just happened to be there at the door to meet him, in the middle of the night no less.

"It was a family of groundlings," the Caretaker continued the story. "She was very pregnant, and he was carrying a little girl, no more than a year or a year and a half old.

"Letting people into my station was strictly against protocol, and worse, there are things I was supposed to do, devices to use, all designed to 'discourage' anyone from coming near, let alone inside, but it was storming out and they were all soaked. I just couldn't do it. So I went up after them and brought them in.

"They were heading downriver, but the little girl was sick, so they ended up staying with me for almost a week. Once she was better, they headed on out, and I thought that was that. Much to my surprise, some six months later, another family showed up at the monument. They were coming upriver, and they weren't there by accident. They'd come looking for me. They'd heard someone lived under the monument who would take care of them, and that's how my nickname was born.

"For a long time, I had pretty regular visitors. Sometimes only a few a year, sometimes a good deal more than that. It got to a point there for a while when it really bothered me. After all, I'd taken that post because I liked to be alone, not because I wanted to run some kind of halfway house or be a station on a modern day underground railroad. Still, when the folks stopped coming, I missed it more than I thought I would. Guess I kind of got used to it."

"Is that how you met my dad?" Jim asked. "Did he come to you for help, like those others?"

"Well, he did, actually," the Caretaker said. "But that isn't how I met him. I first met your dad a half a dozen years after I took this station. I had a huge problem on my main line, and Vista sent your father out to take a look at it. He was their best young robotics engineer and they couldn't afford to have this hub offline for long. He was probably almost thirty, but that was his first time leaving the hive. He got my problems sorted out and fixed up in no time, but he lingered on here a while.

"He liked sitting up above, under the monument, watching the Mississippi River roll on by. He didn't end up leaving the hive for another five years, but I think it all started right there, sitting by the river and watching it roll, just like it's been doing since time began.

"That's when what started?"

"His discontentment with hive-life," the Caretaker replied. "A lot of folks who leave and become groundlings do so because they've been outside and caught a passion for the earth, for the soil, for wind in their hair and fresh air in their lungs. Sometimes that passion fades when they return to the hive, but it doesn't always go away. It didn't for Atticus."

"So when he eventually did leave, he came to you?"

"He did," the Caretaker said. "He knew Vista wouldn't be happy that he'd left, but he also knew he could trust me. So, he took a hovercraft from the hive where he lived in the mountains—"

"Mountains?" Jim said. "Are there mountains near here?"

"No," the Caretaker said. "The hive where your father lived was a long, long way out west—"

"West?" Jim interrupted again. "So the hive where we're headed isn't the one Atticus came from?"

"No, it isn't," the Caretaker said.

"Oh," Jim said. Surprisingly, he felt a little relieved. Maybe Atticus wouldn't have been quite so upset that Jim was going to see a hive if it wasn't the same one he'd left, the same hive he'd hated. "Sorry, go ahead."

"That's all right," the Caretaker said. "Where was I?"

"You were saying that Atticus took a hovercraft from the hive," Jim said. "Did he fly to you?"

"No, actually. That's just it, he couldn't. They would have been able to track him then. He flew south a few hours from the mountains and landed. Then he got out and headed east by foot. It was a long and treacherous journey. There's a lot of open ground between here and the mountains, and it was very risky for him to come this way, but he didn't ever want to be found.

"That, and he'd fallen in love with the river."

Jim thought of a young Atticus, crossing miles and miles of open ground. Even if he'd been careful and only moved at night, it was strange to contemplate. The Atticus he'd known had freaked out if Jim went out in the open at all, even after dark. Here was yet another surprise revelation about his father.

"So he came to you, at the monument?" Jim asked. "How long did he stay?"

"A few months," the Caretaker said. "Those were good times, too. Your dad was good company."

"Why'd he leave?"

The Caretaker stared out the window at the sky ahead, and for a long moment, he didn't answer. Jim turned and searched the horizon himself, thinking that perhaps he'd seen something that had distracted him, but he didn't see anything. He turned back to the Caretaker, "Doc?"

"He didn't leave the hive to only go halfway," the Caretaker replied. "He wanted to live a life that was closer to the land, closer to how people used to live before the hives. And…"

"Yes?"

"Well, we had something of an ongoing argument, and I think it really frustrated him."

"What about?"

"He didn't like that I worked for Vista," the Caretaker said. "He didn't just think that life out here was different, or even better, he thought that life in the hive was wrong. So, my working for Vista and having anything to do with the means by which hive-life was sustained was unacceptable for Atticus. In the end, we reached a sort of truce. Still, it bothered him, and after a while he drifted on."

"You don't think living in the hive is wrong?" Jim asked, hesitantly. Atticus had rarely referred to hive-life or hive-dwellers, but when he had, it had always been with contempt.

"No, I guess I don't," the Caretaker said.

"But what about hunters?" Jim asked. "Don't you think shooting groundlings is wrong?"

"Of course," the Caretaker said quickly, almost dismissively. "But you can disapprove of hunting groundlings and not think living in a hive is immoral."

"But don't the people in the hives know what the hunters are doing? Atticus always said they know and do nothing to stop it, and that knowing makes them complicit."

"Well, he was right in a way," the Caretaker said. "Hunting groundlings is technically illegal, and always has been, but a scandal back when your father and I worked together—involving several prominent government officials hunting groundlings—had the unfortunate effect of making the practice almost acceptable in many quarters. Maybe even most."

"And isn't that wrong?"

"Of course, but that wasn't the question. If you're asking me if everything in the hives is good, then no, it isn't. But every era and culture has its blind spots. Long before the hives, when people still lived on the ground in cities like the one by my station, people did awful things then too.

"You're talking about problems that lie in the hearts of men, Jim, not in the structures of the hive. If you want to talk about whether hives are better or worse than cities, whether it is wise or foolish to live in self-contained towers in the sky, then I'm happy to debate those questions. But I don't see the issue of the hives as a moral question, as a question of right or wrong."

Jim thought about this. He thought the Caretaker had a point, but he remembered how Atticus had always linked the behavior of the hunters with their separation from the earth. "Isn't it possible," he said, as he thought about it, trying hard to frame his thoughts clearly and carefully, "That the behavior of the hive-dwellers is shaped by the fact that they live in the hive? That maybe they don't appreciate life because they experience so few living things around them?"

The Caretaker smiled and turned to look at Jim. He studied Jim's face for a moment, then said, "You sounded so much like Atticus, just then. I had to look and make sure it wasn't him."

Jim felt a flush of pride. He felt sure that the Caretaker had meant that as a compliment, and he took it as one. He didn't have long to savor the compliment, though, as the Caretaker said. "Look. Over there. Can you see it?"

Jim turned, and sure enough, there was the hive.

# The Hive

The golden glass and steel of the immense hive glittered in the bright morning sun. Jim had thought the towers of the ancient city that lay beyond the monument had been large, but they were nothing compared to this. The hive was like a mountain of gold, towering over not just the physical landscape that surrounded it, but over every idea, every memory and every image that Jim carried inside himself toward it.

Not only did the hive dwarf those other buildings he'd gazed upon that morning—in much the same way those buildings had dwarfed the simple structures Jim had grown up with on the island—but those giants from the distant past had all been essentially rectangular, rising in clear, straight lines off the ground. The hive was more than simply huge; it was remarkably complex. One could have called it round, Jim supposed, like a cylinder is round, but their were thousands upon thousands, if not millions of curved nodes extending from it on all sides and at all levels. These gave it the appearance of a simply enormous tree bud that had yet to flower.

"Well," the Caretaker asked. "What do you think?"

"It's astonishing," Jim said. "How could men build something so vast? How…?"

"I know," the Caretaker said. "It beggars the imagination. And it isn't even an especially large hive. All the inland hives are pretty modest."

Modest? Jim wondered if that word meant the same thing to him that it did to the Caretaker. How could anyone refer to what he was looking at as modest? Even if this was the smallest hive in existence, it could never be considered modest. Maybe less imposing, less vast, or less astonishing, but never modest.

Jim noticed for the first time that they weren't the only hovercraft flying near the hive. The closer they got, the more he noticed many, many others going to and from the great structure, and suddenly he saw with unmistakable clarity the similarity between the hive and its natural namesake. The hovercrafts, like small swarms of bees, were concentrated in specific areas, near what appeared to be larger than normal nodes with open spaces in them like gaping mouths. He pointed this out to the Caretaker, who explained what he was seeing.

"Those are the public hangars," the Caretaker said. "About half of the traffic in and out of the hive goes through them. The other half goes in and out of private hangars like mine, which isn't as noticeable of course."

The Caretaker was circling around the hive to the west, and suddenly he pointed at a cluster of nodes about two thirds of the way up the hive. "My place is up ahead," he said. "I wanted a western-facing view, because I like to watch the sun go down when I stay here overnight. At my station, I can see the rising sun in the east just fine, but the city obscures the setting sun pretty much completely."

The Caretaker took the hovercraft in closer, though Jim had no idea how he distinguished any one particular node from another. Perhaps something in the controls of the hovercraft was fixed on its position, Jim thought. He couldn't imagine any other way, once having left, that the Caretaker could ever find his way back home.

Jim shuddered. Home. The hives were home, not just to some who had chosen a different way, but to the vast majority of all people. This was where, with the exception of the small and scattered groundling population, the world lived—or at least, in places just like this one. He was the outsider, the exception, living like the ancients in what he could see now were dramatically primitive conditions.

He'd always known this was the case, but as he watched the hive come closer, it occurred to him for the first time that it was no wonder so few people, comparatively, ever left the hive. Life on the ground was not just simpler, harder, it seemed inevitably that it must also be less glorious. If the luxury within matched the splendor without—and Atticus had never pretended that it didn't—who would ever leave?

Why had Atticus left?

Jim felt a twinge of guilt. He had second-guessed Atticus before on many things, but usually on things of little real consequence. Never on this—on his choice to leave the hive and become a groundling. He had trusted that decision as implicitly as he trusted Atticus. But now, gazing with his own two eyes on the world his father had left behind, he felt doubt, doubt fed by the growing misgiving raised by all the things Atticus had failed to tell him.

Maybe his father's judgement wasn't as impeccable as he had always thought.

"Here we go," the Caretaker said, and the hovercraft veered in toward the hive. Jim could feel the hovercraft decelerating, but as the enormous structure loomed closer and closer, it still seemed to Jim like they were moving awfully fast.

Up ahead, a section of one of the nodes in front of them began to open up, revealing a brightly lit interior room, and the Caretaker flew straight toward it. As they passed inside, the hovercraft came to complete stop in midair, then gently settled onto the ground.

By the time Jim had followed the Caretaker out of the hovercraft, the section of the exterior wall that had opened to admit them had closed again. In fact, Jim couldn't tell which part had opened in the first place—the entire exterior wall appeared to be a single seamless piece of gold, translucent glass.

The Caretaker extended some cables from the hovercraft to a large machine on the back wall of the room, connecting it to recharge, he said. Then, he led Jim through a door that whooshed open as he approached it, revealing the larger living space of the Caretaker's hive abode.

Jim was struck by the contrast between the Caretaker's hive home and the tiny, simple living space underneath the monument. The main living space was round, ornate and full of beautiful furniture and other objects of curious design. Pictures of moving, interconnected shapes and abstract images hung on the walls, but at a word from the Caretaker, each of them sprang to life, revealing varied scenes of people talking—primarily—but also of a host of other things.

It was common in houses like his cabin back on the island to have old television sets, and Atticus had explained what they were and how they worked. Still, it was surreal to be confronted by so many disparate images and sounds flooding over him all at once. The Caretaker scanned them, seemingly unfazed by the confusion and cacophony flowing out of them, and a moment later, said "Schedule." Immediately it all disappeared, replaced by a single graphic on each screen that revealed the details for his various meetings and appointments that day.

"This is what I'm here to do," the Caretaker said, motioning to the nearest screen. "You can come with me, if you really want to, but I'm guessing, now that you're actually here, you might be having some second thoughts about having come. If so, I want you to know I understand, and I'd recommend staying here until I'm finished. If you decide you want to see more then, I can still show you around a bit before we have to get back."

"That's fine," Jim said, feeling guilty, but nodding as though that was exactly what he'd been thinking.

Actually, he hadn't been feeling any reservations about coming. Quite the contrary, since boarding the hovercraft back at the regional hub, he hadn't second-guessed the decision at all.

"Besides," the Caretaker said with grin, "whether you go out into the hive or not, you really can't go back without spending some time in my Dream Pod."

Jim felt goosebumps. Only once in his entire life had he ever heard Atticus say anything remotely positive about hive-life, and that had been about Dream Pods. He had been teaching Jim about geography, and Atticus had expressed wistfully how effective Dream Pods were for giving someone a feel for the beauty, variety and grandeur in the world.

"I'd love that, Doc," Jim said, eagerly, thinking about all the places in the world Atticus had described visiting as a kid in his family's Dream Pod.

"Well, O.K. then," the Caretaker said, his grin widening. "Follow me."

Jim trailed close behind, down a small hallway to a simple door at the end. It opened and the Caretaker stood aside, letting Jim enter first. The room lit up as Jim entered, but he had no idea where the light actually came from. The floor, walls and ceiling were all white, if indeed those words even applied. The room might have been spherical, as Jim thought he could detect curvature in the floor beneath his feet and the room around him, but the entire room felt seamless and 'of a piece,' just like the exterior walls of the rest of the hive seemed to be.

The Caretaker followed him in, and immediately the door closed. He said, as though speaking to the empty room itself, "Loch Ness."

The white room disappeared. Jim was now standing up high somewhere, looking over a large lake. A swath of bright green grass lay before him, and ahead, on a ridge overlooking the dark water, the ruins of some very old structure, maybe a castle, sat empty.

Jim looked up and studied the dark clouds moving quickly overhead. He almost thought he could feel drizzle as he looked at them, and a cool wind made him rub his arms and brace himself against the chill.

"This is Scotland?" he said, turning to look at the Caretaker, who was glancing around at the beautiful scenery.

"It is," he said. "Would you like to walk around the lake? Go to the ruins? Go somewhere else entirely?"

"Show me something else," Jim said, almost unable to control his excitement. The feel of peeling back the veil and peering into the unknown was intoxicating.

"Uluru," the Caretaker said. At once, the verdant Scottish landscape and the gloomy skies disappeared. A giant, red rock rose up before them, surrounded by harsh red soil out of which tough, scraggly desert bushes grew. The sky was bluer than any sky Jim had ever seen, clear and open as far as his eye could see.

And he was warm. Very warm. The earth beneath his feet radiated heat, and he stripped off his fleece and stood, as sweat began to form on his skin. The dry desert air welcomed the moisture, and a breeze like hot breath kissed his forehead from the direction of the mammoth stone before him.

"It's amazing," Jim murmured.

"That it is," the Caretaker concurred. "And it's all yours. I have to go."

"I just tell it what I want to see?"

"That's right. Tell it where you want to go, and you'll go. And remember, once you're there, you can explore to your heart's content." The Caretaker turned away from Jim and added, "Exit."

"Amazing," Jim said, as the door opened, revealing a hole in the Australian bush that led out into the Caretaker's apartment.

"Have fun with it," the Caretaker said, and the door closed. Jim was alone inside.

Jim stared around him at the vast expanse of deep red earth, over which Uluru towered every bit as much as the wishbone monument towered over the Mississippi. He took a few steps forward, his left arm held out in front of him as though expecting at any moment to hit the wall of the Dream Pod—surely the landscape and great red stone were projections meant to create and sustain the illusion of actually being in the Australian outback.

He didn't run into the wall, though, and he stopped, confused, turning back to look over his shoulder at the landscape behind him. It also stretched forward as far as the eye could see.

He looked down at the ground beneath his feet. Did the floor of the Dream Pod move as he moved? Was it some kind of moving walkway? The Caretaker had said that Jim could explore any of the places he visited, so the Dream Pod must somehow be designed to accommodate motion by its occupants, but how? Jim couldn't imagine.

As he turned back around to face Uluru, he saw a handful of animals out of the corner of his eye, leaping across the barren landscape in the distance. Atticus had told him about kangaroos when he was a boy, and he watched in wonder as this group of them used their powerful legs to leap across huge stretches of land with apparent ease. Jim had watched deer in the woods, back on the island, running gracefully beneath the trees, but he didn't know how deer would fare here. As strange as the kangaroos looked to him, they seemed to fit this rough terrain. They exuded a power that must be necessary in a hard land like this one.

As the kangaroos moved on, Jim looked back at Uluru. It was so big, and yet it still seemed to be a fair distance away. He wasn't sure he wanted to go trudging all that way just to get a closer look. He thought of other places he could visit, and then suddenly blurted out, "Grand Canyon."

# A Perfect Day

Jim stood, looking out over the Grand Canyon, trying to catch his breath. Whereas Uluru had been large and round and red, rising up from the Australian outback into the blue sky, the sides of the canyon were variegated with various shades of red and brown and white. And instead of looking smooth, there appeared to be a million different strata with ridges and ledges running parallel to each other all the way down to the canyon floor.

Down below, the Colorado River rolled lazily along its winding way. It didn't seem as broad or mighty as the Mississippi, and yet it had cut this vast gorge. How long had this water been carving its passage through this rock?

Vegetation was sparse, both up here at the canyon's edge, but also on the sides and down below. Spots of green from bushes and the occasional tree dotted the landscape, but there was precious little of it that Jim could see. Thick cumulus clouds moved across the sky, and their great shadows glided along the canyon walls.

Jim gave a little more thought to exploring here, but the canyon was so vast he didn't really know where to start. Atticus had told him once that it could take a whole day to get down into the canyon from the outside, and there were other things Jim wanted to see.

Just then, he had an idea, but he wasn't sure if it would work. "Beach," he said, wondering what the Dream Pod would do with that.

Any doubts he had about the Dream Pod working with such vague direction disappeared with the Grand Canyon, as a great sandy beach appeared under his feet. It stretched out on both sides, while behind him rose large dunes with sporadic tufts of grass. Ahead, the bright blue of some very large body of water sparkled in the sun. Jim assumed it was an ocean, though which one he couldn't have said. He had always wanted to see an ocean, and now that he finally saw one, it didn't disappoint.

Here, too, large white clouds billowed overhead. Jim looked at them meandering across the sky as he listened to the rhythmic sound of the waves crashing in front of him. After a few moments, he closed his eyes and just listened. The ocean was singing its eternal song, and Jim thought it might be more than all right just to listen to it all day long.

And why not? Jim's eyes opened at the thought. Sure, he could have the Dream Pod take him to every famous place Atticus had ever told him about. He could hop through space from spot to spot, seeing all the things he'd only ever seen in a picture or heard Atticus describe. Or, he could stay right here, at the beach, beside the ocean. Really soak in its beauty. True, he might not ever see the inside of a Dream Pod again, but he might never see a real ocean either, and he didn't feel inclined to leave just now.

His mind was made up. He tossed his fleece down on the sand beside him, then slipped off his shoes and socks. He wasn't sure what to expect, lowering his bare foot onto what appeared to be a sandy beach. He knew it must be an illusion of sorts, optical or tactile or both, but to his surprise, he felt the welcoming embrace of fine, white, soft, warm sand.

"Amazing," he said out loud again. There was no one there to hear him this time, but he felt compelled to say it nonetheless.

He sat down and drew his knees up under his chin. The sky above, the sand below, the water and the waves repeating their ceaseless dance in front of him—it was a place of perfect tranquility.

He was exposed beneath a vast and empty sky, and he felt no fear.

Had life really been like this, once upon a time? Had people really moved about beneath the open sky, unafraid of what might lurk above them? Had people really moved freely across the surface of the earth, going wherever they wanted, enjoying the beauty and the bounty of a majestic world? And if they had, why had they left it and retreated into the hives? Atticus had always spoken of this move with scorn, but it had happened long before he was born. He'd never explained to Jim why it had happened. Maybe he couldn't, but maybe the Caretaker could.

Jim lay back in the warm sand. He put his hands under his head and closed his eyes. Even so, he could feel the brightness of the sun through his closed eyelids. He stretched his legs out and felt sand fall from between his toes onto his bare ankles. This, Jim thought, might just be a perfect day.

Some time later, Jim woke with a start. He blinked as he opened his eyes in the brightness. As he grew accustomed to the light, he stared around at the beach and ocean. His disorientation from finding himself in so foreign a place was thankfully brief. He yawned and stood, stretching.

He had no idea how long he'd been asleep, and it occurred to him that before the Caretaker returned, he had at least one more stop to make. "Mountains," he said, thinking that if his vague request to see a beach had worked, this should too.

He wasn't disappointed. No sooner had the word slipped from his mouth than he found himself standing on a rocky ridge, overlooking a steep drop, facing a whole row of high peaks. He realized as he looked around him and surveyed the line of mountains across the way, that he must be above the tree line. Snow and rock were all he could see, unless he looked downward, where he could see the green tops of scattered fir trees far below.

He shivered in the crisp mountain air, and looking around him, was relieved to see his fleece lying beside him on the rocky ledge. He picked it up and pulled it on, surprised to see puffs of his own breath as he exhaled. How the Dream Pod changed so fast, completely altering the illusion in every sensory detail as it did, was simply baffling. If only Atticus could have been there, he could have explained how it worked.

He sat back down, this time on the hard rock. Being in the Dream Pod had pushed the jumbled and confusing emotions he'd been feeling about Atticus away for a few happy hours. Now they were back. Thinking about him now made Jim both sad and angry, and he felt inclined to indulge both emotions.

An eagle flew overhead, and Jim stared as it wheeled around, its wings spread out wide in its seemingly effortless gliding.

"I wish I could do that," Jim said to the distant eagle in the sky, watching it with envy. He'd love to soar above the river, so high that no hunter in a hovercraft would see him there. So high that he could see everything there was to see for miles in every direction. He'd never have to worry about what he couldn't see above him again. He'd be safe—safe and free.

Jim heard the door open behind him and turned to see the Caretaker framed in the doorway where a chunk of the mountain should be, silhouetted by the interior light of the hall behind him. "Enjoying the view?" he asked.

"Yeah," Jim said, a kind of awed reverence in his voice. "It's pretty spectacular."

"I thought you'd like the Dream Pod." The Caretaker stepped inside and looked around. "The Rockies, huh?"

Jim shrugged. "I don't know where I am, exactly. I just asked for mountains."

"Ah, I see," the Caretaker said. "When you give general directions like that, the program picks from among its compatible files at random. I think you're in the Rockies, but I could be wrong."

"Do we need to go?" Jim said, disappointment in his voice.

"We should, especially if you'd like to see some of the hive."

Jim looked around at the mountain scene, inhaling the cool, pine-scented air. "All right," he said.

"But first," the Caretaker said, "you might like this one—Mississippi Paddleboat."

The scene changed again. This time, he was standing on the wooden deck of a large boat chugging along the Mississippi River. They appeared to be heading upstream. Ahead he could see the expanse of the river, flanked on the right by open land, green and fresh, and on the left by bluffs that rose steeply from the shore. Turning to look behind, he saw an enormous paddle wheel churning powerfully through the water and leaving behind a seething stretch of white foam and froth.

"It's a little different from floating downriver on a raft, isn't it?"

"It sure is," Jim said, nodding his agreement.

"And this is nothing, a relic from a forgotten time for history buffs and sightseers," the Caretaker added. "Once, there were boats that could plow up and down the river at remarkable speeds.

"I haven't bought any of those bundles for my Dream Pod," the Caretaker added a moment later, almost apologetically. "They appeal to a younger crowd, mostly."

"Don't apologize," Jim said. "This is great."

He leaned over the rail and looked down at the water. It seemed a long way down. "It's strange to be so high."

"The program always puts you on the upper deck first," the Caretaker said. "We can go down if you want."

"That's all right," Jim said. "I like the view from up here."

"Me too."

They leaned against the rail, gazing at the river and listening to the turning wheel. It wasn't as hot here as it had been at the beach, but it wasn't as cool as it had been on the mountain, either. Jim thought about peeling his fleece off, but he left it on, figuring he'd need it once they went back into the cooler internal temperatures of the hive.

Finally the Caretaker said, "Ready?"

"Yeah," Jim said, reluctantly, turning all the way around to get one final panoramic view of this artificial world before it disappeared.

"Finished," the Caretaker said, and the Paddleboat and the Mississippi disappeared, replaced by the plain white of the Dream Pod. The door opened, and Jim followed the Caretaker out.

# Sycamore Street

Jim stepped out into the hive.

Technically, he'd been in the hive since landing in the Caretaker's private hangar, but now that he'd left Doc's personal living space behind, he felt like he was really in the hive. It wasn't anything like he'd expected.

He'd expected, not tunnels exactly, but lots of halls and corridors, certainly. The hive was a vast enclosed space, so he'd expected smaller enclosed spaces. The hive felt surprisingly open and roomy. In fact, rather than feeling more carpet or wood or tile outside the Caretaker's door—like the flooring in the halls of the Lodge, for instance—there was a broad concrete sidewalk there. Equally surprising, on the other side of the sidewalk was a streetlight, and underneath it, a fairly large tree.

Jim walked over and touched the bark, feeling its rough surface under his fingertips. It looked like a tree, felt like a tree, even smelled like a tree. "Is it an illusion, like the Dream Pod?"

"No, that's a real tree," the Caretaker said. "The hive has an extensive and advanced hydroponics network. Helps keep the air fresh and the residents happy."

"Hydroponics?" Jim asked.

"A way of growing things in water instead of soil," the Caretaker said. He smiled as Jim started to follow up with another question. "You can ask me more about it, but that's really all I know."

Jim looked beyond the sidewalk. The hive looked less like a glimpse into the future and more like a glimpse into the past. Something very like a street ran parallel to the sidewalk. On the other side of it was another sidewalk, along which were several places of business, their storefronts colorful and bright. Jim looked up at the ceiling, which was fairly high above them and the stores across the way, and it was a vibrant, sky blue.

"It changes throughout the day," the Caretaker said. "Eventually, it'll go dark and show stars. Then the streetlights will come on."

Jim looked up and down the street. On this side, were lots of painted front doors with addresses painted on them in a vibrant, bright yellow paint, like the one on the Caretaker's door that said "1212 Sycamore Street." On the other side were the storefronts, like the Ice Cream Parlor and Shoe Store directly opposite. The trees and streetlights were evenly spaced, the street and sidewalks neat and clean, and here and there, people strolled along lazily.

The people. Jim hadn't looked carefully at the people walking around yet, but now that he did, he realized that he'd been expecting the hive to be more crowded. He knew millions and millions of people lived here, and as big as the hive appeared from the outside, Jim figured that many people had to be enough to crowd any space.

"Where is everybody?" Jim asked.

"Everybody," the Caretaker echoed, quietly. "Well, most of them are probably home or at work, which for most people is the same, I guess, since most of them work from home. As the sky dims and the lights begin to come on, more of them will come out. They'll sit at the tables outside the cafes and visit with friends, or perhaps walk down to Main Street and spend the evening there."

"Main Street? Sycamore? What's that about, Doc?" Jim said, looking back at the Caretaker. "I don't understand. This isn't what I thought the hive would be like. Is it all like this?"

"Yes and no," the Caretaker said. "There are thousands of communities like this one, throughout the hive, laid out like towns with streets and shops and more. They're all a little different, though, with different themes and feels. And of course, there are lots of places in the hive that aren't residential. They support hive-life in other essential ways."

"I figured that. I just don't understand this," Jim said, waving his hand as though to take in everything he could see around him. "I thought there'd be halls and corridors and vast public spaces bursting with people, lots of things like small hovercrafts or something, zooming around, taking people wherever they want to go. You know? I thought the inside would look more like the outside—more grand, I guess you'd say."

"Oh, it's pretty grand," the Caretaker smiled again. "The transportation system would astonish you. It's a wonder, can be very crowded—depending on the time of day—and it moves very, very fast."

"Where is it?"

The Caretaker pointed up at the ceiling, then down at the sidewalk. "Above. Below. There are entryways located strategically in every community, but the system is always out of sight. Like the water and the heat and the rest of the hive infrastructure. It's there but you don't see it."

"Or hear it?"

"No, the walls are soundproofed to keep the communities quiet."

Jim was still shaking his head. "I still don't understand, Doc. Sycamore? Main Street? They just replicated the world they left behind."

"In some ways, that's exactly what they did," the Caretaker said. "The earliest hives weren't that different from this, but they were divided into numerical levels, not named communities. People lived on floors, like the hive was some vast hotel.

"But it turns out people don't want to live on floor 954 of an overgrown hotel. They don't like being reminded how far above the ground they are. They don't like the feeling of transience that a numbered floor and hotel-like existence gave them. They wanted something more solid and permanent.

"So the hives evolved, using names and streets instead of numbers and floors, making the residential sections feel more like independent towns than interconnected networks. That's why they look and feel like this, but under those carefully designed and executed facades, they still offer what drew people to the hive in the first place."

"Technology? Like the Dream Pods, you mean?"

"Yes, that and other things. I'll explain it, at least as much as I can, on the way back if you'd like. But if you want to explore some of the hive with me, we should do it now. I want to leave soon, so we can be back by dark."

Jim looked around again at the street, the stores and the people. He didn't especially care to see more of this part of the hive. Now that he was here, it seemed vaguely disappointing. The transportation system that the Caretaker described sounded more interesting, but the thought of crowds made him uncomfortable. He understood that not every person who lived in a hive was a hunter, but some were. He didn't much like the idea of being jammed into a small space with people who might be planning to go out in a hovercraft and hunt groundlings tomorrow.

That thought made Jim shudder even as he looked at the handful of people moving down Sycamore Street.

"We can leave now," Jim said. "I've seen enough."

# Strawberries

Jim watched the hive grow small in the distance as the hovercraft flew south, racing the failing sunlight. He'd watched for quite a long time, and now the hive was little more than a golden blip on the horizon.

He turned around to face out the front. The Caretaker gave him a brief look and said, "I'm glad you came."

"Me too. I would have always wondered what it was like."

"I'm glad you got to see a Dream Pod, too."

Jim nodded. "That was amazing. I'd like one of those. Don't you miss it when you're at your station?"

The Caretaker shrugged. "Sometimes, I guess. I've already seen most of the things I wanted to see, though. And if I get a strong urge to go somewhere while I'm away, I just jot it down, and I go when I'm back."

Jim looked out the window toward the west, at the orange and red light shining through the thick bank of clouds. "Think we'll be back by dark?"

"Probably not," the Caretaker said. "I left it too late."

"Is that a problem?"

"Not really, but Shep doesn't like to be alone after dark," he said. "Guess he's not alone, though, with your robot there."

"No, I guess not," Jim said, agreeing, "though HF isn't exactly a great conversationalist. He might not interact much with Shep."

"He might like to talk more than you think," the Caretaker said. "He just might need to be prompted by a question or two to get going."

"Maybe so," Jim said. He waited a moment, still watching the sunset, then decided he wouldn't wait any longer for the Caretaker to remember his promise. "You said you would tell me about the hives, about their history and stuff?"

"Speaking of prompting with a question," the Caretaker laughed. "I suppose I did. We don't have enough flight time left for the long version, so I'll try to make it quick.

"Believe it or not, the story of the hives begins with robotic strawberry harvesting."

"What?" Jim said, confused. "I don't understand what that means."

"Of course not. I haven't explained anything yet. You do know, though, that agriculture once upon a time wasn't entirely automated, right? In fact, very little was robotic. Most people got their food from people called farmers, who worked their land like you do, as a groundling—only they had specialized tools and equipment to help them work lots and lots of it."

"Sure, Atticus told me that," Jim said. "He was very proud of the fact we grew our own food. Said that was one way a groundling regained some of the humanity lost in the hives."

"Well," the Caretaker said, "I don't know about regaining lost humanity. But it's certainly true that the world was once very different in that respect.

"Anyway," he continued. "A long, long time ago, a small engineering company named Vista pioneered a new kind of machine—a robotic strawberry harvester, and it revolutionized farming. Strawberries are very delicate, and the machine's ability to find and harvest ripe ones without damaging them encouraged more and more companies to get into robotic agriculture.

"The technology boom that followed brought the United States out of a prolonged recession. When the dust settled, decades later, every phase of agriculture was almost entirely automated."

The Caretaker paused, and Jim thought he was expecting some kind of reaction, but Jim didn't know what it was supposed to be. He knew the people in the hives survived on food that was grown, processed and shipped via automated robotic systems, but how did that explain the rise of hive-life in the first place?

"I'm still not sure I understand what this has to do with the origin of the hives."

"It was one piece of a much larger puzzle," the Caretaker said. "Think about it this way. For most of Earth's history, the essential resource has been land—arable land and sufficient water. People spread out because they had to—we each needed our own land to grow our crops and raise our herds.

"As time went on, fewer and fewer people could produce more and more food, so lots of people were freed up to move and live wherever they wanted. That led to larger and larger cities, as fewer and fewer people were tied to life on the land. When the revolution in agricultural robotics took place, the last link in the chain that bound man to the soil was finally broken. Everyone could go where they wanted."

"So why not just live in the old cities, like the one near the monument?" Jim asked. "Why turn from cities to hives at all?"

"Ahh, well, a lot of that had to do with a sense many people had, a sort of movement that had been growing for a long time, that man had made rather a mess of the earth. The early proponents of the hives suggested that moving up into the hives and letting the natural processes of the earth flow unhindered and untouched by man—except obviously, for the vast and essential network of robotic farms—was the right thing to do for the long-term good of both mankind and the planet. In short, if man was ruining nature, perhaps the solution was to separate them as much as was reasonably possible.

"So the hive movement gathered steam, but I don't think hives would have replaced the old way of life so thoroughly, so completely, had it not been for the Dream Pods."

"Because people could live in the hives, away from nature, but still see and experience it when they wanted?" Jim asked. The pieces of the puzzle were beginning to come together.

"Exactly so," the Caretaker said, looking excitedly over at him and pointing forward as though to emphasize every word. "You see it now. The Dream Pods were the perfect answer and the final step in man's journey toward the hive. You could go wherever you liked and see whatever you wanted, and there were no ecological consequences. No plastic bottles left in the ocean to be washed out to sea and eaten by a dolphin, and no aluminum cans beside the highway to be chewed on by a deer. No harmful effects from tourism would ever ruin the natural wonder and beauty of the world again."

"So just like that, people pulled up stakes and moved to the hives?"

"No, not just like that. It was a process that took generations," the Caretaker said. "The early Dream Pods were good, but not like the one you saw. They were very strong, visually speaking, and they improved quickly with smells and sounds, but the feel of a place was much harder. You mentioned visiting a beach today, right?"

"That's right," Jim said.

"How'd the sand feel?"

"Great," Jim answered, then added, "but I've never felt real sand, so I guess I wouldn't really know.

"Well," Doc said, "the early Dream Pods struggled with the feel of sand beneath your feet. That's a big reason why most of the hives are coastal, since the early hive-dwellers wanted to be near the real thing so they could walk on the beach and feel the waves swirl around their legs.

"Even now, long since the Dream Pods mastered replicating even those sensations, most of the hives are still on the coast, since those early ones were already there. Inland hives like the one we just visited, or like the one in the mountains to the west that Atticus came from, are very much the exception."

"And all this started with strawberries?" Jim asked.

"It sort of did," the Caretaker mused. "But that's not as strange as it sounds. The history of the world is full of turning points like this. From the invention of movable type to the electric light bulb to the robotic strawberry harvester, small changes can and do change the world."

"So the world changes, but people don't?" Jim asked, thinking of their conversation on the way to the hive that morning.

"No, not much they don't," the Caretaker agreed. "If history tells us anything, then surely it tells us that."

# Terra

Jim followed the Caretaker down out of the Hovercraft. Shep bounded over and barked as he reared up on his hind feet to greet his master. Doc caught Shep's front paws and gave them a playful shake. "I know, I know," he said. "I'm late. Sorry, boy."

"Hey, HF," Jim said, greeting the robot as he walked over to meet them too. "Have a good day?"

"Tolerable good, I reckon," HF said. "Shep's a playful fella, and strong—he knocked me over this morning."

"Shep," the Caretaker said, speaking with mock sternness to the dog. "Naughty boy."

HF missed the playfulness in the Caretaker's rebuke, and he quickly jumped to Shep's defense. "Oh, that's all right. We were playin' a game and I think I got him kinda worked up. He didn't mean nothin' by it."

"No," the Caretaker said kindly, "he wouldn't have."

Supper was a scrumptious affair, with plenty of fresh beef, corn and beans, and big thick slices of bread with all the butter Jim wanted. After weeks and weeks of careful rations, mostly cold biscuits, since even before Atticus' fever, Jim almost didn't know what to do with so much food. It seemed that he'd been hungry for a month, and now with food before him in abundance, he wanted to eat with abandon. But having gotten by on so little for so long, he found himself getting full way too soon and felt almost angry at himself that he couldn't eat more.

"Slow down, Jim," the Caretaker said, looking over at him as he shoveled another forkful into his mouth even though his stomach told him that doing so was a bad idea. "There's plenty to go around, and there still will be tomorrow and the next day, and the day after that."

Jim nodded as he took up the large glass of milk the Caretaker had just poured him and washed his food down. It was his third glass. The thought of the next day and the day after that reminded Jim that finding the Caretaker wasn't his ultimate goal. As exciting as seeing the hive and experiencing a Dream Pod had been, they weren't why he'd come either.

"I don't know what I'm supposed to do now," Jim said, swallowing and sitting back in his chair.

"Have some apple pie, if you've saved any room," the Caretaker said.

"I don't mean right now," Jim said, wishing he'd saved room for the pie. "I mean in general."

"I know," the Caretaker said, taking his plate over to the sink to rinse it off. "I've been wondering since you asked about Florence when you'd want to talk about the 'what now' question."

"Well," Jim said. "I assume Atticus must have meant my Aunt Flor when he told me to find Florence. But even if finding you meant finding out about her, how does that help me actually find her? You don't know where she is, do you?"

"I don't know, Jim. I know where she was when your father passed through here when you were little."

"Where's that?" Jim asked.

"The same place where Atticus and your mother lived before she died. The same place where you were born."

The Caretaker watched Jim carefully, perhaps to see if that would trigger anything, but it didn't. Jim knew Atticus had moved to the cabin on the island when Jim had been a little boy, but he didn't really remember ever living anywhere else, and Atticus hadn't ever really talked about life before coming there.

Jim shrugged his shoulders and said, "I don't know where Atticus lived before he came upriver."

The Caretaker nodded. "It was a settlement of groundlings. More than a settlement, a town really. Atticus said they called it Terra."

"Terra?" Jim said, "That's a terrible name. Sounds like terror."

"No, terra, that's—"

"Latin," Jim said. "I know. Atticus did teach me that. Terra firma, solid ground. He liked saying that a lot."

"That's right, Jim," the Caretaker nodded. "You can see the appeal for a community of groundlings."

"Sure, but it's still a terrible name," Jim said. He thought for a few minutes. "You have any idea where this Terra is?"

"Downriver," the Caretaker said. "A fair piece. That's all I know for sure, though I had the definite impression it was on the Mississippi, or close enough to it anyway. You should ask HF, Jim."

Jim looked over his shoulder at HF, sitting quietly on the couch beside Shep. The robot didn't appear to be paying their conversation any attention, though Jim knew he would have heard everything that had been said at such close quarters. "How about it, HF? Do you remember Terra?"

"Sure, Jim," HF said. "Terra was a real nice place to live. I was kinda sorry we had to leave after your Mom died."

"She's buried there?" Jim asked quietly.

"Yes sir, she sure is," HF said.

Jim nodded, and he knew. Even if Atticus hadn't sent him to find Florence, and even if she wasn't in Terra, Jim had to go there. "Do you think you could find Terra again, HF?"

"Well, I don't know, Jim," HF said, scratching his head. "I didn't pay no nevermind to where Terra was, exactly. Directions and such-like have never been something I was much good at."

"Was it close to the river?" the Caretaker asked.

"Sure was," HF said. "Just a hop, skip and a jump from the old rail bridge."

"Do you think you'd recognize this rail bridge if we were on the raft?" Jim asked, growing excited.

"I reckon I could. I remember it pretty well."

"Even if it was nighttime and dark?" Jim added.

"Sure, Jim," HF said. "I've seen it in the dark before."

"Well," Jim said, turning back to the Caretaker. "I guess I've got a plan. I'll head downriver until HF spots this rail bridge, then I'll head ashore and look for Terra."

"Seems simple enough," the Caretaker said.

"You've no idea how far downriver I'm heading?" Jim asked.

"No," the Caretaker said. "But I'd be prepared for weeks on the raft, Jim. We'll need to see you well-supplied before you go."

"I'd sure appreciate that," Jim said. "I'm getting a little too used to eating well. It'll be hard to leave that behind."

"Well, you're welcome to stay on as long as you like. I'm enjoying the company."

"Thanks," Jim said. "Maybe I will rest up a day or two, enjoy a bed and regular meals for a change. But then I should be on my way since I don't know if Florence is still in Terra, and if she isn't, then my job won't be done when I get there."

"Jim," the Caretaker said, almost reluctantly. "Florence was your Mom's older sister. Now, your Mom was a good bit younger than your Dad—I'm not sure how much younger, actually, but it was a lot. Anyway, it's been a long time since Atticus came upriver. I just think you should be prepared, you know, for whatever you might find. A lot could have happened over the years."

"It's all right, Doc," Jim said. "I know she might not still be alive, but I have to find out, and not just because Atticus told me to. She's my Aunt, she's family—the only family I have."

The Caretaker smiled, sadly it seemed to Jim, then nodded slowly. "I understand. Well, like I said, stay as long as you like."

"Thanks," Jim said.

That night, Jim went to bed thinking about his Aunt Flor, about what she would be like, and about Terra, and how long it would take to find it. But as he drifted off to sleep, his thoughts drifted north, not south, to the shimmering, golden hive, and the remarkable if alien world that lay within.

# What's in a Name?

Jim's couple of days became almost a week, until he finally announced one morning that he had to be getting underway. The Caretaker had been pulling supplies and setting them aside, so there was a substantial stack of various foodstuffs for Jim to choose from, and he packed a large canvas bag with the things he thought would keep the best and laid it out, ready for departure.

It was evening. They sat together, sipping a drink that the Caretaker called hot chocolate, a drink Jim thought might be a close second to the Dream Pod as a reason to go live in a hive, and Jim said, "Isn't it a little strange, Doc?"

"Isn't what strange?"

"Terra—I mean the fact that groundlings would form a town," Jim clarified. "All the groundlings I've known avoid settling in groups so they won't attract attention from hunters or packs."

"Most don't," the Caretaker said. "But banding together might provide a sort of protection, too. Staying isolated could make you harder to find, but you're also weaker when you are found, because you're alone. I guess there are pros and cons, either way."

"True, but a large settlement or town would be easily detected from above," Jim said. "I'd be worried about hunters going back to the hive and coming back in greater numbers later. They'd probably see it as some kind of perverse challenge, and then what good would your numbers be? The easiest settlement to defend is the one they never find."

"That may be true," the Caretaker said, "but Terra might be harder to find from the air than you think. Atticus said one of the first things he did at Terra was help design a kind of defense system. I don't really know how it worked, exactly, but he said it interfered with the systems of any hovercraft—even the steering—that got within miles of Terra. That would be a good reason for any hovercraft to avoid the area."

"Atticus built that?" Jim asked.

"Not alone, I don't think," the Caretaker said. "There were a handful of people with technical backgrounds involved in founding Terra. They even scavenged a fair number of high tech tools and materials from somewhere, though I never knew exactly how they pulled that off. That's how Atticus had the materials to put HF and all his predecessors together."

"He never told you where they got the stuff to do all that?" Jim asked, wondering for the first time how a groundling came by the tools and equipment necessary to make a robot, not to mention a defense system for an entire town.

"No," the Caretaker laughed, "He didn't. I understand why he didn't, though; the gear was no doubt acquired from Vista one way or another, and I still work for them. I wouldn't have said or done anything, of course, even if he had told me, but as you've gathered, Atticus was pretty secretive."

"Yeah," Jim said. "I've gathered."

The Caretaker sighed. "I know some of those secrets have hurt you, Jim, and now Atticus isn't around to give you the answers you want... not just that you want, that you deserve. Still, leaving the hive and all he had ever known behind was a big deal. Who can say what Atticus went through to leave? It's tough to judge a man when you've never had to walk in his shoes."

Jim nodded because he knew the Caretaker was waiting for some sign of assent. He still wasn't sure how he felt about all the secrets Atticus had obviously been keeping. He'd been focusing on the future and finding Terra and hopefully Florence as a means of keeping his mind off the questions that lingered about his past. It took a moment for Jim to realize that the Caretaker was talking again.

"I don't know a lot about what your father's life was like in the hive, Jim, but I think his departure was pretty hard on him for a variety of reasons, which I guess is why he changed his name—"

"Why he what?" Jim cut in, staring at the Caretaker with lips trembling. "What did you say?"

"I ..." the Caretaker began.

"Atticus changed his name?"

The Caretaker looked startled, taken aback. "I'm sorry, Jim. I thought you knew."

Jim didn't have any words. He just shook his head, mechanically, as he stared off into space.

"But surely, Jim," the Caretaker continued. He was talking softly now, gently. "You must have wondered at some point about the remarkable coincidence that your Dad shared a name with one of his heroes."

"No, I didn't," Jim said, matter-of-factly. "I guess I just always thought he'd been named for the real Atticus, like he named me for the real Jim."

"Yes," the Caretaker said, his brow knitted, still looking confused. "That makes sense, but the last name too, Jim? Didn't it ever seem strange that his complete name was Atticus Finch?"

Jim suddenly felt very foolish. He'd never questioned that Finch was his real last name. Now he understood that it wasn't a happy coincidence at all. It was a fiction, a lie. Atticus had made it up when he left the hive. Just one of the many things Atticus had hidden from him.

Atticus. Jim had no idea what his own father's real name was. For that matter, he had no idea what his own name was.

"What's my name?" he asked the Caretaker. "Who am I?"

"You're Jim Finch," the Caretaker said.

"What's my real name?"

"Just because Atticus adopted Finch as his new name—"

"Doc," Jim said. "Can I get a straight answer? Do you know what my real name is, or will I have to find my Aunt and ask her?"

"Stewart," the Caretaker said finally. "When I first met him, Atticus' name was Tom Stewart."

"Stewart," Jim said, repeating the name, trying to wrap his head around what the Caretaker was telling him. "My name is Jim Stewart."

The Caretaker was frowning again. "Your Dad had been Atticus Finch for years when he met and married your Mom, Jim. She embraced Finch as her real name when they married. Isn't that good enough for you too?"

Jim shrugged his shoulders. "I don't know, Doc. I feel like I don't know anything anymore. Not about Atticus, not about me—not about anything."

For a long while, Jim sat staring into his drink, neither he nor the Caretaker saying anything. A myriad of thoughts swirled in Jim's head; mixed in and around them all was this strange new revelation. Tom Stewart. The name didn't fit his Dad. He pictured Atticus in the cabin, lying dead with the candle on his chest. Tom Stewart. No, his name was Atticus. That was who lay buried in the glade.

Then a thought occurred to Jim, and a shiver ran down his spine. His hands began to tremble. He knew he had to ask, but he was afraid of the answer. He stalled. "Doc, how old was my Dad when he left the hive?"

"About thirty-five or so," the Caretaker said.

Plenty old enough. He took a breath. "Was he married before?"

The Caretaker looked off through the doorway into the large, dark chamber beyond. He looked like he wanted to escape through that door, but Jim's hunger for truth, his need to know, blocked the exit from the room. "Yes. He was."

Silence. Jim leaned forward and placed his forehead on his fingertips, with which he massaged his hurting head. His father had been married before he met his mother. He'd left a wife in the hive. "Were there kids?"

"Honestly, Jim," the Caretaker said, "I don't know. When we first met, he wasn't married yet. We kept up a while after he went back to the hive, long enough for me to know he'd gotten married, but we lost touch for a few years before he just appeared on my doorstep again. He only mentioned his wife once, saying he'd begged her to come but that she wouldn't. More than that, I just don't know."

Jim nodded and stood. It was time to leave.

"It's probably dark out by now," Jim said. "We should be on our way."

"Jim," the Caretaker said, "let's talk about this for a—"

"No, Doc," Jim said firmly. "Whether I stay here five more years, or five more minutes, I'm done talking about this."

Jim reached over the table and shook the Caretaker's hand. Whatever he thought of the things the Caretaker had told him, the man had been candid with him, and Jim was grateful. "Thanks for everything."

The Caretaker nodded slowly. "Anytime, Jim."

Jim moved to collect HF and his things.

"Gonna make our getaway now, Jim?" HF asked.

"Yes, HF, we are."

"Are you planning to come back upriver when you're finished?" the Caretaker asked as they walked out into the big room, Shep padding along quietly behind.

"I don't know," Jim said.

"Promise me, if you do, that you'll stop in and tell me how it went."

"Sure, Doc," Jim said. "I'll be hungry anyway, probably."

"I'll stock up," the Caretaker said, trying to lighten the moment. When he continued a minute later, he was serious again though. "And if Florence isn't in Terra?"

Jim shrugged. "That'll depend on what I find out there, I guess."

Outside, the night was clear. The stars were out, and a bright moon hung low on the horizon, its lesser light reflecting in its own way as brilliantly off the gleaming city to the west as the morning sun.

Jim had come for answers. He'd found more than he'd bargained for, a lot more. Even so, as he headed to the raft, he felt that what he had really found were questions. Did he have any brothers or sisters in a hive? If so, how old were they now? Why had Atticus hidden so much from him?

Not knowing so many facts about his father's past wasn't nearly as disturbing to Jim as the thought that maybe Jim hadn't known his father. Not really, anyway. And if he hadn't known his father, could he really know himself?

Jim stood at the top of the stairs, gazing at the river rolling slowly by, the moonlight shining on the water. The river had brought him here, had brought him to the questions. Maybe it would take him to the answers, too.

# The Robot

# Broken Bridge

Jim brooded silently through the first several nights of their journey south from the Caretaker. For his part, HF seemed content to leave Jim alone with his quiet meditations, taking seriously his charge to look out for the rail bridge that would signal their approach to Terra. Had HF been prone to fatigue— physical, mental or otherwise—Jim might have told him to relax during these first nights, since by all accounts Terra lay a fair distance downriver. However, Jim was glad of the opportunity to consider all that he'd learned from the Caretaker.

The approach of April brought several changes, some welcome, some not so much. Rain was more frequent, which made Jim feel less exposed out on the river, and as the days were growing warmer too, the rain was less uncomfortable to travel in.

Along with the warmth, though, came longer days, which meant shorter nights and less travel time. Jim figured it didn't matter too much in the long run, but since he had to wait longer each day for dark to come, he found his patience being sorely tried by the boredom and monotony of his daytime imprisonment in strange house after strange house.

What's more, the spring rains, combined with the melting that must have been going on further up north, were having their normal effect on the river, which was swelling higher with each passing day. The current was stronger and the raft more difficult to navigate.

As the river rose, Jim figured the increased volume and speed would either get them wrecked and him killed or shave several days off their journey, he couldn't tell which.

One evening, as Jim ate salted pork in the kitchen of the small yellow cottage in which he'd taken shelter just before dawn, he looked up from the table at HF, who stood by the sink staring out the kitchen window at the river. "HF?" he asked. "What was my mother like? Do I look like her?"

"Well, Jim, let me see," HF said, turning away from the window. "Your mama was real pretty, sure 'nough. And she was dark. *Black as midnight,* Atticus used to say."

"Darker than me?"

"Sure," HF replied. "She was darker than you, but that didn't bother her none. She called you her 'brown sugar,' said you was a 'sweet little thing.'"

Jim nodded as he chewed, massaging his sore arms that had spent the night trying to steer the raft on the rushing waters of the river. "So we don't look much alike," he said after a while, feeling disappointed.

He had realized, the older he got, that he was darker than Atticus, and that his curly black hair didn't look much like his Dad's straight, white locks. That had disappointed him, since he admired his father so. But as he mulled over his time with the Caretaker, he had started to wonder if that didn't help to explain some of his father's reluctance to talk about her. Maybe it had been too painful. Maybe looking at Jim was kind of like looking at her. Not that this would have excused it; he was still angry about the things Atticus had kept from him. But he found himself searching for an explanation nonetheless.

"Well," HF said as he studied Jim carefully. "I wouldn't say that. You look plenty like her, I reckon. You got her curly dark hair, for one thing, and even though you don't smile much, when you do, you sure look like her to me, Jim."

"Did she smile much?"

"All the time," HF said. "She was the smilingest lady I ever met, her and Aunt Flor. They smiled and laughed all the time."

"Did Atticus use to smile and laugh a lot, too?" Jim asked, curious, wondering if his serious father could ever have been like that.

"Well now, he smiled at your mama a lot, I reckon, but no, Atticus wasn't much of a laugher." HF reached up and scratched his head, like he was thinking carefully about it all, and then he added, "They always said they was opposites, your folks. Your mama was young, dark and playful, and your daddy was old, pale and serious, but that didn't seem to bother them none."

Jim thought about that a lot as the raft continued on its tumultuous way after dark. Living alone with Atticus all those years, he had learned to subdue and curtail his natural gaiety, and he wondered what his childhood would have been like with his mother around, with the sound of laughter in the house. He wondered what Atticus would have been like? What would he be like himself, if he had been raised by a such a happy mother?

They had only been on the raft a few hours when the light rain that had been falling when they set out began to clear up. The cloud cover became intermittent, and the first few hesitant stars began to peek through. Jim was glad for the starlight, despite feeling a little less safe; the night had been awfully dark so far.

Jim was watching the surface of the water, mesmerized by the widening and narrowing of the "V" made by a bobbing snag, when HF called from the front of the raft. "Jim, you better take a look at this."

Jim scrambled forward until he was beside the robot. He peered ahead, but at first, he couldn't see anything in particular.

"Up yonder," HF added. "Looks like something big in the river."

Jim peered forward again, and gradually he thought he could make out what HF was talking about, a large object up ahead in the distance, angular and enormous, jutting up out of the water. Though the shape was dark, down closer to the surface of the water it glinted with reflected starlight. "What is that, HF? What do we do?"

"I don't know what it is," HF said, "but I suggest we paddle like crazy, otherwise we might get a look that's a little too close."

"All right," Jim said, scrambling to the oar bench at the back of the raft and calling to HF, "let's make for the western shore, it's closer. I can't believe the whole way ahead is blocked, but we can put in there if we need too."

Jim fought the current, straining into the oar sweep with all his weight and strength, but the raft was being swept downstream so fast, he felt he wasn't getting anywhere. The object that had been a vague shadow in the distance was beginning to take firmer shape. It looked to Jim like a bridge that had broken in the middle, and the half on the near side of the river had slid sideways into the river, where it now stood, leaning against the massive pylons that had once held it. Whatever had happened, Jim was staring at a great block of concrete, several times wider than the raft, looming directly in front of them, and all his efforts to get the raft far enough into the shallows to slowly and safely bypass it were going for naught.

He worked the sweep with all his might, and HF paddled heroically on the port side. Maybe they'd have been all right, but the great shaft of old bridge wasn't the only thing looming up ahead. Not as clearly visible in the dim starlight, were the half submerged cars and trucks hung up on the angled piece of broken bridge, some bobbing slightly in the flowing waters, extending out in a dangerous flotilla of metal. It was against this dark island that the raft actually struck; the impact was hard and the consequences immediate.

Jim was thrown down and went scuttling across the raft, barely managing to keep a hold of the oar sweep. When he finally slowed to a stop, he realized the raft was hung up on the interlocking mass of metal, itself hung up on the concrete. Water from the swiftly flowing river was running over the raft, pushing the wood down as it continued on its way down south. As Jim got his bearings, he realized suddenly that he was alone on the raft. HF was no longer on board.

He stared around frantically, seeing no sign of the robot. "HF! HF!" he called over the rushing waters. "HF! Where are you?"

"Jim?" came the answer from somewhere up ahead. "I'm tryin' to hold on."

Jim moved forward to the edge of the raft and gazed out in the direction of the concrete slab, where the words had come from. He couldn't make out HF, but he had to be out there, clinging to one of the submerged cars or perhaps part of the bridge itself.

There wasn't much time to think. If the river pulled HF free of whatever he was clinging to, Jim's chances of catching up and finding him in the dark weren't good. At the same time, if Jim went in after HF, then the river might well break the tenuous connection between the raft and its current mooring. If it did, then the raft would likely be lost to him forever.

Either way, there wasn't really any deliberating to be done; HF was all Jim had left in the world. He couldn't let the river sweep him away. Jim leapt off the raft, clear, he hoped, of the island of cars.

He hit the cold water with a splash, and his legs didn't strike glass or metal. The current grabbed him immediately and began to sweep him downstream. He hadn't been quite prepared for the strength of its pull, and he struggled against it, reaching out desperately for something solid to hold onto. His fingers found the open door of a car, and he grabbed unsuccessfully, cursing his ill fortune as it slipped from his grasp.

The next thing he felt was not metal but concrete, and Jim knew he had been pushed up against the side of the slab of bridge itself. He grabbed hold of its rougher surface, holding on for dear life. He came to a stop, and the next thing he knew, he heard HF say, "Jim? You all right, Jim?"

There, bobbing just up ahead, clinging to the same large piece of concrete, was HF. Jim held onto the concrete with both hands but let the water pull his legs and body downstream. "Grab a hold of a foot, HF," he called.

HF did just that, and a moment later, Jim was fighting the current as he tried to get a grip on the nearest car in the water to move upstream from the concrete slab. He finally got a solid grip and let go of the bridge piece, regretting it almost immediately. The car wasn't nearly so solid as the concrete, and with Jim pulling on it, it dipped up and down in the water. Fortunately, however, it was hung up on the other cars beneath and around it, and all of them were hung up on the concrete, so it did not dislodge.

Jim worked slowly, painstakingly backward, upstream. He prayed the raft was still there, but he couldn't see it in the darkness. It was all he could do to keep his head above water and make out something else solid to grab as he moved, hand over hand, with HF holding desperately to his ankle and foot.

It seemed to take forever, but then, out of nowhere, there it was—the rough, wooden edge of the raft. It was on an angle now. The water moving downstream had been pushing it sideways, gradually off the island of automobiles. Jim grabbed hold of it, and using the foot that HF wasn't holding onto, he pushed off the windshield of the car next to the raft and scrambled up onto it. He lifted his leg and HF as far out of the water as he could, and soon the robot had scrambled onto the raft beside him.

As Jim lay there panting, exhausted, he felt the raft slide free of the island of cars. He braced for another bump, but it never came. As they passed by, he saw the looming, dark form of the leaning slab of concrete overhead. They cleared it quickly, leaving behind the bridge and the strange collection of cars attached to it.

Jim gazed up at the sky. All he could see were the same scattered stars, and fewer of these than before. Large, cold raindrops began to splash on his face, and lightning flashed in the distance. He thought about crawling under the tarp, but he felt exhausted. He closed his eyes and let the quiet world drift by.

# Burning Up

Jim hadn't slept very long when a loud peal of thunder woke him with a start. It was raining hard now, and he reluctantly crawled across the raft, under the tarp. He wasn't sure why he bothered. He was already soaked to the bone.

The rain didn't let up, and he passed a restless night, shivering in the middle of the raft. He curled up into a ball, trying to stay warm, but to no avail. He grew aggravated with an annoying clicking sound coming from somewhere nearby, and he was just about to yell at HF to knock off whatever it was, when he realized it was the sound of his own teeth chattering.

When the time came to put the raft into shore and get off the river before daylight, Jim struggled even to lift himself up onto all fours. His arms and legs felt rubbery and weak. Fortunately, the raft had stayed close to the western shore since bypassing the collapsed bridge, and Jim was able with HF's help to get in and tie up before sunrise.

Wobbling up the bank, feeling suddenly flushed and warm despite the cold rain, he followed HF to a faded grey house they had noticed from the river. No sooner had they opened the door than a strong odor of decay wafted out to meet them. Jim slid down to his knees and retched on the wooden porch.

"I can't go in there," he said, looking up at HF, who was looking down on him in concern. "It's foul."

"You don't look so good, Jim," HF said, glancing sideways, almost longingly at the cozy interior that he couldn't smell. "But we can find someplace else if you'd rather."

The closest house was a short walk inland from the river, and once inside, Jim sank down onto a couch on the main floor, unable to face the stairs up to the bedrooms. "I think I'll just sleep here," he said to HF. "Could you pull the curtains to, so the light doesn't wake me?"

"Sure, Jim," HF said, moving quickly to do as Jim had asked. "Don't worry about nothing. Just get some sleep."

Jim didn't need to be told twice. He buried his face in a musty sofa cushion, closed his eyes, and slipped into a world of troubled dreams.

The hovercraft zoomed over a bleak landscape, and Jim found that looking down made him feel sick. He tried to keep his eyes forward, but that didn't help much. Lightning flashed in the clouds ahead, and he could feel the small craft wobble up and down as it flew on into the storm. He closed his eyes.

When he opened them again, he wasn't in a hovercraft at all. He was in the cabin, and he was freezing cold. The fire had gone out, and he could see that the windows were broken. The wind blew rain in onto the cabin floor. He pulled his heavy comforter tight around him, but it was no match for the wicked draft blowing in from the outside.

He looked at the bed next to his, at the dead body lying there. He didn't recognize the man, though the name, Tom Stewart, seemed vaguely familiar. He couldn't remember how the man had come to be there, or how he'd died.

The storm had stopped. Jim was still cold, but maybe not quite as much. He looked back out the window, and he was startled to see the golden sheen of a hive shining just beyond the cabin outside. He rose weakly from his bed, the comforter still draped over him, and walked to the cabin door.

Only a few feet lay between the cabin door and the base of the hive. Jim crossed it and reached out, feeling the cool, smooth metal. It occurred to Jim that maybe it was warm inside it, so he thought he might try to find a way in. The base extended as far as the eye could see in either direction, without any visible entrance. Jim picked a direction and started walking. On and on he went, searching for a way in, but no door, no window, not even a crack appeared anywhere along the solid foundation.

"Jim?"

He opened his eyes. HF was sitting in a chair, leaning over him, watching his face intently. Outside, the sky was dark.

"No dawn, yet?" Jim asked softly, his voice strangely hoarse and raspy.

"It's come and gone, Jim," HF said. "Sun went down about an hour ago."

It took a moment for this to register with Jim. He'd slept through the whole day. He shivered. Why was he so cold? He looked down at the mass of blankets piled over him. There were several, they were heavy, and he had absolutely no recollection of having them when he lay down. He looked up at HF. "Did you put these blankets on me?"

"Yup," HF said. "You kept mumbling about being cold, and you were shaking so, I thought I'd better scare up something to put over you. I brought down all the blankets I could find."

"Thanks," Jim said. "I must have a fever."

"I reckon so, Jim."

"We might need to stay here a while, let me rest."

"That's probably wise. You ain't in no shape to be on the river tonight. Can I get you something to eat?"

The thought of food wasn't appealing, so Jim shook his head. "I don't think so, HF. Not right now, anyway."

HF leaned back in his chair, and Jim wondered if the robot had been keeping watch over him the same way he'd kept watch over Atticus. Perhaps in answer to his unspoken question, HF asked. "Are you gonna die too, Jim?"

"I don't think so, HF," Jim said. "I sure hope not."

"Good, 'cause I'd get awful lonesome if you died."

Jim looked at HF sitting there, thought of him watching him shiver all day long, worrying he'd lose Jim the same way he had lost Atticus. It occurred to Jim that he might be worse off than he'd thought.

Jim didn't necessarily feel any sicker than he had felt when he had a fever before, but how would he know if this fever was different? Had Atticus known? By the end, maybe, Jim thought, but not at first. Maybe he should make amends with HF, just in case.

"HF, I'm sorry about yelling at you for not telling me about the monument, or the Caretaker, or my Aunt, I shouldn't have…"

"Aw, shucks, Jim," HF said, literally waving away Jim's words as though they were flies buzzing over the couch. "You still worried about that? Don't give it another thought. Friends don't worry none about that kinda stuff, do they? We're friends, ain't we, Jim?"

HF peered at him in the dim twilight, and Jim thought that perhaps he saw a hint of anxiety on the robot's usually inexpressive face.

"Yeah," Jim smiled, and a coughing fit overtook him. For a few minutes the conversation was suspended. "We are friends,

HF. You're the best friend I've got. My only friend, now that Atticus is gone."

"The Caretaker's our friend, isn't he?" HF replied. "And the Murphys, right?"

"I suppose so, but they aren't friends like we are."

"No, I reckon not," HF said, and Jim could have sworn, whatever he had or hadn't seen before, that he heard something a lot like happiness in HF's voice.

Even just that little bit of talking had worn Jim out, and he settled back onto the couch and closed his eyes. HF was content to sit and wait while Jim got some more sleep, and all through the long night he sat in the chair next to the couch, his legs rocking silently back and forth.

When Jim woke again, not long before dawn, the fever had broken. He ate some then, and he and HF passed a boring day in the house, waiting for night to come again. When it did, they set out eagerly for the raft.

As glad as Jim was to find it still tied up and waiting, his elation was dimmed somewhat by the discovery that his .22 was gone. He remembered thinking in his muddled state when they tied up, that he should grab it when they left to seek shelter in the grey house, but he hadn't, nor had he realized that it was missing. Jim figured it had been thrown from the raft like HF when they struck the island of cars that surrounded the downed bridge.

Nothing else was missing, though, and Jim felt too glad to be well again and back on the river to dwell on it. There might come a day when he was sorry it was gone, that was for sure, but there wasn't anything he could do about it now.

The days drifted on with the raft, and Jim and HF floated right into April. Jim had never been this far south, so he had no idea if it was unseasonably warm or not, but it was certainly warmer than he was used to for this time of year. He spent most nights in short sleeves, enjoying the warm spring air after the long cold of winter.

One gorgeous, near perfect night, not long before dawn, they were drifting close to the western shore. Jim intended to put in soon, whenever they found a suitable place. Up ahead, though, a flickering orange light attracted HF's attention.

"What do you think it is?" Jim asked after HF pointed it out to him.

"Looks to me like a fire," HF replied, "but if it is, it must be awful big. It ain't no camp fire, that's for sure."

"Good," Jim said. "A campfire would probably mean people, but a natural fire means we should be OK."

As they got closer, Jim could see it was indeed a fire. A large house on a bluff, overlooking the river, was burning out of control. Massive waves of flame were rolling up the outer walls and across the roof. Even in the general darkness, Jim could make out how much darker the thick plume of black smoke was as it billowed up into the warm, peaceful night.

Jim was struck by the sharp contrast between the idyllic feel of the evening and the usually terrifying sight of a big fire out of control. He wondered what had started it, since lightning, the usual culprit for natural fires, was clearly not the cause here. He'd dismissed the possibility of a human origin almost out of hand, because it didn't seem likely anyone would be so careless as to set ablaze the place they were sheltering in, but he wondered what else it could have been.

Jim suddenly felt naked and exposed as the raft drifted past on the river below the burning house. The flames were more than big enough to cast flickering shadows across at least half the river, making Jim and the raft easily visible to anyone who might be up on the bluff, near the house.

He scanned the horizon quickly, and sure enough, he saw the silhouette of a man. He was standing just south of the burning house, so close that the heat of the flames must have been almost unbearable. Jim took a deep breath, hoping the man's attention would remain fixed on the vivid conflagration.

The raft drifted on, and they had almost slipped out of sight. Almost, but not quite. The man turned, enough that Jim could make out some of his strangely lit face in the fiery light.

That face was mad with delight, and two pools of flickering red glinted in eyes that stared right at him.

# Laying Low

"That feller saw us, Jim."

"I know."

HF had slipped quietly across the raft as they drifted below the bluff on which the house was burning. The crackling fire continued to cast dancing shadows across the river. Jim was turned away from the house and the man with his glowing red eyes, pumping the oar sweep as hard as he could. He was no longer primarily concerned with moving quietly, and he tried unsuccessfully not to think about how much those red eyes reminded him of the terrible griffin painted on the rock wall upriver. "Is he still watching us?"

"Yup," HF said, "but he hasn't moved a hair."

"That's good," Jim said, but he didn't slacken his pace.

"You got the .22 handy, Jim?" HF asked. "I was looking for it to bring to you, but I couldn't find it with the gear."

"I think we lost it in the storm, when we hit the cars and you went overboard."

"I'm sorry, Jim," HF said contritely.

"Not your fault we crashed," Jim said.

"Well, we might be in a pickle without that .22," HF said. "And no mistake. That feller looks like trouble."

"Has he moved?"

"No, but he gives me the fantods, got fire in his eyes."

"That's just a reflection," Jim said, but he shared HF's unease, and he paddled even harder. Dawn was close at hand, but he resisted putting in and going ashore, even when a handful of reasonable places presented themselves. He wanted to put as much distance between himself and that man as possible.

The dim rays of first light stole across the raft, and still Jim paddled hard downriver. It was a clear morning, with few clouds in the sky—the kind of morning he'd normally have been petrified to be out in the open. HF was watching the sky and both shorelines nervously. "Don't you think we ought to call it a night, Jim?"

"Yeah, I guess. The next place you see that looks good, let me know."

"There's somethin' up ahead, like a road winding down to the riverside," HF said a moment later. "Think maybe a ferry used to dock here, perhaps. Otherwise, it was a powerful silly place to put a road."

"Tying the raft here would be a bit obvious, wouldn't it?" Jim said, looking downstream at the place where the river lapped up onto the asphalt road. "Couldn't it be seen pretty easily?"

"Well, there seems to be some kind of alcove just on the other side," HF said. "We could paddle in there and hide the raft tolerable well."

HF turned out to be right about the alcove. It was well hidden from the western bank of the river upstream, and only someone who was actually looking to find a raft moored down there would even have been likely to find it from the downstream bank. Of course, that didn't comfort Jim completely. After all, if the man—and any friends he might have with him—came south along the river, looking for the raft, he need only cross over the road and keep going southward to find what he was looking for.

"I'm half-tempted to keep going awhile, HF," Jim said. "At least, far enough for us to work across the river so we can put in on the other side."

HF glanced out across the river and turned back to Jim, "I don't know, Jim. It's mighty wide. We'd be out in the open for hours."

Jim scanned the river too. HF was right. The current was strong and the river wide. It would be the work of several hours to get all the way through and across.

"Well, how about we just stay with the raft today," Jim said, looking up at the brightening sky. "Even hovercraft coming from the west or north would have trouble seeing us here."

"That's a terrible idea, Jim," HF said, sounding horrified. "We're completely exposed to the east and south, and—"

"I know," Jim said a little indignantly. "I didn't say we would stay, only that it's tempting. I just want to stay close to the raft so we can shove off if that guy comes looking for us."

"Well, you ain't asked me what I think, Jim, but I'm gonna tell you anyways," HF said. "If I had my druthers, we'd stay farther from the raft than usual, today, not closer, so if that feller finds it, it won't be so easy for him to find us too."

Jim thought about this for a moment, and then he nodded. "You're right, HF. It's probably safer to put some distance between us and the raft. We're what matters. If we absolutely had too, we could continue downriver toward Terra on foot. We can't be too far away, can we?"

"I don't know, Jim, but I think we must be close. Feels like we've already come a powerful long way."

Jim gathered up everything but the paddle, the sweep, and the pole they used to push off each morning, leaving them under the tarp, and he and HF stole quickly up the bank below the place where the road dipped down to the riverside. The sun was peeking up above the eastern horizon, and as he looked at its brightness, Jim found himself wondering how wise he had been to stay on the river so long just to avoid the attention of what had appeared to be a solitary man. Now he and HF were running across a largely open landscape, more exposed to the skies in daylight than he had ever been.

Even so, they bypassed the first few buildings they found along the road, knowing they'd be the most logical places to check should someone find the raft. Eventually, they came to a crossroads and an old gas station, less picturesque than the one they had to pass on the island when going to the Murphys', but situated at the corner in much the same way. He led HF inside.

The storefront was a mess of empty shelves and the abandoned detritus of yesteryear, having long ago been stripped of anything of use. Jim pushed though it, aware that the large glass windows made it a bad place to hide anyway. He was more interested in the state of the interior. He found a small storeroom with no windows at all and a sturdy door, and he and HF slipped inside.

The door had a working lock, which they used, and then they moved the few heavy objects they could find up against it too, just in case someone tried to force his way in. Jim curled up on the floor with his fleece wrapped round his backpack for a pillow. HF sat beside him on the floor, his knees drawn up under his chin, staring at the storeroom door.

HF was still staring at the door when Jim woke up several hours later. He yawned and sat up, stretching. "Anything unusual?" he whispered.

HF shook his head.

"Good," Jim said, standing. "What time do you think it is?"

"From the light coming in from under the door," HF replied, "I'd say mid-afternoon."

Jim groaned. He'd seen the light and known it wasn't dark yet, but mid-afternoon meant several more hours cooped up in this glorified closet. In fact, Jim began to realize, he might need to wait even longer. If the man did come looking for them, only to find the raft but not them, he'd probably figure they'd gone ashore to hole up in daylight, and he might well stake out the raft.

Jim ran his fingers worriedly through his curly hair. How long would he have to wait to make sure it was safe? How would he know? If the mystery man cared about finding them enough to come downriver and stake out the raft, would a few hours be long enough to wait him out? Could they ever risk going back?

Jim shook that thought off. He was being paranoid. For the man to stake out the raft during daylight, he would have to be willing to be out in the semi-open, and Jim didn't know many groundlings bold enough to do that. Maybe they should leave their hideout at dusk, bypass the buildings they'd passed on the way here in case the man was lurking in one of them, and try to get to the raft first. Another full night on the river should put enough distance between them that they'd be safe from a lone traveler on foot.

At first, HF didn't like this idea very much, but he conceded that running back to the river at twilight wouldn't be any more dangerous than running away from it at dawn had been. "Of course," he added, "Just because we got away with a fool thing once't, doesn't mean we ought to try the same fool thing twice."

Jim had made up his mind, though, and when the shadows had grown long on the floor outside the storage room, they moved the small barrier they had erected and slipped back out through the gas station into the fading daylight. Once outside, they ran back the way they came, only they gave the few structures along the road an even wider berth than they had that morning.

They neither heard nor saw anything unusual. Jim could have hoped for more cloud cover as they ran, but he was pleased that the moon was up and casting its soft, gentle light down upon them when they reached the river. He could see the raft tied and unattended, just as they had left it.

"He's not here, Jim," HF said, as they gazed down from up on the bank. "Ain't that a relief!"

"It sure is," Jim said, and they scrambled down the bank excitedly. HF waded out and climbed aboard the raft first. He crawled over to get the pole for pushing off. Jim was about to follow when he saw something move out of the corner of his eye, over near the place where the road sloped down.

He turned to see the man from the night before moving swiftly toward them. He was closing the distance between his hiding place and the raft quickly, revolver in hand. In the silver moonlight, the man's eyes had lost their eerie red glow. But, as his face grew clearer, Jim saw deep, terrifyingly intense eyes and a wicked grin.

Jim froze, trembling.

"Hey Jim, I think—"

Whatever HF had been about to say, he swallowed it.

"Well," the man said in a quiet, even tone as he stopped not five feet away. "I thought you two would be along presently. Good thing I decided to hang around."

# The Duke

Jim stood, stock still. He had thought he was being paranoid, worrying about the man following them. Really paranoid, worrying about his staking out the raft. To actually find the man here was stunning. He was having trouble breathing.

"Well," the man said, almost expectantly. "Aren't you going to ask me aboard?"

"Aboard?"

"The raft," the man sneered. "What else?"

Jim blinked, then turned and looked at the raft. HF was kneeling near the center, staring at the scene unfolding before him.

"You want a ride?" Jim asked, turning back.

"For starters," the man said.

"What else do you want?" Jim said, emboldened a little by the combination of the strangeness of the request and the odd sense of humor, even playfulness, in the man's tone.

"Why don't we discuss this while we're on our way?"

"All right," Jim said, and he motioned to the raft as though the man was welcome to it.

"Please, after you," the man said, and he waited as Jim waded out and climbed aboard. "Now, if you and your electronic friend would back up a bit, I'll come on out."

Once all three were aboard, Jim pushed off and paddled out from the shore as the current pulled them on their way southward. The man sat, backpack in his lap and gun in hand, several feet away, watching quietly. When they were well underway, Jim put the paddle down and turned toward their visitor.

"That's close enough," he said, and Jim sat down, some half a dozen feet away.

"I'm guessing that if you were planning to shoot me, you would have," Jim said, matter-of-factly, and far more calmly than he felt.

The man shrugged. "I've never shot anyone I didn't think deserved it, and I don't know you well enough yet to know if you do."

Did that mean the man had actually shot someone? Perhaps many someones? Jim had hoped for more reassurance that the fellow had no hostile intent. He moved on. "If you wanted the raft, why didn't you just take it?"

"If I'd wanted the raft, I would have."

Jim felt confused. Behind the mysterious stranger, the moonlight twinkled playfully on the river. The air was warm and the evening pleasant. The tranquility of the setting clashed with the oddness of the conversation, not to mention the presence of the revolver.

"I don't understand," Jim said.

"I'm not sure I do, either," the man said, examining Jim with those intense eyes. "I had every intention of taking your raft when I found it, but something inside me said, 'Not so fast, Duke, the boy might be useful.'"

"Your name is Duke?" Jim asked, wondering what kind of name that was.

"More of a title than a name," the man said. "The Duke of Destruction, actually. I'm a burner. The burner. The best ever."

"A burner?"

"A pyro," the man said, then added when Jim still looked confused. "I set things on fire."

"You burned that house deliberately?"

"Of course I did," the Duke said, looking a little indignant. "You think a fire that beautiful, that complete, that all-consuming—you think that just happens?"

"Yeah," Jim said, thinking it a very stupid question and wondering if this man was quite in his right mind.

The Duke shook his head. "Then you don't know much about fire, boy."

"I know they're easy to start, so I don't know what you're so proud about."

The man glared at Jim for a moment, and even though there was no fire burning nearby, the red glint seemed to reappear for a moment in his eyes, reminding Jim that the illusion of familiarity on the raft was just that, an illusion. He felt instinctively that he would need to be careful with this Duke, and not let his strange charisma fool him into letting his guard down.

"O.K., you're just an ignorant kid," the man said after a few moments, his voice almost a growl. "I'm going to ignore that."

But clearly, the Duke couldn't ignore that.

"Of course fires are easy to start, and maybe, once in a great while, a fire like the one I created last night might accidently happen. But a fire like that, with the whole house burning together, all the fuel inside and the whole external structure engulfed, all together, a beacon of beauty in the night, that kind of fire doesn't just happen. It needs help.

"I should know. I've burned more buildings than I can count, and it took a lot of practice getting it just right. And what I did last night, that's just a taste of what I can do. With my crew, I can burn a whole town like that."

"Crew?" Jim said. Any hope that he and HF might be able to give this Duke the slip and get away began to fade. A crew sounded like a pack, and memories of finding HF hanging from the rafter at the lodge flashed through his head.

"Well, they used to be my crew, anyway," the Duke said, and Jim could see the man looking past him, gazing southward. His voice sounded distant, as though his thoughts were far away. "And will be again, once I deal with the King."

King? Jim didn't say anything out loud, but he wondered what in the world he had gotten himself into. Atticus had taught him a bit of history, and he knew that once upon a time, long before the hives, there had been kings and queens, dukes and nobles, but their day had long since passed. And yet here he was, with a man who called himself a Duke, talking to himself about something that sounded a lot like revenge against someone he called a King.

The Duke turned back to Jim, as though his attention had suddenly returned to the raft from wherever it had been wandering. "Since it looks like we're going to be traveling together for a little while, you might as well know what you're getting into."

The Duke paused, but Jim had nothing to add to this. He figured being let into the Duke's confidences had to be a good sign, though he felt some trepidation about the way the Duke was talking, as though something unpleasant lay downriver, waiting for them.

"As a sign of goodwill, I'll put this away," the Duke said, lowering the revolver. He tucked it into his pants, leaving the handle out in plain sight, perhaps as a reminder to Jim that it was there, perhaps just for easy access. "For years I've run a crew of burners."

"A pack, you mean."

"Not a pack," the Duke scowled. "A pack is a herd of animals; we're a collection of artists. We didn't leave the hive to kill wantonly and create mayhem. We create masterpieces, while at the same time, we sweep the forgotten places away, burn them clean. You might say we're humanity's cleaning crew, taking care of the trash that was left behind when the world relocated to the hives."

"But what about groundlings, like me," Jim said. "People live in some of those forgotten places."

The Duke shrugged, nonchalantly. "Do you have any idea how few groundlings there are compared with how many houses and buildings are out there? I could burn for a lifetime, and I would barely make a dent in the number of places left vacant.

"Besides, what are you worried about? You live on a raft."

Jim almost objected that he hadn't always lived on a raft, but he didn't want to derail the Duke from telling his story before he'd even really begun. He silently vowed to keep his mouth shut.

"Anyway," the Duke eventually continued, "a few years back, the crew took in a fellow we found living all alone in a place down south on the Gulf, and I took him under my wing. I really invested in him, taught him everything I know about burning. I thought maybe he'd be a good leader for my crew after I was gone.

"Turns out, he thought so too, only he didn't think he'd wait for me to go. He fomented rebellion and discord in my crew, and the worst part is that by the time I got wise to it, he'd been at it for years. Apparently, he'd been sowing his poisonous seed almost from the beginning.

"Well, it all came to a head a week or so ago. We were camped out in a nice little town a few days south of here. I like to get to know a place before I burn it, you see. Anyway, he convinces the rest of the crew that this little town might be a nice place to live, that we don't need to burn it after all, that maybe our lives would be easier if we weren't always burning down the town where we live, if we stopped creating the conditions that required us to move on. He didn't understand, you see, that staying put would make us nothing more than ordinary groundlings, twiddling our thumbs while the world turns to dust and ashes without us.

"So the crew tells me they're not going to burn the town, that they've decided they're wanting a new crew chief, that this fellow's in charge now—and the worst part is, he looks right at me and says that it was time for the Duke to step aside, to make room for the King. The King! Can you imagine that? The gall of that man. After all I'd done for him.

"Well, I made like I would go along with it, all peaceful like, but I had other ideas. That night, when most everyone was asleep, I decided to remind them of the power of fire, of why we were burners in the first place.

"I wanted to burn the house down around the King, and him with it, but he had a sentry guarding his house and I didn't dare risk it alone; burning is a precise business. So, instead, I burned down a nearby place that housed some of the crew that had supported the so-called King most adamantly against me. I burned them good. There was no way out of that place. By the time they smelled the smoke, they were as good as dead. You should have heard the screams."

The red glint had returned to the Duke's eyes, and Jim felt goose bumps up and down his arms. The gleam of delight that emerged as he spoke of killing those men was the most frightening thing Jim had ever seen.

"I had to skedaddle then," the Duke said, "which was fine with me, since it was all part of my plan. How else to draw off enough of the crew to have a chance to get at the King? I've led them on a merry chase, right up the river, stopping just long enough to leave a fresh burn for them to track me with, all the while looking for a way to get back downriver, back to the King. Then you came, you and your little friend, on this beautiful little raft. Providence had smiled on me at last.

"A couple of nights on this raft, moving like this, and we'll get there in no time. The King will still have a guard, no doubt, but you can help me with that. Between the two of us, we'll take care of him. And who knows, if you do good work, maybe I'll let you stay on with me after."

From the way he sounded, Jim knew the Duke believed he'd just made Jim a great offer. Jim didn't want to offend such an obviously unstable man, but he couldn't muster much enthusiasm, so he tried subtly to evade having to fake it.

"How can I help, exactly? I don't have experience burning anything but dinner," Jim said, making a weak attempt at humor.

"Don't you worry about that," the Duke said. "You're with a master. Just do what I tell you, and we'll make a fire to remember, a fire the King will never forget—not that he'll get a chance to."

As he spoke, a grin spread across the Duke's face, and for a long time, they drifted southward in eerie silence.

# A Long Day

The raft drifted through the warm April night. Fireflies danced along the western shore, and Jim watched them glow, wishing he was ashore with them instead of floating downriver with a madman.

"Your robot's not very talkative, is he?" the Duke said, staring at HF.

"Not very," Jim said.

"But he can talk?"

"Sure," Jim said.

"Well let's hear it, little fellow," the Duke said, addressing HF directly. "What do you have to say for yourself? What did you think of my fire last night?"

HF looked from the Duke to Jim, as though unsure if he should answer. "It's all right HF, go ahead and answer him," Jim said gently.

"Well, it was a whopper of a fire, and no mistake," HF said, "but I ain't got much use for fires nohow, unless Jim needs it for cooking with, and then I reckon I can stand 'em if he can."

The Duke looked bemused, glancing from HF to Jim. "Why's he talk like that?"

"That's just how Atticus programmed him," Jim said.

"Who's Atticus?"

Jim hesitated. He didn't guess there was much reason not to answer truthfully, but he felt instinctively that if this question about his story and what he was doing out here on the river turned into many, he'd need to be careful about what he did and didn't tell the Duke.

"Atticus was my father."

"Was?" the Duke asked, fixing Jim with those eerie eyes, the bemusement gone.

"Yes," Jim said quietly. "He died of fever about a month or so ago."

"I'm sorry to hear that," the Duke said, sounding sincere. "And your mother?"

"Died a long time ago, when I was little."

The Duke nodded. "Losing your folks is a hard thing, Jim—the robot did call you Jim, didn't he?"

Jim nodded.

"A hard thing," the Duke continued. "I wasn't much older than you myself when my folks died. Course, that was a long time ago, but I remember it like it was yesterday."

They sat in silence, the Duke seemingly lost in memory. Suddenly he seemed to snap back into the moment. "Is that why you left the hive, Jim? Your Dad dying?"

"No," Jim said. "I've been a groundling all my life."

"Really," the Duke said, sounding surprised. He looked at HF again. "I've not come across many groundlings with a robot, let alone one that's such fine work. You said your dad programmed him? He made him too, I bet."

"He did."

"So he grew up in a hive then."

"Yes," Jim said, wondering why this was important to the Duke. "Did you grow up in a hive? Is that how you recognized HF was a robot so fast, how you know he's well made?"

The Duke nodded. "Seems like a long time ago."

"Why'd you leave?" Jim asked. "Was it because your parents died?"

"Sort of," the Duke shrugged. "That was part of it, but mostly, I guess I left because folks in the hive weren't very keen on fire. It's not really a place where a burner can develop his talents. We're kind of frowned upon there."

"I imagine so," Jim said. He couldn't fathom something being less desirable in a hive than a person who likes to start fires.

"So why are you here?" the Duke asked, fixing Jim once more with his penetrating gaze. "You and your deliberately antiquated robot friend? Where are you going?"

"Nowhere, really," Jim said, hoping HF wouldn't react to the lie. "I just thought it would be nice to go south, where it's warmer. With Atticus dead, there didn't seem to be any reason not to."

The Duke nodded. Jim guessed he found this answer satisfactory enough. "Well," he said, after a few minutes. "Like I said before, help me with the King, and if things go well, you can stay with me, join my crew."

This time there was no avoiding the offer, and Jim managed to say, "Thanks, I'll think about it."

They found a good place to put in just before dawn, and while he apologized profusely this time for needing the revolver, the Duke drew it and kept it out nonetheless. The three of them made their way up the bank and over to a towering house they'd seen from the river.

"She's a beauty," the Duke said as they stood in front of it before going in. Then he added, longingly. "I'd love to watch her burn."

Jim already knew from things the Duke had said on the raft, that he didn't dare risk setting any fires as he doubled back to the town where the King was holed up with the part of his crew that hadn't come north after him. He could see in the pained look on the Duke's face, though, that his resolve was being sorely put to the test.

Once inside they ate, finishing off the last of the supplies Jim had brought with him from the Caretaker. He'd had them rationed to last a few more days, but the Duke didn't seem to get the idea of rationing, and Jim realized he might as well eat as much as he could while any was left, otherwise the Duke would simply eat it all himself. If he hadn't had bigger things to worry about, Jim might have spent the morning wondering about what he was going to do with his food gone and no .22 to hunt with.

As it turned out, there were more pressing things to concern him. Once their meal was complete, the Duke marched Jim and HF upstairs. "You're going to need to shut the robot down," the Duke said.

Jim complied with this demand, and then the Duke shoved HF in what looked to be a walk-in closet in the master bedroom, and then he had Jim help him move a heavy, wooden dresser in front of the closet door. "Just in case he's not as shut down as he appears," the Duke said, eyeing Jim suspiciously.

Then, the Duke led Jim to the smallest of the bedrooms, and with a length of rope scrounged from inside his backpack, he tied Jim good and tight and left him on the bed. Once tied, he gagged Jim too. "I wish I didn't have to leave you like this, Jim," the Duke said from the doorway. "But you'll pardon me, given my recent history, if I have some issues with trust."

Then the Duke produced a book of matches. Pulling one free and striking it, he held the burning match up in the grey half-light of morning and extended it into the room toward Jim. "Now I like you, Jim. I really do. I don't mean no harm to you or your robot, but that doesn't mean I won't burn this house down and you with it if you try anything. Don't make me do that, Jim. I don't like burning women, and I don't like burning kids."

With that, the Duke blew out the match and dropped the smoking remains onto the floor. The door closed behind him with a bang, and Jim listened as the Duke moved something in front of it, just as he had done with the closet HF was in.

Jim was tied, gagged and barricaded inside a house by a crazy man whose favorite thing in the world was setting buildings on fire. Jim wondered how things would have gone if the Duke hadn't taken such a shine to him.

It was going to be a long day.

# Not Again

Jim heard the voice and opened his eyes. The Duke was leaning over him, shaking him gently. After lying awake for what must have been most of the day, Jim had been so tired at the last that he'd fallen asleep, despite the tremendous discomfort of being bound and gagged.

"It's dark, Jim," the Duke said, pulling the gag from his mouth. "Time to go. For now, we float. Later, we burn."

The fiery glint returned to the Duke's eyes as his wicked grin crept slowly across his face. He was leaned over, so close that Jim could smell something potent and foul on his breath. What it was, Jim had no idea.

Soon Jim was untied, and together he and the Duke moved the chest away from the closet door. Once activated, HF looked at Jim and said, "How long've I been out, Jim?"

"Just since morning," Jim said.

"That ain't so bad, I guess," HF replied, then he looked at the Duke who stood in the doorway to the walk-in closet, holding his revolver. "We're coming with you to the raft, mister. There ain't no need for that there gun."

"Maybe not," the Duke said. "But I think I'll keep it handy, all the same."

And that was that. They left the house and made their way back to the raft. Once aboard and on their way, they settled in as they had the night before, the Duke sitting far enough away to be out of reach of the others, his gun tucked into his waistband.

The nice weather continued, but the sky was cloudy, so that the moon only occasionally broke through to shine down brightly on the river. Otherwise they drifted in comparative darkness, and comparative silence, as the Duke seemed to be in a less sociable frame of mind that night.

In fact, Jim figured out pretty quickly that the lack of chatter wasn't the only thing that was different tonight. The Duke was paying a great deal more attention to his backpack—specifically, to a flask that he slipped out every so often and uncorked to sip from before sliding it away again. The odor from the flask was the same foul smell he'd detected earlier on the Duke's breath, so Jim figured that mystery was finally solved.

The further they drifted, the more the Duke seemed to sink into a melancholy silence. Jim had been uneasy the night before, unsure how to reconcile the Duke's almost pleasant manner with the occasional glimpses into the disturbed mind within. Tonight, though, Jim didn't have that problem. The Duke's brooding seemed in keeping with his stated intentions. He was a man making his way through the darkness, carrying out a mission of vengeance.

Having eaten regularly, even if not spectacularly since leaving the Caretaker, Jim felt the absence of food keenly. He asked for and received permission to try his hand at fishing, but he had no luck. He was almost glad for it. The more he thought about reeling something in, the more he disliked the idea of any sudden movement or excitement on the raft. He thought the Duke's silent reverie was best left undisturbed.

It was well past midnight, in the wee hours of the morning in fact, when the Duke rose from his seat and pointed to a dark structure on the western shore. "There it is," he said. "That's the first place I burned as I started north along the river."

Jim peered more carefully through the darkness, and at last he could make out the charred remains of what had, according to the Duke, once been a much larger structure.

"We're close, now," the Duke said, and at his command, Jim worked hard to bring the raft in close to the shore so they could put in as soon as the Duke directed.

Having found the place the Duke was looking for, Jim tied up the raft and the three of them climbed up the bank and gathered on the edge of a small wood. "Now," the Duke said. "Help me gather a stack of firewood."

They scrambled around in the dark, bringing several armloads of wood back to that same spot, and Jim wondered what they were going to do with it all. The branches were old enough to burn just fine, but the pile they were building was far too big for them to carry with them. Even if they took it out to the raft and floated downriver with it, he couldn't imagine that this was how the Duke planned to get his revenge on the King, with a great big stack of firewood.

But the Duke had other plans. As Jim dropped his final armload onto the stack, the Duke seized HF by the ankle and upended the robot, quickly slipping a noose over his foot and tightening the rope.

"What in tarnation!" HF cried, thrashing wildly.

"Hey!" Jim shouted, when he saw the Duke holding HF upside down. "You put him down!"

"Everybody just relax," the Duke said, pointing the revolver deliberately at Jim's chest. Jim forced himself to stand still, despite the anger rippling through him. Even HF, when he saw the gun trained at Jim, stopped his thrashing.

The Duke threw the rest of the rope over the big branch overhead and directed Jim to grab hold of it. "Now pull until your robot pal is dangling a few feet above our stack of firewood. That's right, just like that."

After the Duke had HF secured, hanging upside down above the pile of wood, he told Jim to back up a few steps. He then pulled a small device that Jim didn't recognize from his backpack, adjusted a small dial, and set the thing carefully under the stack of wood.

"Now listen to me, Jim, and listen good," the Duke said, all hints of friendliness, pretend or otherwise, gone from his voice. "I set that timer for an hour. If things go well, we can do what we've come to do, and you can be back here to get your robot friend down before it goes off and ignites this fire.

"You give me any grief, or fail to do what I tell you, as soon as I tell you, I'll make sure you don't get back in time, and that's if I let you live at all.

"Don't let it come to that, Jim. Just do what I say, and you and your robot can be on your way—or stay, if you'd rather. You'd be welcome on my crew. But first, we take care of the King, and we do it now."

Jim looked at HF, dangling over the pile of wood. He thought of how he had found him in the lodge after the pack had left him there. He'd survived that ordeal well enough, but Jim could see HF was precariously close to the pile of wood, and that it was a very large pile. What's more, Jim didn't know what that timer had been attached to, so he had no idea what the Duke was using to ignite this fire or how hot it would burn.

"Time's a wasting, Jim," the Duke said.

"I'll be back, HF," Jim said, reaching out and clasping one of HF's hands. He turned to the Duke. "Let's go."

Then they were running. Jim pushed away all distractions. Fear. Anxiety. Anything that would detract from his ability to recognize the way back. He searched out markers in the dark, landmarks to help him on the return journey. He had come too far to lose HF now. He'd do whatever the Duke wanted, then he would return, rescue HF, and they'd be free of him.

Soon they were approaching the outskirts of a town. Jim wondered where the King and his crew were, but the Duke didn't say anything. He kept moving quickly and quietly, zig-zagging his way through the town. Jim figured the Duke knew which places were occupied, or might be, and so he followed, careful to stay close, but not too close. The Duke still had his revolver out.

Before long they had come through the town, or just about, anyway. The Duke led Jim down a short road that led along the river to a very large, very nice house, surrounded in the back by a series of smaller structures. The Duke left the road once they could see the place, and he began circling through the tall grass in a wide arc, approaching the outbuildings from the rear.

The Duke stopped and held up a hand for Jim to stop. They crouched down. Up ahead, a small building like a shed or a garage lay on the edge of the tall grass. The clouds were thick and there was precious little light to see by, but Jim thought he could make out a figure moving.

The Duke leaned over and whispered. "Circle round, over there," the Duke pointed past the small building. "Distract the guard."

"How?" Jim asked.

"Just do it," the Duke said. "The clock's ticking."

Jim wanted to punch the Duke in the face, but the revolver was a strong deterrent. He ran, hunched over, in the direction the Duke had sent him, his mind racing. He reached a place where the high grass ended at the edge of a gravel driveway that circled around the big place, running past the various other smaller structures around it. Jim saw the gravel, and suddenly, an image of the road running across the island near the cabin flashed through his mind. He knew what to do.

He slipped out from the cover of the tall grass, snatched up a handful of gravel, then darted back. He looked back in the direction of the guard, who was still pacing in front of that other building. He didn't know where the Duke was or what he planned, but Jim couldn't worry about that. He threw a piece of gravel onto the driveway further down, away from where he sat in the grass, and then glanced back. Sure enough, the guard had heard it and was peering through the dark. Jim waited, watching, and when the guard didn't move any more, he lobbed another stone.

This time the guard started away from the small building, walking toward the place where he'd heard the stone. Jim could see the man was carrying a gun, too, and he stayed very still. It wouldn't help HF any if he got shot while trying to help the Duke.

And then it happened. A shadow rose up out of the tall grass beside the place where the guard stood and struck a swift, vicious blow to the back of the man's head. It was quick, and it was silent. The shadow motioned toward Jim, and he rose, following it to the front of the small building.

By the time Jim reached the door, the Duke was already inside. He had lit a match and was holding it up. It illuminated the small space surprisingly well. Rows and rows of large red cans were stacked in there, and Jim could smell the unmistakable odor of fuel.

The Duke turned to Jim, the wicked grin back on his face. "Oh, Jim," he said, rapture in his voice. "It's still here. All of it. Grab four cans. We're gonna make a fire to remember."

# Playing with Fire

"I can't carry four cans," Jim said.

"Make two trips," the Duke replied with barely a glance in Jim's direction. From a large shelf he was pulling down devices like the one he'd placed underneath HF and carefully setting them in his backpack. "Set two up near the back of the house, then come back for the others."

Jim felt a brief surge of hope. If the Duke remained behind while he carried the cans to the house, what was to keep him from slipping away then? He doubted that the Duke, faced with choosing between chasing Jim and pursuing revenge, would choose Jim.

Jim picked up two heavy cans of fuel and started to leave the shed. Just as he was leaving, the Duke said. "Hold on, not so fast," and slipping the backpack onto his shoulder, the Duke followed Jim out into the night.

He had only been hoping to get away for a few seconds, so the despair he felt was completely disproportionate to the hope invested, but Jim couldn't help it. He walked fast, looking straight ahead, afraid that even in the dark the Duke would see his disappointment. Once he had set the cans by the house, the Duke followed him back, though Jim noticed he glanced back frequently at the house.

The return trip didn't take long, and finally they stood together behind the big house, surrounded by the four large cans of gasoline. The Duke leaned in close, the terrible smell of his breath even more oppressive than it had been before. "There's almost certainly another sentry round front. Carry two cans and follow me. Once we've taken care of him, I'll tell you what to do."

Jim followed the Duke, his arms straining with the heavy cans. They kept close to the southern side of the house. Passing the ground floor windows made Jim nervous, but all was dark except for a faint light glowing above the main door around front. They reached the front corner, and the Duke peered around, surveying the scene as Jim set the cans down, glad to give himself a rest. After a moment, the Duke looked back at Jim. "I don't know why there's no guard, but I'm not complaining."

"Give me one of those," he added, holding out his empty hand, "and follow me with the other."

The Duke crept up onto the long, low wooden porch that ran the entire length of the front of the big house. The heavy front door was partially open, even though the outer screen door was closed. The Duke froze when he saw this, and Jim wondered what it could mean. The Duke seemed to deliberate, then suddenly to decide on a course of action, and he stooped, setting one of the devices from his backpack by the door. Then he turned to Jim.

"Pour. Quickly."

The Duke started pouring the gas and walking quickly, quietly, back the way they had come. Jim followed, likewise pouring out the gasoline. They made their way back along the house, stopping just once, ever so briefly, so the Duke could set another device by the south wall of the house.

Around back, they dropped the empty cans. Jim quickly clasped and unclasped his hands several times. His palms were sweaty and his hands sore. The Duke took out another of the devices, set it down carefully, then picked up one of the other cans. Jim took the last one, and they continued along to the back corner and around to the north side, heading quickly back toward the front.

As they approached the porch, Jim began to get excited. His can grew lighter, and so did his footsteps. He was almost finished here. If the Duke was true to his word, he should soon be on his way back to HF. A big if, but he couldn't worry about that now.

How long had it been? How much time had it taken to get here? How long to get back? Would he have trouble without the Duke to guide him? How long had they been at this? Not long, Jim thought. Other than distracting the guard near the shed, which hadn't taken a whole lot of time, they'd been moving pretty steadily and efficiently.

The Duke had set his last device along the north wall, and once more they were walking across the low wooden porch, splashing the last of the fuel generously on it. Once finished, they quickly retreated to the grass beside the house, and the Duke pulled out his matches.

He struck one and held it firmly between his fingertips as it burned. With his other hand, the Duke reached into his pocket and pulled out a dark, slender object. He tossed it to Jim.

It was a pocketknife. Jim looked at it, wonderingly, then looked up at the Duke, his face barely illuminated in the flickering of the match. The Duke reached down and pulled his revolver out of his waistband, and for a moment Jim panicked, thinking that the Duke meant to hurt him, but he never raised the gun.

"I'm going to hang out here," the Duke said quietly, "and give my regards to the King."

"But," he added in the next breath, "if I were you, Jim, I'd run."

With a quick flick of his wrists, the match landed in the pool of fuel near the corner of the house, and bright orange flames leapt up, running instantly in both directions along the side of the house and up onto the wooden porch.

As striking as the image of the burning house was, it was the rapt face of the Duke, soaking in that fiery glow, and those eyes, burning once more with delight at the destruction he was witnessing that struck Jim in that brief instant before the screen door to the house flew open.

He was about to turn, about to run, when the man came out. He was clutching the front of his pants, as though trying to hold them up as he stepped quickly out across the still low-burning fire that was just beginning to really get going on the porch.

His other hand held a gun.

The man looked up, peering beyond the flames on the porch into the darkness beyond, and seeing Jim, standing out in the grass, raised his gun and pointed it right at him.

# Rescue

Jim thought he was dead. He had no gun, and in the flickering light of the rapidly growing fire, he was clearly visible to the man on the porch. But the man didn't shoot, confusion registering on his face. For just a moment he hesitated.

The fire on the porch was growing in intensity, and perhaps it distracted him. He stepped further away from the front wall and the flames already moving up it. As he did, a bang echoed through the quiet evening and the man flew back like he'd been hit in the chest with a sledgehammer.

Jim glanced over at the Duke, whom, the poor soul on the porch hadn't yet noticed. His revolver was still raised. The Duke turned from the now motionless body on the burning porch, looked at Jim, and grinned.

Jim ran.

Behind him, the world erupted into chaos. Several bangs— much deeper in pitch and louder than the gunshot had been— echoed through the quiet night. Even facing away from the house, Jim realized there'd been an accompanying flare up with the fire, as the dark night suddenly brightened and then quickly died back down again.

It wasn't hard for Jim to figure out that the explosions must have been those strange devices the Duke had planted around the house, but all questions of what they actually were disappeared with the exchange of gunfire that now echoed behind him. Jim flinched involuntarily, though by now he was much too far away to be worried that any of the bullets had been aimed at him. Worse to him than the shots were the screams and cries of pain. He reached down and found a gear he didn't know he had, accelerating through the darkness.

He was weaving back through the town, wondering if any of the King's crew were lurking in one of the dark buildings there, and if he would come face to face with any of them. Surely anyone within miles of the burning house had to have heard the explosions. Jim was as careful to stick to the shadows as he could without going too far out of his way, but only speed mattered now.

He had to reach HF before that timer expired.

With a sigh of relief, he left the town behind, and searching in the darkness for any of the markers he'd noted on his way in from the raft, he found one and altered his course accordingly. Unbidden, the image of the man on the porch being shot flashed through his mind. He saw him fall again, saw the blood spread across his chest.

He was responsible. The man hadn't noticed the Duke because he was staring through the flames at Jim. He'd probably expected to find the Duke, and he'd hesitated when what he actually found was a stranger, a kid. That hesitation got him killed, and it was Jim's fault.

And that man wasn't the only one Jim had gotten killed that night. The King, and whoever else was in that house, they were Jim's responsibility too. He had helped the Duke pour the gas, helped him make the fire. Whether they burned in the flames or got shot by the Duke while trying to escape, Jim had aided in their deaths.

Of course, Jim thought, they might not be dead. He didn't know for sure that the shots he'd heard indicated that the Duke had shot them. Maybe one of them had shot the Duke. Maybe the Duke's plan had backfired. He must have been clearly visible from any number of windows. Maybe someone with the presence of mind to do so had shot him out of one of them.

Jim wasn't sure how much better he felt about that. The Duke was a scoundrel and worse, but he hadn't hurt Jim or stolen his raft. And he had, very possibly, just saved his life. The whole thing was a mess, a mess he wanted to put as far behind himself as possible. If he could just reach HF in time, they could slip down to the river and leave the Duke and his fire and all the rest far behind.

He had to be in time. He hadn't let himself entertain the possibility that he might not be. HF was all he had left of Atticus, of the only world Jim had known, a fragile world that seemed more lost to him each day. He'd lost so much. He couldn't lose HF too.

The moon slipped out from behind a thick bank of clouds. The result was a flood of moonlight, illuminating the ground across which Jim was running with startling clarity. Up ahead, he could now make out the edge of the wood where they'd left HF. Jim couldn't see any fires burning. Hope that he was in time grew. He sped on with all the strength he had left.

And there was HF, off to Jim's right, still dangling from the tree over the large stack of wood. Jim veered toward him, calling out, "Hold on, HF, I'm almost there."

"Jim? Get me down, Jim! Get me down!"

"I will," Jim cried, slowing as the moon disappeared once more behind the clouds, bringing back the darkness and making it hard for Jim to see just exactly where the rope was that held HF suspended in mid-air.

In that brief, uncertain moment, the quiet stillness of the early morning was broken by a loud bang, and Jim screamed as a burst of flame erupted up through the stack of wood, engulfing HF. The force of the explosion blew a chunk of wood right past Jim's head. He could feel the breeze as it passed by his ear.

The fire rose and fell, but Jim didn't wait for it to recede. He grabbed the rope near the trunk of the tree, having seen it in the light of the flames, and he yanked hard to the side. As HF swung out of the fire in the opposite direction, Jim cut the rope with the pocket knife. HF kept right on swinging in a slight arc and fell with a smoldering thump in the nearby grass.

Jim was there in an instant. Peeling off his shirt, he dropped it over the smoldering frame of the robot. Using the soles of his shoes as insulation, he rolled HF over and over through the dewy grass as thin wisps of smoke drifted upward.

Jim worked feverishly. HF hadn't been in the flame for more than a few seconds, and being more or less flame retardant, he hadn't actually caught fire. It was still several minutes, though, before he was cool enough for Jim to touch, and in the near complete darkness, Jim just couldn't see how bad or extensive the damage might be. What worried Jim most was the fact that HF was strangely motionless and quiet.

He leaned over the robot, peering down through the dark. "HF! HF!" he said urgently, desperately. "Say something, anything."

"That's twice, Jim!" came the moaning, plaintive reply. "If this is what comes of heading downriver on a raft, I give up. I want to go home. I don't want to be dangled over no fire, no more. No sir!"

The words came all in a rush, and Jim felt HF's evident anguish, but despite his own worry and fear for HF, and his anxiety and guilt over the events of this terrible night, he couldn't help but laugh. He laughed and laughed and laughed. Finally, HF sat up and said. "What's so funny? You're laughing like some fool hyena, Jim, but I was almost roasted alive."

"I'm sorry, HF," Jim managed to get out as he gasped for breath. "I know I shouldn't laugh, but it's just been such a horrible night, and ... and I'm so glad you're all right, I just can't help it."

"Oh," HF said, evidently reappraising the situation. "Well, I reckon that's all right then. Come to think of it, I'm glad I'm all right, too. I thought I was a goner."

"Me, too," Jim said, the laughter going as easily as it had come. He spoke quietly, seriously. "I saw you there—no fire beneath you. I knew I'd made it. Then the fire erupted. It felt so unfair to have come so close but fail."

"I'm sorry, Jim," HF said, "but I can tell already I've got some damage this time. I don't think it's critical, though, not yet anyway. My essential functions seem all right for now, but I think it'll be more than you can handle on your own. I'll need some proper maintenance, Jim, though I guess that's a problem for another day."

"It is," Jim said, helping HF get to his feet.

"What about you, Jim? What happened with that Duke fellow?"

"I'll fill you in on our way," Jim said, the mention of the Duke's name prompting him to action. "We should get to the raft and put as much distance between us and this place as we can."

"Oh, am I glad to see you," Jim whispered to the raft as he climbed aboard and pushed off. He paddled hard, trying to get as far from the western shore as he could. He didn't think there'd be any escaping the light cast across the river from the fire that must be even now engulfing the house, but he wanted to be as far as possible from it and anyone who might be near it—and their guns.

A cool breeze blew across the surface of the river. The sweat that had been flowing freely just moments ago gave Jim a chill on his bare chest. He had a spare shirt in his pack, but he didn't dare stop now. He'd get it out and put it on once they were below the house and safely on their way.

It wasn't long before the orange reflection of the raging fire was visible on the river. As they drew near, Jim thought he could feel the air temperature rise, though he wondered if that was a trick of his imagination. Flames rose high into the air, but Jim forced his eyes away from the fire itself, searching half eagerly, half fearfully for any sign of survivors.

He saw no one moving on the horizon, but a thunderous boom echoed through the night, suggesting that the Duke's work wasn't yet complete. Flaming objects shot into the air from somewhere beyond the house, illuminating the dark sky in the distance.

The shed. The Duke's supplies had also somehow caught fire.

What did that mean? Would the Duke have destroyed his own materials? If not, who would have? The distance between the back of the house and the shed was substantial. Could fire there have really been an accident? He doubted the fire could have crossed the cool, wet grass, though perhaps a flaming piece of the house could have been thrown there somehow.

Whatever had happened, the night sky was alive for a few brief moments with a pillar of flame that stretched up and up and up, before falling back down and being lost behind the more steady fire of the house.

The current pulled them swiftly on, and the burning house faded behind them. Jim, whose hands were sore and tired from gripping his paddle so tightly after carrying those heavy gas cans, sat and watched it disappear. He didn't know if the Duke had killed the King, or if the King had killed the Duke, or neither. Maybe the fire had gotten them both. He supposed he'd never know.

Right then he couldn't say that he cared all that much. He was alive, and he had HF and his raft. That was all that mattered. He'd felt sorry for the King, since he didn't think anybody should be burned in his sleep. In the end, though, he didn't imagine the King was probably any nicer than the Duke. He was just glad to be on his way, without either one of them to reckon with or worry about.

# Fear and Hope

Exhausted, Jim slept like the dead. He had found a tiny but cozy bungalow, a little back from the river, resting idyllically beneath the shade of a beautiful maple tree. There was only one bed inside, but that was all Jim needed.

His dreams were troubled, though he couldn't remember the specifics with much clarity when he woke. There had been a dark pall, a sense of foreboding, draped over them all. The only concrete image that remained with him when he woke, stretched and sat up, was the image of his cabin, back on the island, burning in the night.

The image seemed so real to him in the half-light of evening, that a wave of sadness washed over him as he sat on the side of the bed, staring blankly out the window at the maple. A solitary tear slipped out and made its lonely way down his cheek. He blinked, reminded himself that the dream wasn't real and wiped away the tear. He yawned and stood up. The Duke was gone. The real nightmare was over.

He had slept right through until almost sundown, so that there wasn't much time before they'd be able to get underway again. Not much was still plenty of time to realize he was starving, however, and for all Jim's looking, he didn't turn up anything edible, anywhere in the place.

He felt the absence of the .22 keenly. He didn't know that having it would have changed anything with the Duke. Even if Jim had been carrying the gun that night, the Duke certainly would have taken it off him. But now, facing the prospect of a long and hungry night, Jim wished he had the .22 back again. He felt much more confident about his ability to hunt for his dinner than to fish for it.

So while trying to ignore the rumbling in his stomach, Jim spent the time that remained until sunset examining HF. His head and shoulders and parts of his torso were severely singed in places. Jim was able to clean some of the soot off, but he feared that much of the external damage was irreversible. Without the requisite materials and expertise to replace those parts, HF would likely bear permanent reminders of his second up-close encounter with fire.

As for any internal damage, Jim couldn't worry about that now. He only knew how to do the most basic internal maintenance. He had to seek solace in what the Caretaker had told him about Terra, that Atticus hadn't been the only groundling there who had worked in a hive and had knowledge of robotics. Finding Terra, and soon, was all the more imperative.

As they sat together once more on the raft, Jim shared with HF the new fear that was growing inside him. "Do you think, maybe, with all we've been through the last few nights, or maybe even before, in one of the storms perhaps, that maybe we missed Terra? Missed the rail bridge?"

"I think I would have seen it, Jim," HF said, scratching his chin. "It's real distinctive like."

Jim nodded, somewhat reassured, but unable to shake the fear. "What if we find it, but it's abandoned? That would be even worse."

"I guess anything's possible, Jim," HF said, "but I can't see the whole town up and moving away after all the work Atticus and the others put into it. It was a real nice place to live."

Jim didn't say any more about it, and his futile attempts to catch a fish for dinner pushed the matter from his mind. In the early hours of the morning, they drifted past a decent-sized little town, and Jim decided to put in even though there were several hours of darkness left.

They tied up just south of the town and made their way back up the river to it. As he stood on the outskirts, Jim decided that tired as he was, he needed at least to try to find something to eat. So he started systematically exploring the houses and shops along the southern edge, working north through it. By the time dawn was about to break, he figured he'd been through some fifty buildings, with almost nothing to show for the effort. He had found an old jar with a handful of peanuts in it, but eating them had been like eating gravel.

He watched the sun rise in the east, sitting in a wooden rocking chair in a second floor bedroom in a house that was right smack-dab in the middle of the town. The yellow-orange glow of morning broke over the town, bringing color back into the world. The fears that had plagued him on the raft the night before melted away.

He had survived the pack at the lodge, survived the wild dogs, survived the raft's crash and survived the Duke. He'd find food sooner or later and survive this crisis, too. He just needed to hope and trust to Providence.

Fear and hope were curious things, Jim thought. He loved the one and hated the other, clinging desperately to hope and wishing passionately to be free of fear. Hope energized and fear—run amok—immobilized, but he guessed, in a way, he needed both in due measure.

Still hungry, but feeling more at peace about the world, Jim went to sleep. This time, he had no dreams.

When he woke, a steady rain was drumming against the window of his room and pattering on the roof overhead. For a while Jim lay there, listening to it fall, but then he rose, went downstairs and greeted HF. "Hey, HF, I think we should keep exploring the town."

"I'm sure we got more than an hour until nightfall, Jim," HF said. "I think we should stay put."

"I know," Jim said, looking out through the front window at the steady rain falling on the street. "I just think we should check out some more before we go back to the raft. There were some stores further along the street, and one looked pretty big, like it might be a grocery. I'm really hungry, HF."

HF looked out the window too, also taking in the rain and the street. "I know it's raining, Jim, but we'd be awful exposed. Can't we just look when it gets dark?"

"How about a compromise," Jim said, barely restraining the enthusiasm that even the possibility of finding a grocery and something edible inside it had produced. "Let's go up the street, take a quick survey of the stores, and if the big one is a grocery, we'll go in and stay there until dark, even if we don't find anything for me to eat."

"That don't sound like a compromise to me," HF said. "Sounds like we're going outside and walking down that open road like you suggested in the first place."

"Yes," Jim said, "But only so long as it takes to scout one street and examine one store. Any further exploring can wait until dark."

HF still hesitated, and Jim leaned forward, getting closer to the window and staring up at the darkening sky. "Come on, HF, there's quite a storm brewing out there. I think it's just getting started. Odds aren't good anyone is out in this weather."

"I can tell you've got your heart set on it," HF said with a sigh, "and I sure don't want you to be hungry, Jim. I guess we can go if we have to. Do you promise it's just the one store?"

"I promise," Jim said eagerly.

A moment later, as they stood at the front door with what was left of their gear in hand, Jim pulled his fleece out of his pack and over his head, then leaned over and said to HF. "If there is a grocery, maybe it'll have some of that hot chocolate the Caretaker had. That would go nice with some dinner."

"Don't get your hopes up too much, Jim," HF said, but Jim had already opened the door and stepped out into the rain.

The evening was warm and the rain steady as Jim made his way up the street. He darted from building to building on his side of the street, scanning the stores they were approaching. They were on the other side, but Jim thought he wouldn't risk the crossing until he found the one he wanted and hopefully some evidence it was what he wanted it to be.

The first few stores were small, and obviously had been dedicated to selling things that had nothing to do with food. That was all right, Jim thought, since he hadn't expected anything from them anyway. The larger building was a little farther along, and that was another story. The name had faded from the big wooden sign above it, but the signs inside it—stuck up on the glass windows at the front—they were all advertisements for things to eat. Jim smiled. He'd been right.

"Come on," Jim said to HF enthusiastically, breaking out from the cover of the building beside him and jogging out into the middle of the street.

"Hold on, Jim!" HF called from behind him, but it was too late.

The hovercraft zoomed overhead.

# Sacrifice

For the briefest of moments, time seemed to stop. The world around Jim froze in an awful stillness. He blinked, his eyes peering upwards. Hard, driving raindrops struck his forehead and cheek, splashing water into his eyes. Still he stared, disbelieving, at the sleek hovercraft flying right over the street. Right over him.

It was the remotest of possibilities—stepping out into the street in an abandoned town, far from any hive, only to find a hovercraft patrolling the same town, the same street. It was also a groundling's worst nightmare. He'd been seen, he was unarmed, he was far from any place that might offer relative safety, and he was, except for HF, completely alone.

The flash that glimmered for a moment through the rain and the bullet that ricocheted off the street beside his foot snapped him from his reverie. He turned, took three or four long strides, and dove between the two houses closest to him. HF was there just ahead of him. They half-ran, half-scrambled along the wall toward the back of the house in a desperate search for a place to hide.

At the back corner, they looked at the avenue of overgrown backyards that ran between these homes and the ones of the neighboring street. It was open, but not nearly as open as the street. There were trees and bushes and patches of waist-high grass. Jim scooted out to a big evergreen bush, and he and HF pushed under its full, prickly branches. They lay, listening intently, and sure enough, a moment later, the unmistakable sound of the hovercraft buzzed overhead.

The hunt was on.

Jim supposed, in a way, it was good the hovercraft was still in the air. Yes, it was harder to move without being spotted, but at least the hunters hadn't gone aground yet. The visibility issue went both ways. Hovercrafts were easier to spot than individual hunters.

Suddenly, the steady rain became torrential. It was as though someone turned a valve and opened the great deep of heaven. The rain poured down with a renewed vengeance. Jim welcomed the fury of the storm, hoping that it would not only hide him from watching eyes, but maybe even encourage those eyes to go home. Jim leaned over and whispered in HF's ears.

"We need to try to make our way to the raft. We can't stay here."

"I'm scared, Jim," HF said. "That fellow took a shot at you."

"I know," Jim said, beginning to move. "I'm scared too. Come on. We can't stay here."

Jim scrambled out from underneath the bush, peering up through the sheets of rain, searching for any sign of the hovercraft. Seeing none, he ran, bent over, through the tall grass to the nearest house in the direction of the raft.

He paused there, squatting against the back corner of the building, staring up into the sky. He almost missed it. The rain was falling so hard he almost didn't see or hear the hovercraft, but there it was, returning above the open backyards. It dropped down out of the sky, landing not far from the bush where he'd just been huddled with HF.

He fought the strong impulse simply to run, fearing that even through the storm, pronounced movement of that kind would be visible to the hunters. Instead, he dropped down and crawled quickly but steadily through the high grass, up along the house and away from the hovercraft. Near the front, he saw an opening leading to a crawlspace under the front porch. It was small, but so were he and HF. He slipped through the opening and as far under the porch as he could. HF followed, and they lay on the hard-packed dirt there, as still and as quiet as could be.

Then, the real waiting began. Jim felt cramps forming in his muscles, but he didn't dare move at all or change positions to alleviate the soreness, not in the slightest. He concentrated on breathing evenly, regularly, quietly. A few feet away, HF lay utterly motionless too, though he alternated between staring out through the wooden latticework and staring at Jim.

Being watched by HF was unsettling. Jim knew HF was looking to him to get them out of this, but Jim had no idea what to do next.

Movement caught Jim's eye, and at the same moment, both he and HF looked to the side so they could watch two feet in black boots walk past. They stalked, really, more than walked, and Jim could tell the hunter that went with those two feet was taking his time, studying his surroundings, looking for any sign or evidence of his prey. Jim held his breath, hoping he wouldn't notice the crawlspace or the small opening through which they had entered it.

If the hunter did notice, he didn't bother to check. He moved out beyond the house into the street, and Jim watched him turn away to move past the neighboring house. He allowed himself softly to exhale the breath he'd been holding, and he went right on, waiting some more.

The moments stretched on, until it seemed to Jim that quite a bit of time had gone by. There had been no further sign of hunters looking for them, and the rain still fell heavily. He began to toy with the idea of crawling over to the opening, slipping out if the coast looked to be clear, and trying to see if the hovercraft was still there. Perhaps the hunters had been turned away by the ferocity of the weather.

As though in confirmation of his hope, a bright flash rippled through the air, and a few moments later, a terrific peal of thunder roared in the sky above. Surely hunting some unknown groundling couldn't mean so much to these hunters that they would persist through daunting conditions like these.

Jim started slowly to turn around so he could crawl back to the opening. HF leaned in close and whispered, oh so quietly, "Jim, what are you doing? I reckon we should just stay put 'til nightfall, then try to slip away under cover of dark."

"Maybe, HF," Jim said, just as quietly. "I just want to sneak a peak and see if the hovercraft is still there."

"I haven't heard it leave, Jim," HF said. "I've been listening for it, too."

"It'd be hard to hear over the storm," Jim said. "I'll just take a quick look."

Jim started crawling toward the side of the crawlspace, but he stopped instantly when another pair of boots, a different pair, moved past the side of the porch. He watched them, holding his breath, and panic seized him when they stopped just a little past the opening. He had barely heard HF from a couple feet away. Had he been as quiet? Had the hunter somehow heard their exchange?

"Say that again, Pete?" The voice of the man was audible though not especially loud, clear enough over the pattering of the falling rain. Jim didn't hear anyone answer, but a moment later, the hunter spoke again.

"No way," he said, adamantly. "Nobody got past me. He's still here. You know the drill. Just patrol your sector of the town like you're supposed to."

He. Either they'd gotten a good look at them both and knew HF was a robot, and so were only worried about tracking Jim, or they'd missed HF all together.

"Of course I let the others know," the hunter went on. He sounded annoyed, indignant. Jim held his breath as the feet of the man shifted around, indicating he was turning slowly in a circle. Jim didn't know how the hunter was doing it, but he realized the man must be talking to another hunter who was somewhere else. "Don't worry, Pete. The others'll be here before dark, and then we'll tear this town apart. We just need to make sure he doesn't get past our perimeter before then. He won't get away."

The hunter started walking again, moving slowly away from the house, and Jim lay still, trying to keep despair from washing over him. Others? It sounded like more hunters were on their way. How many? Another hovercraft full? A whole fleet? And if so, what chance did they have?

He'd come all this way, through so much, and now he was going to die in this wretched little town. He was going to be shot like an animal by a hive-dweller who thought killing a groundling was great sport.

He hit the hard-packed dirt with his fist, struggling to hold back the tears. They had to go. They couldn't wait. He didn't know how many hunters were out there, patrolling the town to make sure he didn't escape, but they had to go now, before the odds got even worse.

He crawled back to HF and whispered. "Did you hear that, HF?"

"Yeah, I heard," HF said. Jim noted that the fear and agitation that had been in HF's voice just a moment ago was gone. His voice was soft but clear.

"We can't wait until dark now," Jim said, hoping HF had understood what he'd heard and could see this. "We can't wait for them to find us here. We have to go for the raft while we still can."

"No," HF said, stirring finally and crawling past Jim so that he was between Jim and the opening to the crawlspace. "We're not."

Jim was taken aback, not just by HF's words, but by their quiet adamancy. He spoke with a forcefulness Jim had never heard from him before.

"HF, we have to go, we can't stay—"

"We're not staying," HF said. "We're just not gonna go for the raft, not both of us anyways."

Jim frowned. His eyes narrowed as he stared through the dim light at HF's strangely intense look. "What are you saying, HF?"

"I'm saying this is what we're gonna do, Jim," HF said in a tone that suggested he'd brook no argument. "I'm gonna climb on out of here in a moment, and then I'm gonna run down that there street, and I'm gonna shout and make a ruckus just to be sure they see me, and then I'll lead them as far away as I can take them."

"No, HF—"

"And then," HF said, completely ignoring Jim's attempt to countermand his plan. "You're gonna run right the hell out of this town, all the way to that raft, and you're gonna get on it and slip away downriver, and when you see a big 'ole railbridge, with pylons of red-brown stone, you're gonna find Terra and your Aunt Flor. You're going to find her, and you're going to be happy again, Jim. Do you hear me?"

"HF," Jim pleaded, his voice cracking. "Don't. You don't have to do this. We might be able to get through together."

"Maybe," HF said. "Maybe not. We ain't gonna find out, cause this is what we're gonna do. You heard them, they're looking for one person. They're gonna find one person, and then maybe they won't look no more."

"No, no, HF," Jim whispered. He was frantic. "We have to take care of each other. Atticus said … "

"We have taken care of each other, Jim," HF said. "And I'm real sorry it's come to this, but now I have to take care of you."

Jim had been lying on his stomach, up on his elbows so that his head and chest were just barely off the ground, and HF reached out, across the small intervening distance. Gently, he placed his hand on Jim's chest, so that it rested over his heart.

"One battery, Jim," he said quietly. "You only get one."

Without another word, HF crawled quickly to the opening of the crawlspace. He looked briefly out, to make sure the immediate coast was clear, and without looking back, he darted out into the pouring rain.

# In the Storm

Jim blinked. HF was gone.

There was no time to process what had happened. He heard HF's voice call out above the din of the storm. "Ain't no hunter from no hive gonna get me!"

Jim sprang to life. He slipped his head out of the opening and peered toward the street, straining to see or hear anything. He caught a glimpse of a hunter running out from between two houses further up. The hunter turned and disappeared up the street. Jim couldn't see HF from where he lay.

He didn't know if it was safe. He'd never know. He could only hope that the diversion had worked and go, otherwise it would be wasted and HF's sacrifice would be in vain.

He slipped out, sprang up and ran with all the strength in him. He crossed the street in a flash, ran madly through front and back yards, leapt over a leaning, rusted metal fence almost in a single bound, and hoped against hope that HF might be able to elude his pursuers.

He had reached the southern edge of town and could see up ahead the fields of grass in the distance through which he needed to make his way to the raft, when a distant shot rang out. He faltered for a second, the image of HF stumbling and going down like a buck, suddenly burnt indelibly into his brain. He felt a searing, terrible pain in his own gut, and he clutched at it desperately. A second shot echoed across the bleak landscape, and Jim was back at full speed.

He broke through into the tall grass of the field, pumping his arms vigorously as he ran, wanting something or someone to hit. Something to destroy. Tears mingled with raindrops on his face, but he did not slow down. More hovercraft were coming. Even if he'd gotten past the hunters in the town, he had to get to the raft, had to get underway.

Up ahead, he could see the river, but he wasn't yet close enough to see the raft tied up at the base of the bank. The sun was very low in the west, and Jim knew night wasn't far away. That meant the other hunters had to be close. Hopefully, they weren't coming from the south.

He crested a slight ridge before the riverbank and saw the corner of the raft a little farther downstream. He tore straight toward it, scrambling down the riverbank in a couple of quick strides. In a flash he had opened the knife the Duke had given him, and in another flash the rope holding the raft had been cut and he was pushing it out into the river. He was about to climb on when he noticed the small dark shapes moving through the sky up ahead.

He cursed his terrible luck. They were hovercraft, and they were coming from the south. He'd be as visible here on the river as he had been in the streets of the town. There was no time to go anywhere else. There was no cover nearby.

Without even really thinking about what he was doing, he took a deep breath and ducked down below the surface of the river. He swam under the raft, moving up along it until he was near the downstream end. Suddenly, he had a crazy idea.

Murphy had done an excellent job picking logs that were fairly straight, smoothing them out and lashing them tight.

Even so, they weren't a perfect fit and they weren't perfectly tight. There were gaps here and there between them. If Jim could just manage to grab hold somehow and smash his nose and mouth up into one of the cracks between two of them, he might be able to breathe and stay under the raft long enough to drift unnoticed past the hovercrafts.

He'd spotted them while they were still a long, long way away. They were large, shiny and moving quickly across the sky. There was no reason to think they had yet been able to see him, a solitary figure standing waist deep in the river a long way off through a terrible storm. Maybe, just maybe, they would see the raft drifting with no one on it and think nothing of it.

He rolled onto his back and reached up, his hands feeling frantically for some way to grab hold of the raft. He found a place where Murphy had lashed some of the logs of the raft together and grabbed hold of the rope. He pulled his face up and pressed his nose and forehead up into the small crack between those same two logs. His eyelids fluttered open and water didn't seep into his eyes. He started to open his mouth to breathe, but water did splash in there. He swallowed it awkwardly, then tried to breathe, just through his nose.

It worked. Air swept in and he clenched the slippery, wet rope even tighter. The raft drifted on, and Jim drifted with it. He couldn't see anything but the dark shape of the logs right above his face. His ears were below water, and other than the muted sounds of raindrops splashing down, he heard nothing.

His fingers started to ache, and still he held on. He held on until he couldn't hold anymore, but still he made himself hold on. His fingers were somehow both cold and numb, but also on fire. Still he held on.

He thought perhaps he was imagining it, but he began to think the air he was breathing was stale, less refreshing. He knew there was no way the seal between the logs was perfect. Fresh air had to be coming down into the small gap where he breathed, but that knowledge didn't alleviate the sudden and growing panic that he was going to suffocate if he had to stay much longer.

His fingers slipped. He clutched for the rope, but he couldn't catch hold again. The raft began to move over him. He had no idea how long he had actually been under the raft. However, he hadn't taken an especially large gulp of air, so he began frantically to turn over and swim backward to get out from under the raft. He felt burning in his lungs. At last, the dark swath above him cleared and he could see the surface of the river. He rose, head plunging up as he opened his mouth wide to swallow the air. He gasped as he drank it in.

No sooner had he done so, than he searched the sky in every direction for signs of the hovercraft. He saw none.

The raft was slipping away from him, being carried by the current more swiftly than he. He swam to catch up, but he didn't climb on. Instead, he grabbed hold of the side and let it pull him along as it continued downstream.

The rain beat down on his head. The river was choppy and the current really, really strong. The swirling waters bobbed the raft up and down, and Jim with it. Holding on was no easy task.

Sunset came and went, and only after it was completely dark did Jim climb up onto the raft. He was spent. Physically. Emotionally. It took all he had left to crawl to the boarded floor in the middle of the raft and slide under his tarp, and there he lay.

Perhaps there was something he should have been doing to try to steer the raft through the turbulent waters, but he didn't think he had the strength, and furthermore he didn't care. It didn't really matter what happened now. Nothing mattered. Everything had gone wrong. He'd lost everything.

He lay motionless for hours under the tarp. He blinked and stared in the darkness. His mind was blank. There were no words, no thoughts, no feelings. There was nothing. He was empty.

Then, without warning, he saw the cabin. He saw Atticus lying asleep in his bed, in the grip of fever. He saw HF sitting in his chair, keeping his vigil, legs rocking rhythmically back and forth. He saw, and he wept. He didn't cry; he sobbed—great, heaving, body-wrenching sobs.

All gone. All lost. Atticus, his father. HF, his robot.

No, not his robot. His friend.

He wept until his body ached, until he thought he must not have any tears left, and still the tears poured from him. He clasped his arms tightly around his trembling body, trying physically to restrain his shaking. He couldn't.

Then the raft hit something very, very hard. Jim felt himself just about lifted up and off the raft and flung forward. His head and shoulders also hit this cold stone object very, very hard. Pain radiated through his neck and down his back. His head felt like it had been struck by a hammer.

He dropped into the cold, swirling waters, and as he drifted down, down below the surface, he felt darkness washing over him. He felt the darkness, and he thought, *so, this is what it is like to die.*

# Reunion

Blueberry Muffins. That was the smell.

Jim's eyes fluttered open. If he could smell blueberry muffins, then he wasn't dead.

He was inside, in a cozy bedroom with walls and ceiling painted yellow. He was in a warm bed, in dry clothes that weren't his own, with a thick comforter over him. There was a large, comfortable looking armchair with blue and white plaid upholstery sitting in the corner by the room's solitary window on the wall opposite the foot of the bed, and the sun was peeking in through the window almost hesitantly. The armchair was empty, though a ball of yarn and knitting gear suggested it had perhaps been recently occupied. For now, though, Jim was alone.

And hungry. Really hungry.

His stomach rumbled and growled, and he felt embarrassed, even though there was no else one around to hear it. Jim hoped desperately that the enticing smell of the blueberry muffins meant the real thing was around here somewhere—wherever here was.

Where was he? Slowly, memory washed back over him. The hunters. HF. The storm. The crash. The river. None of those things explained how he'd gotten here.

He tried to sit up and thought better of it as both his head and neck complained mightily. His head throbbed and his neck was so sore that turning his head even just a little bit to either side was painful. He guessed the crash hadn't been a dream, since he thought he remembered hitting his head pretty hard.

And if not, then none of the rest of it had been a dream either. The hunters had been real, and HF was really gone. *"Ain't no hunter from no hive gonna get me!"* He thought of HF's final words and wondered how HF had felt as he ran down that street. HF had never been particularly brave. In fact, he'd always been pretty timid, which made his calm, decisive action in the midst of their terrible predicament that much more remarkable. He'd seen a way to save Jim's life, and he hadn't hesitated. Much like his actions at the lodge, Jim realized, when HF had buried Jim and Mr. Murphy with leaves and left himself exposed.

The door to the bedroom opened and light flooded in from the hall. Jim started to turn to look, but the pain in his neck radiated down his back. He winced, stopped and turned back.

"You're awake," came the soft words, and right behind them came a short woman with mostly grey hair, though some patches still retained what had probably been her original, dark black color. She was older, but not as old as Atticus or the Caretaker, and she wasn't a whole lot taller than HF had been. She had a kindly face, though, and her fingers were gentle when they touched Jim's shoulder. "Does it hurt very much?"

"A fair bit," Jim said, looking up at her as she leant over him, smiling.

"I'm not surprised," she said, "you have an impressive lump on your head. Whatever happened, you took quite a blow."

"We crashed," Jim said, before he could catch himself.

"We?" the woman said, looking suddenly alarmed.

"I mean me," Jim said, not sure he was ready to talk about HF. "I crashed, my raft I mean. It hit something hard in the storm."

"Ah, one of the bridge pylons, I bet," the woman said. "That storm last night was a doozy. Tough weather to be out in."

"Had no choice," Jim said quietly.

The woman looked like she wanted to say something then, but she must have decided against it. Jim was glad. There'd be a time for explaining things, but not yet.

"Are you hungry?" she asked instead.

Jim nodded gently, not wanting to hurt his neck further. "I haven't eaten in days."

"Well," the woman said, standing up straight. "That, at least, is something we can take care of."

"I'm Mary," she added, almost as an afterthought.

"I'm Jim."

"Nice to meet you, Jim," she said. "You just lie down and I'll be right back."

Jim wasn't disappointed. There was hot tomato soup with soft warm bread. There was an apple cut up into slices and even a little bit of cheese, and there was soft butter with a basket piled high with still-warm blueberry muffins. Along with it came a tall glass of fresh milk to wash it all down. Mary sat on the edge of the bed and helped Jim balance the tray while he tried to eat without lifting his head up too far, staying as still as possible.

When he was finished, she whisked the tray away, returning a little later to sit in the armchair by the window. Soon the click-clacking of her knitting echoed rhythmically in the little room. Jim found it comforting, a reminder that he was not alone.

"How'd I get here?" Jim asked.

"My Thomas found you," Mary said, without looking up and without pausing in her work. "You were lying facedown, washed up on the side of the river. When he saw you there, he figured you were dead, but when he walked over to you, you groaned and he knew you weren't."

"Nothing left of my raft, I guess," Jim said, his heart sinking.

"Not that I know of. Thomas didn't say anything about finding a raft nearby, and I think he would have."

Jim sighed. He guessed he'd have to start numbering his raft among the things he'd lost. However far he still had to go, he'd be going on foot. Once he could walk again, that was.

"You won't be well enough to go anywhere for a while, though, I imagine," Mary said, as though reading his mind. "But if it's a raft you need, and you have a little bit of time to tarry while you mend and rest up here a bit, there might be someone in town who could help you with that."

"Town?" Jim said, propping himself up slightly and ignoring the pain it caused him. "This is a town?"

"Well, we're not right in town," Mary said. "We live kind of on the outskirts, out here by the river, but —"

"Is this Terra?" Jim asked, not really daring to hope but unable to help it.

"It is indeed," Mary said, looking up from her knitting then, but still not slowing down any. "You've heard of Terra?"

"I have," Jim said, excited. "This is where I was headed. My Aunt lives here, or she used to anyway."

For the first time since she'd sat down, Mary stopped knitting. Her hands just hung, in midair, and she leaned forward, peering across the room at him, as though seeing him for the first time. "Jim Finch," she said softly. "Jim Finch. I don't believe it. You're Bryn and Atticus' boy, aren't you?"

"I am," Jim said, wondering how long it had been since he'd heard someone say his mother's name out loud. Atticus never referred to her as Bryn, only ever speaking of her as "your mother."

"Does my Aunt still live here?" Jim asked, again trying unsuccessfully to stifle the hope rising inside, while at the same time trying to banish the terrible fear that he'd come all this way for nothing.

"She sure does," Mary said, rising from her chair and putting her knitting back down on the seat. She crossed over to the bed and stood beside him once more, reappraising him. "And my, oh my, Jim, won't she love to see you."

Jim let his head settle back into the pillow. He closed his eyes—joy and gratitude and relief washing over him.

He'd made it. He'd found Florence.

In less than an hour, Mary returned to his room, followed by his Aunt Flor. Her coal black eyes sparkled with tears as she entered. She was tall, towering over the much shorter Mary. Her face and hands were darker than his own light brown skin, just as he had always pictured his mother, but two swaths of white hair at her temples kept her short hair from being entirely black. When she saw him she smiled, a radiant smile that stretched from ear to ear.

"Oh, how I've prayed I would see this day," she said, her voice clear and strong, but trembling as she went on. "How I've prayed I would see you again."

Jim wasn't sure what to say. Until a few weeks ago, he hadn't known his Aunt existed. Now that he was here, though, he did feel strangely emotional. He searched for words to suit the occasion but found none. In the end, he just looked up at her and smiled.

Flor bent over and kissed him gently on the cheek. Her soft lips lingered there, and Jim closed his eyes, imagining that his mother's lips had probably felt much like this. He wondered what it would have been like to grow up with a mother's hugs and warm embraces, a mother's smile and comforting kisses—not instead of Atticus, but along with Atticus. He guessed it would have been pretty great.

Mary had dragged the big armchair over to the side of the bed, and as Flor settled into it, giving Mary's arm an appreciative squeeze, Mary excused herself from the room, murmuring, "I'll just go check on my Thomas."

Left alone, Flor gazed at Jim, as though trying to read in his face his entire history since leaving Terra as a toddler. Jim lay back, awkwardly, trying to keep his neck still while peering sideways at his Aunt. "I'm sorry, but my neck hurts," he said after a moment, trying to explain why he didn't turn his head to look at her directly or roll on his side so she could see him better.

"Never you mind," Flor said. "Mary told me about your crash, and I can see well enough for myself that you need to keep still."

And that was all anyone said for a while. Flor seemed content to sit and stare, and Jim was content to be stared at. After a little while, Flor said, "You know what I see?"

"What?"

"I see Bryn's beautiful eyes staring at me out of Atticus' thoughtful face—a browner, younger version of Atticus' face."

Flor's eyes twinkled at him when she said that. Jim wasn't used to that twinkle, and he wondered if his mother had had it, too. What he said, though, was, "Atticus always said I had Mom's eyes."

"Oh, you do," Flor said, nodding, "and they're beautiful, just like hers."

"Atticus is dead," Jim said starkly, figuring it needed to be said, even if he didn't know the best way to say it.

Flor nodded, her eyes glistening again. "I wondered," she said quietly. "Mary said you'd come alone. How long ago?"

"Not long," Jim said. "Month and a half, maybe."

"I'm sorry," Flor said. "He was a good man."

Jim nodded, but he didn't comment. Flor prompted him to tell her more, and before he knew it, he was telling the whole story. He told her about the fever and about burying Atticus in the sunny glade on the island. He told her about his last words and going to the Murphys' with HF. He told her about building the raft at the lodge and about narrowly evading the pack. He told her about setting out with HF, about the wild dogs and even about the horrible, painted griffin. But, when he got to the Caretaker, he omitted the trip to the hive.

It wasn't like he planned to omit it, but when it came right down to it, he decided to bypass that particular part of the story. He didn't know how folks in Terra, and his Aunt in particular, felt about the hives, and he didn't want to make a bad impression right up front. He felt kind of bad about skipping over that part, but he figured there were lots of things he was leaving out, so it wasn't lying, not exactly.

When he got to the Duke, he also decided to omit telling his Aunt about helping him burn the King's house. He just said he'd given the Duke a ride downriver, and that he'd been glad to get the raft back, moving on quickly to the episode with the hunters and losing HF.

Aunt Flor seemed familiar with the town where this had happened, saying it wasn't all that far upriver, though it was on the western side and Terra was on the eastern side. "Maybe when I'm well enough," Jim said, "I can go back up there. Perhaps they left him when they realized he was a robot. Perhaps he can be fixed."

"Perhaps," Flor said, but Jim could tell she was just saying that, like adults sometimes did when they didn't want to upset you. He didn't care, though, it would be worth the trip to find out.

When he was finished, Jim lay there, thinking it was quite a story, all put together like that. Flor seemed to agree. "Well," she said, "it sure sounds to me like Providence has had a time of it, watching over you."

Jim frowned. "I'm not sure I believe in Providence."

"No?" Flor asked, watching him carefully. "Why not?"

Jim shrugged. At least, he started to shrug before it hurt too much and he had to stop. "I don't know," he said. "I guess I think that if Providence really wanted to watch over me, HF would still be here, and Atticus too for that matter."

Flor sat in the armchair, nodding quietly, but then she said. "I know what you mean, Jim. Sometimes it doesn't seem like life makes any sense. It doesn't feel fair."

Jim didn't answer. There wasn't anything to say. She was right. Never knowing his Mom. Losing his Dad at only fifteen. Being hunted just for being a groundling. Losing HF. It wasn't fair. Not any of it.

"There is another way to look at it, though," Flor said.

"How?"

"Providence doesn't keep death away forever, Jim," she said quietly. "In fact, Providence is bigger than death. It includes it. Our appointed time is part of Providence. Losing Atticus was hard, I'm sure, but he must have been about sixty-five. That's not bad for a groundling that chose the life of a hermit.

"And from the story you tell, it sounds like you had several close calls on your way here. It doesn't seem like too much of a stretch to think an invisible hand was on you, guiding and protecting you."

"Well, then I wish that invisible hand had seen fit to protect HF too."

"I know," Flor said, reaching down and taking his hand in hers. "But maybe Providence wove the tapestry of history in just such a way that HF would be with you yesterday, be there to lay himself down for you. Maybe that's what HF was made for, even if Atticus didn't know it. I think he'd consider it a fair exchange, don't you? Losing his robot to save his only son?"

Jim lay still, thinking about that. He thought maybe he was going to cry, and he didn't want to do that in front of his Aunt. So, he thought he'd move the conversation along. "Is my mother buried nearby?"

"Yes."

"Will you take me?"

"I'd love to," Flor said. "But not until you've had time to rest and heal some. I promise you, though, when you're able, we'll visit her."

Mary and "her Thomas" spoiled Jim for several days, until Jim was able to move to Flor's house in town. The lump on his head had gone down, leaving behind an ugly bruise, but his neck remained stiff and sore. Aunt Flor brought a man by to see him, the closest thing Terra had to a doctor. He said he thought Jim had some damaged vertebrae. More to the point, there was nothing to be done about it except give them time.

Gradually, the pain decreased until Jim could sit upright for longer periods of time and even stand and walk. Turning his head to either side, though, required him to turn his whole body in what felt like an incredibly awkward manner. He started to despair of ever being able to turn his head without pain, but he made slow progress and was comforted one morning, about ten days after arriving at Terra when Flor said, "How about today, Jim?"

And that was how Jim found himself, about an hour later, standing over his mother's grave.

It was one of many in the Terra graveyard; his mother wasn't the only resident the town had lost over the years. The grave lay beneath the shade of an oak tree, and Jim stood beside it, looking down at the smooth stone that bore the simple inscription, "Bryn Finch."

And there it was again. The image of a grave, Atticus beside him, tears on his face, the sensation of hands on his shoulders.

"Aunt Flor, were we, were you, here with me when we buried my Mom?" Jim asked. "Were you standing behind me? Hands on my shoulders?"

"Yes, I sure was," Flor said. "You remember that?"

Jim nodded. "I do."

They stood in silence, as Jim stared at the stone, mesmerized almost by the sight of his mother's name. "I remember that, but I don't remember her," he added. "I can't. I never have."

Flor, who was standing beside him, slipped her arm around Jim's shoulders. "I'm sorry, Jim. I wish you'd known her. She loved you, very much."

"Will you tell me about her? Maybe not now, but while I'm here?"

"Of course," Flor said. "I'd love nothing better."

They lingered in silence, and in the end, it was Jim who took the first step away. They walked together, through the grass, and Jim said, "Was she sick a long time?"

"Yes," Flor said. "Bryn had her good days, of course, but she was sick more often than not. She was fragile, Jim, all her life, like the beautiful flower that she was. Atticus knew, of course, when he married her, but I think since he was so much older, he wasn't really prepared for her to go first. He was devastated."

"Is that why he left Terra?"

"I think so. He never liked to talk much, but the waters in Atticus ran deep. I think the memories of her here were just too strong for him to bear."

"His name really wasn't Atticus, you know," Jim said suddenly. "It was Tom Stewart. Did you know that?"

Flor laughed. "Yes, I did, but I'm a little surprised you do."

Jim tensed, but he kept walking, trying not to let it show. He asked, hesitantly. "Why are you surprised?"

"Well," Flor started, "I shouldn't say I'm surprised, I guess. I'm probably making too much of it … "

"Too much of what?" Jim prompted.

Flor walked on with Jim, and he waited in agony. He felt the myriad of questions about his father and the secrets that he'd kept for so long, roiling below his calm surface.

"When Atticus showed up in Terra," Flor said, "and he introduced himself as Atticus Finch, it wasn't hard to figure out that wasn't the name he was born with. But he wasn't the only one who'd changed his name when he left the hive, so no one thought much of it. He was just Atticus to us, and that was fine.

"As he started getting serious about Bryn, though, I think he felt like he was keeping something from her, that she needed to know his real name. I was there when he told her, and I don't know why we thought it was so funny, but we did, and we laughed our heads off.

"Tom Stewart just felt like such an ordinary name. It didn't fit him at all. Atticus was much better, and we told him so.

"The laughing, though, it embarrassed him. His face was so red—I don't think a face can get any redder. We didn't mean to, it wasn't malicious, but Atticus always was a sensitive soul, God bless him. He'd gone and opened up about himself, which understanding him better now, I'm sure took some doing, and we had rewarded him by laughing.

"Later, of course, I understood what that laughter had cost him. We tried to repair the damage, but it was clear that bringing it up again, even to apologize, was almost as painful as our laughing in the first place had been. In the end we dropped it, and that was definitely that."

They had come to the top of a small rise, and the main road leading into Terra lay on the other side of it. Flor stopped, gazing down that road. "So, anyway, that's all I meant. I think Atticus had buried 'Tom Stewart' for himself, long before he met us, and after our reaction, I figured he'd buried 'Tom Stewart' for everyone else too."

They headed down the rise to the road and turned back toward Terra. Thick white clouds floated in a blue sky. A faint scent of mint wafted over from the fields on the other side of the road.

Jim's mind raced. Was that it? Was it that simple? Of all the wild and crazy explanations Jim had dreamed up on the raft to explain the inexplicable—the secrets his father had kept from him—it had never occurred to him that Atticus had been ashamed. For all Jim's fears and insecurities, it might not have had anything to do with him after all.

Of course, Jim thought, that didn't explain why Atticus had never mentioned Flor, but that explanation might be fairly simple and straightforward too. If living in Terra had been too painful and had conjured too many memories of his mother, then maybe talking about Flor had been too hard as well.

Perhaps that was it. Perhaps his father's perplexing silence, in the end, boiled down to two things as simple as shame and pain.

"What now, Jim?" Flor asked, and Jim could hear an unusually tentative note in her inflection. "You've found me, seen your mother's grave—what are your plans?"

Jim shrugged. "I don't know. Just getting here was all I've been focused on."

Flor nodded. "Well, I hope you know how I feel. I'd love for you to stay."

"Thanks," Jim said, but Flor's question had stirred something else in him. "You know, it's not what I expected."

"What isn't? Terra? The grave? Meeting me?"

"No," Jim said, "None of those things, exactly. More of the whole thing, I guess. I'm not sure how to say it."

"The future never turns out quite like we expect," Flor said.

"No, I guess not," Jim said. He gathered his thoughts as they walked, and Flor waited quietly. "I've been so focused on where I was going—first to find the Caretaker, then to find you. I don't think I understood, not really, not until now, just how much I was banking on finding more than that."

"What do you mean?"

"I don't know, answers I guess? I think I was hoping for some answers."

"But you haven't found them?" Flor asked, looking over at Jim and studying his face.

"I've found some," Jim said. "About Atticus, and about my mom…"

"But?"

"But, I think," Jim stopped in the middle of the road and turned toward Flor, "I think this started out as something about Atticus, about his last words. And then, later, when I found out about you, it also became something about my mom. But really, deep down, perhaps even right from the beginning, it was about me."

"What answers were you hoping to find?"

"I don't know," Jim said, and they started walking again. "Something that would tell me who I am, I guess?"

"Ah, I see," Flor said, nodding.

"But, even though I found the Caretaker, and found you, and found out things about my mom and about Atticus that I didn't know, I don't think I know much more about who I am than I knew when I set out."

They walked on in silence. A pair of cardinals flitted playfully in front of them. Jim realized that his attempt to describe what he was feeling was incomplete, like the discoveries he had made on this trip, so he kept silent.

"I think, Jim," Flor said, "that the journey every person takes to find out who they are is never really finished. I'm older than you—a lot older—and I haven't figured out who I am, not completely anyway. Maybe I never will.

"It's a journey that takes a lifetime. In fact, it's not a journey, it is the journey. So, I'm sorry, but the answers you're after probably can't be found.

"At least, not here."

• • •

Jim's neck continued to heal. He could turn his head without pain, and he felt more comfortable with the idea of going out and about in Terra, now that he felt more himself.

The May weather was spectacular. For once in his life, spring wasn't completely consumed with farming and hunting and the hard work that the coming of warm weather had always brought on the island. There was plenty of work to be done around the town, but he was still being treated like a patient who needed to take it easy and had barely left Aunt Flor's house. That meant lots of free time, something he'd never really experienced before.

It was midmorning, and Jim was sitting on the wooden steps in front of Aunt Flor's house. He was still getting used to looking up at an open sky in broad daylight. The system Atticus had helped develop twenty years go still kept the hunters away. Jim leaned back on his elbows, face turned up, eyes closed, enjoying the warmth on his face without fear.

Aunt Flor had been suggesting all week that Jim should meet some of the teenagers that lived in Terra—hinting none too subtly that there were some rather pretty girls among them, and it looked like today might be the day she followed through on this. She just had some errands to run first.

The thought of there being several kids about his age, all in one place, was almost as strange as the thought of walking outside in broad daylight. He wasn't quite sure what to make of it, and he was too embarrassed to admit his anxiety to his aunt.

He took refuge in the same daydream that had been a place of frequent retreat of late. He thought of Sarah Murphy's shy smile, thought that maybe he already knew the only pretty girl he needed to know, and he figured that whatever the future held, at some point he'd need to make his way back upriver, back to the island.

Along the way, he'd drop in on the Caretaker and Shep, and visit a while. He felt bad about the way he'd left and wanted to let the Caretaker know everything was all right. He wasn't mad at Atticus anymore, not really.

But before he could really give any serious consideration to heading back to the island, Jim had to go back to the town where he had left HF and see what he could see. Now that he was better, there wasn't any good reason why he shouldn't. Only the fear of what he might find held him back. It might be a long shot—that HF would still be there and be reparable—but Jim had to go.

HF had sacrificed himself to save him. Jim owed him this.

The sound of wheels on the sidewalk in front of the house snapped Jim out of his daydream. Opening his eyes in the bright sunshine meant some quick blinks and a moment of rapid adjustment as he made out the blur on the sidewalk. His heart skipped a beat and he leapt up off the stairs as he began to make out the small figure pulling a wagon past the house.

"HF?!"

The figure stopped pulling the wagon and turned. Jim froze. It was HF, but it wasn't. There were striking similarities and subtle differences. The synthetic hair was different, not quite lying flat, his nose was a little more bulbous, and there were too many freckles on the robot's face. And when he spoke, his voice was much, much too shrill.

"You talkin' to me, Mister?"

"Yes, sorry," Jim said. "I thought for a second you were someone else."

"That's OK," the robot said cheerfully. "Could happen to anyone. All of us look more or less alike."

"All of us," Jim murmured, repeating him. "Atticus made you."

"Of course," the robot said.

"How many of you are there?"

"Thirteen."

"Thirteen."

"That's what I said," the robot answered and leaned forward to peer at Jim. "You having trouble with your hearing?"

"No," Jim said, as he walked out to stand beside the robot. "It's just that Atticus was my father, and I grew up with a robot named HF."

"Seventeen!" the robot said. "He was the last of us, one of the four we lost, though I reckon we didn't exactly lose him, since he left with Atticus."

"And me. I'm Jim. I was a little boy back then."

"Well I know that," the robot said. "You were just a little feller when your Daddy left. I'm Six, by the way."

"Hello, Six," Jim said. "What happened to the other three, besides Seventeen?"

"Well, Four never worked quite right, so eventually Atticus just took him apart and salvaged what he could when he built Eight. Nine washed away when he fell in the river several years back, and of course, Atticus never made a Thirteen—that would have been bad luck." Six looked around, like he was making sure no one was listening, then he leaned over and whispered, "Atticus was a bit superstitious."

"I know," Jim smiled.

"So, are Atticus and Seventeen around here somewhere then?" Six asked, looking past Jim at Flor's house.

Jim wasn't sure how Six would take the news that his maker was dead, so he just said, "No, I'm sorry. Just me."

"Oh," Six said, sounding a little disappointed. "That's too bad. We'd love to have seen Seventeen. We helped design him you know."

"Did you?"

"Yup," Six said, standing tall and looking proud. "Atticus knew he was close with Sixteen, and we all made lots of suggestions for Seventeen, and even though Atticus couldn't use 'em all, he told us we'd been real helpful. Said it right out loud."

Jim smiled as he nodded. "I'm sure you were."

"Well," Six said, looking down at the wagon. "I'm supposed to deliver this here wagon-load of stuff to the General Store. I better get going."

"Can I come along with you?"

"That's fine with me, Jim," Six said enthusiastically, looking delighted to have been asked. "I would enjoy the company."

Six started pulling the wagon, and Jim thought of walking through the snow with HF, pulling the sled, piled high with firewood. The memory wasn't happy or sad. It was both.

Kind of like life, he thought.

He walked beside Six, the wheels of the wagon squeaking on the pavement. The sun was warm, the day beautiful.

"Would you like to meet the others?" Six asked.

"Yes," Jim said. "I think I'd like that."

## THE END

# Afterword &
# Acknowledgments

The story of R3—how I refer to *The Raft, The River, and The Robot* with friends—begins with a single, dominant image: a boy and his robot on a raft, floating down the Mississippi. Where that image came from in the first place, I have no idea.

I was captivated by it, however, and immediately the image raised some fascinating questions. Who is this boy and why was his robot programmed to sound like Huck Finn? If this is the future—which clearly it must be if a boy has a very lifelike robot for a companion—what led them to travel the Mississippi in this archaic way? And why was the world around the river so empty and deserted?

The pursuit of these questions took over my mind, and while I was writing *The Darker Road* at the time, it was not yet under contract, so I had the freedom to do what I generally advise writers never to do—namely, to lay down the book I was working on to start working on another one. And so for a time, my work on TDR ground to a halt and R3 became all-consuming.

My first thought was that the world was largely empty because it was post-apocalyptic. Something had happened to destroy the world as we know it, and that was how 'largely empty' and 'archaic' could also fit into the future.

I didn't like this answer though. It felt too predictable.

So I kept looking—always a good idea when you haven't yet found what you are looking for—and the answer I eventually arrived at was much more satisfying. The world wasn't empty because of an apocalypse, because the world wasn't empty. It just *felt* empty. But why did it feel empty?

That question led to the hives. I imagined them as cities that grew up, rather than out, and part of the growth of the hives was the abandonment of the towns and cities that you and I inhabit. Of course, I now had to figure out both why people would want to live in a hive, and just how this would be possible.

I won't retrace all those steps here, but the key step came in a casual conversation with my good friend, Ben Wickham, where he mentioned a project his older brother was working on: developing a robotic strawberry harvester. Of course, if you've read the book, the penny has now dropped for you. (And if you haven't, why are you reading this first? Go read the book!)

With that conversation, the vision of a future where farming is managed almost entirely through robotic means, breaking the last link in the chain tying mankind to the earth and freeing him to reach for the skies and move into the hives was born. And with the hives and the story of how they became both possible and desirable figured out, I was then free to focus on the groundlings who rejected the hives and on Jim, HF-17 and their story. Voila, R3 was born.

Before turning more directly to my acknowledgements, I'd like to say a word briefly about R3's relationship with *The Adventures of Huckleberry Finn*. I am an avid fan of Twain's original, as I trust will be clear to the careful and casual reader alike, and there are many allusions to people, events and even specific quotes from this great work. These are deliberate, and I don't apologize for it, since I believe R3 is creative and original in its own right and stands alone very well as a separate story.

Having said that, I know that for many people, what they remember best about Twain in general and *Huck Finn* in particular is the humor, and R3 is not especially funny. This was a deliberate choice, on my part, and again, I don't apologize for it. Twain is one of the great, truly original voices in American literature, and while I had no qualms drawing from his story as I created my own, I felt any attempt to even try to be funny in a Twain-like way would be disastrous for me. My own writing voice is so different from his, it would have been futile and, I think, a colossal failure.

While the book came out in a flood—a veritable torrent, in fact, the likes of which I've never experienced before—turning R3 into a finished, fine-tuned product took a good bit more time. I want to thank two friends in particular for their work on the text. Jonathan Rogers is the best writer I know, and if you've read his *Wilderking Trilogy* then you know why I had to get his help fine-tuning HF's voice for R3. Also, I am as usual, very much indebted to my friend Matt Crossman, who was once again one of the first to see R3 and provide feedback, even as he was the last to look it over and help me find mistakes I'd missed.

I am again grateful to 52 Novels for their excellent work on the interior design for R3, and likewise to Abe Goolsby, who created the cover. It may not be the cover *greater than which none can be conceived,* but it is pretty close.

Lastly, many thanks to my family, for their love and support. In the writing of the book, I thought often of my father, and of my too-often flawed attempts to be a father to my own children, and I am greatly comforted that the Providence that the original King & Duke mock in *Huck Finn,* but is taken a bit more seriously here, is very, very real.

# About L.B. Graham

L.B. Graham writes fantasy/sci-fi and contemporary adult fiction. His novel *Beyond the Summerland* was a finalist for a Christy Award in 2005. Check out his website www.lbgraham. com for more information on his previously published works and his forthcoming titles. He lives in St. Louis with his wife and two children.

# Also by L.B. Graham

**The Binding of the Blade**
A five volume, epic fantasy series, consisting of...

 *Beyond the Summerland*, Book 1
 *Bringer of Storms*, Book 2
 *Shadow in the Deep*, Book 3
 *Father of Dragons*, Book 4
 *All My Holy Mountain*, Book 5

**Avalon Falls – A crime novel for adults**

**Coming Soon from this Author**
*The Darker Road* – Book 1 of a new fantasy trilogy called *The Wandering*. (Spring of 2013. Books 2 & 3 of that series will follow in '14 and '15)

*The Promise* – The first book of an adult contemporary trilogy called *These Three Remain*. (Release Date to be Determined)

A *not yet* BOOK

We live in the Already. We wait for the Not Yet. We write about both.